A Texas Ghost Story

A Novel

By

Arley Owens, Jr.

SHORTY MAE PRODUCTIONS

A Texas Ghost Story

COVER ART:
Front: The Author
Back & Spine: CL Owens

Editor: Pitman Sanders

First Printing March 2013
Printed in the U.S.A.

Soft Cover Edition
ISBN: 978-0-9848195-5-3

SHORTY MAE PRODUCTIONS
P.O. Box 81102
Midland, Texas 79708

Amarillo By Morning
composed by Terry Stafford and Paul Fraser

The Wind Cries Mary
composed by Jimi Hendrix

Horse With No Name and *Ventura Highway*
composed by Dewey Bunnell

Peggy Sue
composed by Buddy Holly, Jerry Allison,
and Norman Petty

You Can't Always Get What You Want
composed by Mick Jagger and Keith Richards

The Times They Are A Changing
composed by Bob Dylan

To everyone who loves
The Lone Star State
&
Ghost Stories

Special Thanks to Dylan J Morgan
& Sue Smith.

1

Jasper Miller rose from the squatting position he'd assumed to repair the bottom strand of a barbed wire fence. Squinting against an approaching sunset, he pulled a leather work glove off his right hand and tilted his hat back to scratch away an itch. He thought he'd heard a woman cry out for help from a small valley lying west of the hill he stood on, but couldn't see anyone there. Black Stetson once again covering his temples, he re-sheathed his fingers and hadn't gotten the cowhide pulled tight against his fingertips before hearing the troubled voice a second time. Still unable to spot the crier, he figured she must be injured or in some other way immobilized behind a patch of sunflowers at the far rim of the valley, since there was nothing else to block his view. The four stretches of wire above the broken one wouldn't bend enough to step through, so he climbed over at a post, careful not to catch his jeans on a barb. A bum knee making a full sprint impossible, he jogged towards the tall yellow blooms. When he got to the bottom of the basin she cried "Help! Help!" in rapid succession, sounding more woeful than frantic, as if pleading for the sake of someone with her. Forming a megaphone with his hands he hollered, "Help's on the way . . .!"

Now standing on the other side of the sunflowers, Jasper scratched his head again, but in bewilderment rather than to sooth an irritated scalp. Impatiently tapping his hat against his thigh, he scrutinized the westward landscape. A breeze came up, slicing through his sweat-dampened hair, but it carried no sound. He called out again and waited.

Still nothing.

After several more attempts, he gave up and walked back to the fence. Arriving at the post, he turned towards the valley one last time. The prairie grass was too short to conceal anyone unable to rise from the ground. He had to have been hearing things.

The fence encircled seven thousand acres of North Texas ranchland owned by his employer T. Wayford Cross, a billionaire with many successful business concerns, but whose pride and joy were his seven steakhouses located in the Dallas-Fort Worth Metroplex. His spread, named The Double Cross Ranch, helped keep those restaurants supplied with beef and pork. The valley Jasper had just traversed belonged to the Canton Ranch, owned by T. Wayford's cousin Willis Canton. Willis inherited fifty thousand acres when his dad died, and sold T. Wayford the land that became the Double Cross. He also allowed T. Wayford to hire away his daddy's foreman, Red King, because Willis wanted to get out of the cattle business and raise thoroughbred horses. Jasper had been a rising rodeo star before a bull tore up his knee, ending his career. Red, who'd been a big fan, offered him a job as a ranch hand. He'd started out riding fence and shoveling manure, but soon moved up to more important duties when Red saw he had a natural eye for livestock and a flare for handling them. Everything Jasper knew about ranching he'd learned from Red King. When the old cowboy died of natural causes seven years ago, the job of foreman fell to him.

The fence repair had been delegated to Drake Jensen but his father passed away before he finished the job. He'd left to attend the funeral, and the other hands had chores of their own they couldn't be cut loose from. Jasper didn't lack much wrapping it up, but suppertime drew nigh so he decided to call it a day. He climbed back over the fence, gathered his tools, dropped them in the back of his pickup, and got behind the wheel. His dark eyes glanced at him from the rearview mirror before he backed up. Faint character lines at the corners were the only thing betraying he'd recently turned forty. Not only did he not have a lick of gray anywhere, his curly brown hair hadn't thinned, and nary an ounce of flab had gathered on his lean six-foot-two muscular physique. Since boyhood his mother had proudly claimed he looked like Errol Flynn but his sister maintained he was uglier than sin. If anyone else shared either opinion they'd kept it to themselves.

He drove to the ranch house. As foreman for T. Wayford, or T.W. as a lot of folks called him, he got to live in the two bedroom hacienda rent free. Unlike the four cowboys working under him, who resided in the bunkhouse, he lived alone. Banger, a big mixed-breed hound, wagged his tail once while raising a sleepy eyebrow in greeting as Jasper stepped out of his truck and ambled to the porch.

Closing the front door behind him, he hung his hat beside an empty holster dangling from a coat rack affixed to the immediate right of the entrance. He kept his three-fifty-seven revolver locked in a desk at the far end of the same wall, separated from his gun cabinet by a window facing the front yard. Sitting at a right angle to his desk, situated behind a plain wooden coffee table, a long couch faced an entertainment center on the opposing wall which ended at a short hallway. A fireplace with an easy chair on either side occupied the wall to the left of the hall entrance. Except for the kitchen appliances and a bedroom suit in the spare room, the furniture was his.

Passing the entertainment center, Jasper entered the hall and turned right for the kitchen. He set a bowl of leftover potato salad on the cabinet near a small electric grill and portable timer, then fetched a steak from the fridge. Hooking his fingers in a fold of butcher paper, he ripped it open and unwrapped a twenty ounce rib eye. With the top part seasoned, he left it breathing on a plate, plugged in the grill, and held his right palm over the element until sure it was heating up. Sometimes he had to jiggle the plug to make the damn thing work. Feeling it grow warm, he set the timer for six minutes. Back at the refrigerator, which he often called an icebox, he grabbed a bottle of Lone Star beer, twisted off the cap, and downed a hefty swallow on his way to the table. Salt and pepper shakers, and a roll of paper towels standing on end, adorned the center of a circular tabletop built to accommodate four diners. Close to one edge sat an ashtray, butane lighter, and a ten-pack of Swisher Sweet cigars. Sitting down in front of them, he lit up his first stogie of the day. Afterwards he alternated between puffing and sipping until the timer alerted him it was time to put the steak on the cook.

The perfectly marbled rib eye came from an Angus steer raised on the ranch and would have set him back over fifty dollars if he'd ordered it at one of T. Wayford's restaurants. Using a fork, he placed the seasoned side over the heat, salted and peppered the other, set the timer for eleven minutes, and returned to his chair. Three of the kitchen walls were exterior and had windows, as did the backdoor. Idly staring towards one of them, he couldn't stop thinking about the cry for help and trying to figure out what could have made the sound if he hadn't been hearing things. With no one there it couldn't have been a real woman.

Maybe the wind somehow produced it, he thought unconvincingly. Pondering that possibility took him to Jimi Hendrix's *The Wind Cries Mary.* He'd always loved that song. Unlike the cowboy buddies he grew up with in Waco, he'd never thought it blasphemous listening to anything other than Buck Owens, Merle Haggard, Johnny Cash, George

Jones, or other country musicians. And though he liked ol' Buck and Merle and Johnny and George as much as the next goat roper, he relished rock and roll.

Nostrils starting to get titillated by the savory aroma of sizzling beef, he swallowed a gulp of Lone Star while rising from the chair, and strolled to the window he'd been blankly eyeballing. A row of tall elm trees separated a backyard of Bermuda grass from pasture stretching into the darkening horizon where a line of fence prevented cattle from intruding on the living quarters, slaughterhouse, smokehouse, barn, feed shack, stables, and silo. His thoughts drifted back fifteen years to Pecos, Texas and the last rodeo he'd ever be a participant in. Diablo Toro was the name of the bull that obliterated his knee. The physical pain he'd endured had meant nothing compared to having his lifelong dream annihilated on the chilly arena dirt. That agony would linger until he drew his last breath.

His dark musing came to a screeching halt when something white suddenly appeared near the trees and abruptly vanished, sending goose bumps all over him. A second later it happened again—a flash of white composed of something material rather than some type of light. It was there, then it wasn't. Jasper blinked his eyes and squinted hard but couldn't see a thing besides the usual landscape. Stomach twisting with fear that he might be on the brink of losing his mind—first hearing things and now having hallucinations—he stood there gaping through the pane, wondering what the hell was going on.

The timer dinged, forcing him away from the window . . . .

After eating supper—barely tasting the tender steak, due to preoccupation with the mysterious cry for help and what he'd seen through the window—he stretched out on the couch and watched a rerun of Bonanza which had Hoss Cartwright in it.

Of course he'd never seen any of the episodes that weren't reruns, being he was born after the show ended its run. He didn't particularly enjoy any of the ones made after Dan Blocker passed away. To his delight an old black and white episode of Rawhide followed Bonanza. Had it ever been in color? He wasn't sure but thought some of the last shows might have been. Either way it had the original cast. Poor Eric Fleming, who'd played trail boss Gil Favor, drowned in the prime of his life, but Clint Eastwood had done real good for himself since his Rowdy Yates days. He wondered whatever became of Wishbone and Mushy. While part of him focused on the cattle drovers, another kept reflecting on a frightened feminine voice and the peculiar flash of white.

A western romance followed Rawhide. Unable to get interested in it, he flipped through the myriad channels available to him by the satellite T. Wayford provided. His gut soured as he clicked past one preacher after another trying everything under the sun to fleece their flocks for cash. Disgusted, he turned off the TV and aimed the remote at his CD player. He spent the remainder of the evening with Lone Star beer, The Rolling Stones, Bob Seger, The Who, Bruce Springsteen, Linda Ronstandt, Bob Dylan, and George Strait.

George Strait's *Amarillo by Morning* closed his night. Like always, when George crooned about breaking his leg Jasper started bawling, for it took him painfully back to the end of his rodeo career. Gathering up ten empty bottles of Lone Star—a few in the kitchen, the majority on the coffee table—would be his first chore in the morning before finishing off that section of fence. He drifted to sleep still thinking about the woman crying for help and that oddball flash of white.

2

Jasper had the beer bottles put away and breakfast cooked before daybreak. The sun peeped over the horizon shortly after he sat down to eat. A few minutes later someone banged on the door. Sitting with his back to it, he swallowed a bite of fried egg and hollered, "Bring it!"

Useless Horton, a lanky cotton-haired puncher with a ghostly complexion and rawboned face, walked in.

"Get that hat off."

"Sorry, Boss . . ." Useless snatched a confederate-gray Stetson from his head. Though five years younger, he'd been on the Double Cross longer than Jasper, and like Red, had been a fan during his rodeo days.

Jasper cut off a wedge of sausage from a large patty and brought it to his mouth. "Been to breakfast?"

"Just finished, but wished I hadn't since I see you made sausage. Will take some coffee though."

He'd modified his grandmother's recipe for pork sausage and had never tasted better. Neither had anyone else who'd tried it, or so they said to his face. "What did you boys eat?"

"Dree favored us with his biscuits and gravy, along with ham and eggs."

"That hoss is darn near as good a cook as myself. And since I don't make biscuits, he tops me on that."

Useless set his hat on the table and headed for the coffee maker. "His biscuits *are* dandy but they can't touch your sausage."

"My grandma would be proud to hear you say that, rest her soul. Of course she might turn over in her grave if she knew I tampered with it."

"So what's your secret?" Useless filled a cup as he spoke.

"It's mostly her secret, and if I told you, I'd have to kill you."

Chuckling, he sat down across from him and winked. "Well in that case, keep your damn secret."

"Sure you won't have some?"

"I'm full as a dog tick." He patted his stomach for emphasis and slurped a gulp of coffee.

"I'll finish up Drake's fence chore then be down to give you boys a hand. How many did you get done yesterday?"

"Thirteen Durocs and ten Blue Butts."

"Everything go okay?"

"Yep, scraped 'em and sprayed 'em. No serious bleeding."

"What did you do with the balls, give them to the cats?"

"Yep."

"This time save some for ol' Banger." He capped the sentence with a sip of coffee.

Useless shot him a rankled squint. "That worthless mutt? At least the cats earn their keep around here eating mice. He's about the sorriest excuse for a ranch dog I've ever seen."

"He is for a fact, but he was Red's pet. Once in a while I like to spoil him. Hate it Red didn't get to train him the way he did ol' Bastard. That was the smartest damned dog."

"How old is that mongrel getting to be anyways? Hell he must be a hundred in dog years."

"Seven years old, though he lazes around like he's a hundred, I'll grant you. It's easy for me to remember his age since he was born the same year Red died."

A gloomy sigh escaped the cotton top. "Yeah . . . that was a cold, dark day. There'll never be another Red King."

"Nope, sure won't." He split open a store-bought biscuit, swabbed its insides with grape jelly, and consumed it in three bites.

"When's T.W. coming?"

"Tomorrow."

"Hope he doesn't bring Ginny with him. She hasn't been out here in a long time and I'm afraid we're about due for a visit."

Scooping up the last of his eggs, Jasper winked at him while forking them into his mouth. "What's the matter, you don't like good looking women?"

"You know what I mean. She's the bossiest bitch I've ever seen."

"She is for a fact."

"At least T.W. never stays long when she tags along. That time she came by herself was about the longest workday of my life."

"That's why I suddenly remembered I had to go to town for supplies."

Thin lips forming a sly grin Useless sniggered, "You did squirrel out on that one, didn't you."

"Can't blame me. I got stuck with her once back when she was a teenager. T. Wayford asked me to chaperon her on a shopping trip in Dallas. I thought that day was never going to end."

"When was this?"

"My second year working for Red. You were on vacation at the time. I told T. Wayford if he ever asked me to do that again I'd quit."

"You got balls—" Useless turned up his cup and swallowed

"—bet he hit the ceiling."

"Nope. Told me he respected my honesty and let it go at that." He got up and put the dishes in the sink. "Well, we'd best get to it."

* * * *

The fence didn't take long and Jasper would have driven to the hog pens to help castrate the remaining boars if he hadn't heard the woman cry out again. It came from the same direction as yesterday, and he again didn't find anyone there. Nonetheless there was no longer a doubt in his mind he'd really heard the voice.

"Somebody's fucking with me!" he shouted angrily, pushing through the sunflowers, fully expecting to find a tape recorder or walkie talkie—some sort of sound-transmission device. He kneeled down and spied a horny toad, who eyed him for a cautious moment before scurrying away. Then he located a gopher pile. Though a varmint had obviously created the mound, he smoothed the silky soil with his hand, making sure nothing manmade lay beneath. Gingerly, he rose to his feet, careful not to make his right knee catch. If he came out of a squat the wrong way, the joint locked up, effecting the sensation of a hot chisel being driven beneath his kneecap. This time he succeeded without discomfort, and made his way back towards the fence.

* * * *

Tray Walsh headed towards him as Jasper got out of his pickup. He was the same age as Useless and sported a bushy coal-black handlebar moustache that gave the lower part of his face a walrus appearance whenever it spread with a grin.

The wiry puncher claimed he didn't color it, despite the fact his hair was brown. "Morning, Boss."

"Morning. How you boys getting on?"

"We're done. Just got through as a matter of fact." He held up a plastic bag containing pig testicles.

Jasper was relieved to hear it. Of all the chores on the ranch, he liked castrating pigs the least. Separating baby males from their gonads was practically effortless, but they grew faster with their balls intact. On the Double Cross, boars got to keep their jewels until they reached four months. By then they weighed well over a hundred pounds and required three men to cut them. While two held the wriggling, screaming pig's hind legs in the air with a death grip, the other sliced open the scrotum, removed the glands, and sprayed antiseptic on the wound. Everyone vied to be a leg holder. Jasper didn't like being the surgeon either but never asked anyone to do something he wasn't willing to do himself, so he always took the knife when helping out.

"Useless said you wanted some nuts for Banger. Here's four. Hope that's enough for that lazy hound." He handed over the bag.

"Four'll do."

Tray eased his hat back. "What you want us to do now?"

"Two of you start worming calves and have the other get the bunkhouse spic-and-span for T. Wayford's visit tomorrow."

"I'll let ol' Dree do the cleaning. He's a much better housewife than cowboy."

"He is for a fact." Jasper grinned, looking towards Dree Gillis, walking up from the hog pens, the brim of his black hat shifted low over his eyes. "Speak of the devil."

"Morning, Boss," said Dree.

"Morning."

The youngest of the hands working the Double Cross,

muscular with yellow hair hanging to his shoulders, Dree was one of those handsome cowboys women swooned over. He wore a full beard, a shade darker than his hair, and stood an inch taller than Jasper. His big blue eyes always seemed filled with childlike curiosity. Useless had nicknamed him Thor because he looked like a bearded version of the comic book hero.

Dree wound up a ranch hand the same way he had, but a neck rather than knee injury ended his sports career. For two years he'd played backup tight end for the Miami Dolphins, but at the beginning of his third season he got blindsided by a safety and cracked a vertebra in his neck when he got slammed to the turf. Grateful the hit hadn't paralyzed him, he swore off football and moved back to Texas. Instead of squandering the money he made as a professional ball player, he'd stashed it back and went to work in the oil patch after discovering he wasn't cut out for business administration, which he'd studied in college. Working as a floor hand on a drilling rig suited him until a fellow roughneck lost an arm in an accident, causing him to look for safer employment. He drifted through several odd jobs and wound up slinging hash on a ranch in central Texas. Tired of being kidded about how a cook wasn't a real cowboy, he started learning the ropes.

Mistakenly thinking he'd gained enough experience, he sank his football cash into a cattle spread that he had to sell at a loss only a short year later, leaving him broke by the time he paid off his creditors. After that he took to cooking in restaurants and met T. Wayford at a steakhouse in Fort Worth. Checking out his competition, T. Wayford wanted to meet the cook who'd grilled his steak, which happened to be Dree. They got to trading stories and T. Wayford learned he wanted to go back to ranching. Because they were expected to help outdoors as well as prepare meals, cooks came and went at the

Double Cross, and Jasper had to man the kitchen on top of his usual chores whenever one bailed. Being they'd been in such a situation at the time, T. Wayford had given him a call and asked if he'd be interested in letting an ex pro football player try his hand as full time cook and part time cowboy. Thanks to Dree, Jasper hadn't prepared a meal in the bunkhouse kitchen for almost two years now.

Useless came ambling up. "Got 'er did already, Boss."

"So I'm told."

"What now?"

Tray grinned. "You and me'll worm calves the rest of the day."

Useless pulled off his hat and wiped his brow. "So what's Thor get to do while we're doing that?"

Patting Dree on the back Tray said, "Ol' Thor here gets to clean up the bunkhouse for T.W."

Dree winced. "Aw come on, it's clean enough as it is. I don't want to do house work, that's woman's work."

Jasper smiled at him. "A woman's work is never done."

"Thanks a lot, Boss," he grumbled. "But why do I have to do it?"

"Seniority," said Useless.

"Seniority?"

"Yeah, as in you ain't got none."

That brought a guffaw from Tray.

"Get to it, boys . . ." Jasper held back a laugh as he got in his pickup—Dree looked *some* pissed off. Pig balls resting on the dash, he drove to the ranch house.

Banger raised a wrinkled eyebrow to acknowledge his presence.

"You're in luck, ol' boy. Brought you a surprise."

Lounging just outside his doghouse, the hound eyed the bag and actually wagged his tail more than twice, a rare show of excitement. Jasper emptied it on the ground and grinned as the slothful mutt started gobbling his pig treat. He tossed the baggie in a metal barrel by the front porch. Once used as a fifty gallon oil drum, it now served as a trash can. He gave Banger a pat on the head and got back in his pickup.

They had ninety pounds of bacon curing and two dozen hams marinating in brine water in the smokehouse. After checking their progress Jasper went next door to the slaughterhouse and entered the carcass storage section, constantly kept at a temperature of forty degrees. He walked down a line of hanging beef severed at the spine. Each had a tag denoting the slaughter date. They needed to rest fourteen days afterwards before being processed. Six of them would be ready for butchering in two days. With that part of his daily routine completed, he locked the door and headed for his pickup.

"Help!"

He froze in his tracks.

"Help!"

The cry came from behind the slaughterhouse.

"Help!"

Trotting around back and finding no one there, he scanned the horizon yelling, "Where are you?!"

The woman cried out once more.

A shallow stream that served to water the cattle lay beyond a cluster of trees fifty yards from the slaughterhouse. That's where she had to be. He headed that direction, climbed over the fence, and made it all the way to the brook without seeing anyone. Standing on the bank, looking across the water, he gritted his teeth with anger, again certain the voice wasn't a figment of his imagination. Someone was making a fool of him. "Well I won't bite next time dammit!"

Almost at his pickup, he heard it again. Instead of seeking

out the voice, without looking back he raised his right hand, gave the finger, got behind the wheel, and peeled out.

* * * *

Straddling his cutting horse, Useless herded calves through a chute where Tray forced de-worming medication down their throats with a syringe-gun. Jasper pulled up close to the corral and rolled down his window. "You boys all right?"

Tray raised his hat just enough to run a hand over his scalp. "Doing fine, Boss."

"Got to butcher day after tomorrow."

"How many?"

"Six halves of beef."

Useless galloped over and reined to a stop.

Jasper winked at the cotton top. "Some people always take the easy job, don't they."

"It was Tray's choice."

"I doubt that."

Tray donned a walrus grin. "At least my butt ain't sore."

"Well I'll let you boys get back after it. I'm going to check on Dree."

"Tell him we want chili for supper." Tray shoved the gun into the corner of a young Angus bull's mouth as he spoke.

"Will do . . . ."

Veneered with red brick like the ranch house, the bunkhouse could accommodate up to ten men. The large living room had a massive fireplace, comfortable furniture, and a wall phone for which T. Wayford paid a flat monthly fee so the boys could call anywhere in the country toll free. A long oak table, with a bench on either side and a chair at each end, stretched across the center of the dining room. Swinging doors led to the kitchen. A deep freeze, industrial-sized refrigerator, and humongous pantry stored the food. Two wall ovens and a six-burner stove were used to cook it. Sleeping quarters consisted of five bedrooms, each outfitted with a pair of comfortable beds and two closets. The immense lone bathroom had two showers and a tub for bathing in addition to a whirl pool for soaking sore limbs. Ten lavatories, with a mirrored medicine cabinet above each, afforded every hand his own storage area for dental products and shaving gear. Sanitary needs were met by a full length urinal standing out on the open and two toilets enclosed in metal stalls, beside which sat a washer and dryer.

Jasper stepped inside the facility to find Dree had it gleaming and was working on one of the mirrors. "Looks good, hoss. The boys asked me to pass on they want chili for supper."

"They're getting spaghetti . . ." the big blonde continued wiping.

"Like to live dangerously, don't you."

"They don't scare me. Care to join us?"

"Don't mind if I do."

* * * *

The bunkhouse smelled of meatballs. Jasper took a big pleasant whiff as he hung up his Stetson and went into the dining room where Dree was tossing a huge salad sitting next to the main course.

Useless got up from the end of the table nearest the entrance. "Sit here, Boss, I'll take the bench."

He complied with a thanks.

Tray sat at the other end, still wearing his hat. Jasper wanted to tell him to take it off but didn't as this wasn't his house. As if reading his mind, Tray jerked the brown straight-brim from his head. "Sorry, forgot I still had it on."

"Wearing a hat indoors is akin to blasphemy, it's so ill mannered," Grandpa Miller had always said. The old man had never bothered trying to fart silently though.

Dree situated himself on the bench across from Useless. "Who's gonna turn thanks?"

"I will," said Tray.

Everyone bowed their heads.

"For what we're about to receive may we be truly grateful, amen."

Dree dished out a generous portion of meat-laden noodles on a plate and handed it to him. Then he filled a bowl with salad, doused it with vinegar dressing, placed two slices of toasted garlic bread, smothered with butter, on a saucer, and passed them on. "There you go, Boss. Eat hearty."

"Gracias." Jasper wound spaghetti around his fork and brought the dripping spool to his mouth. It was down right lip smacking. "Damn, Dree. This is outstanding."

"Thanks, Boss. Anywhere near as good as yours?"

"Nobody cooks as good as Jasper Miller," said Useless.

"I know that, but let the man speak for himself."

The expectant look the big blonde was giving him made Jasper feel like a judge at a cook-off. "The only pasta I ever mess with is macaroni and cheese from a box. I've never tasted better than this though."

Dree beamed with elation. "You just made my day, Boss."

"Well you'd have made mine if you'd whipped up a batch of chili and cornbread instead," Useless complained. "If the boss had ever tried some, he'd say the same." Despite appearing so disappointed, he served himself a heaping helping.

"Load me up while you're at it." Tray shoved his plate down the table.

Looking more irritated, Useless ladled spaghetti on the

platter and slid it towards him. "I'm taking your seat next time the boss comes for supper."

Tray shuffled his salad bowl and bread dish down for filling. "Quit your bitching and give me four pieces of toast. I want a full dose of salad but go light on the dressing, I'm watching my figure."

"Yeah, you wouldn't want to mess up that beanpole frame of yours."

"Fuck you, Useless!"

"I ain't piped right and you ain't no plumber, walrus mouth. Here—" Useless fired the toast and salad down the table. Tray barely caught the salad bowl before it sailed off the edge.

Jasper imbibed a scrumptious meatball and took a sip of tea. "Any of you boys been hearing someone cry for help the last day or so?"

"For help?" said Dree.

"Yeah."

"Where at?"

"Anywhere."

"Not me, should I have?"

Useless snickered. "I've been wanting to ask for help but it warn't me."

"No, I mean a woman crying *Help*."

Tray furrowed his brow. "Drake said he was hearing things the other day."

"Where at?"

"On the fence I reckon."

"Did he say what sort of things he was hearing?" Jasper bit off a hunk of garlic toast and started chewing.

"No. Just told me he was hearing things and it was worrying him a little. Said he might ought to get his hearing checked. I told him it was probably just the wind whistling through a tree, but he said he knew that wasn't the case. You think you're hearing things too, Boss?"

He swallowed and began twirling spaghetti for another bite. "I heard a woman cry out for help while I was finishing up Drake's repair on the rim of the Canton ranch where that valley is with the patch of sunflowers. I looked all over but there was no one there. Then today while I was checking on the bacon I heard it again, only this time it seemed like it came from behind the slaughterhouse. It was the eeriest damn thing."

"Sounds eerie," said Tray. A second later his moustache widened with a grin. "Maybe there's a ghost haunting the Double Cross."

"That's sure what somebody's trying to make me think apparently. So none of you boys have heard anything?"

Dree shook his head but Useless shot him a worried frown. "I haven't heard anything, but last night I saw something white come out of nowhere and a split second later it was gone. Figured my eyes were playing tricks on me after being out in the sun all day, but hearing about that mysterious woman, now I ain't so sure."

"There you go," Tray taunted. "There's a ghost haunting the Double Cross all right. Ol' Useless just provided the proof."

Jasper thought about what he'd seen. "What time was it when this happened?"

"Just before supper. I was out on the porch having a smoke and *SWISH!* it came and went."

So something really *had* manifested. "I saw it too."

"You did?"

"Yep." He swabbed his plate with a last bite of Dree's perfectly toasted homemade Italian bread. "Something white just appeared then disappeared, quick as a camera flash, then did it again."

Useless raised his brows warily. "Same thing I saw. Wonder what the hell it was?"

"Couldn't say, but I think someone's pulling a practical joke. It wouldn't be one of you boys now would it?" He popped the toast in his mouth, chewed, and washed it down with a swig of tea.

All three denied having anything to do with it. Seeing they were all serious, he believed them. "Whoever it is, they're slicker than greased snot."

Dree laughed. "Now there's a concept. Greased snot."

"Please, I'm still eating," groaned Useless, face knotted with a sour pout.

"Well I'm done. Dree, it was great . . ." Jasper rose from the table.

"Yeah, you really outdid yourself, Thor. But dammit, can we please have chili and cornbread tomorrow?"

Tray chimed in with Useless, pleading like a child.

A reluctant grin overtook Dree, who'd apparently planned on not giving in. "Oh all right. Chili it is, unless T.W. decides to stay for supper. He told me chili gives him heartburn."

"If T. Wayford stays for supper it'll be a first. You boys enjoy your evening, I'm heading back to la casa."

3

T. Wayford arrived at ten. Thankfully Useless's fear that Ginny might tag along this visit turned out to be groundless. Jasper smiled with relief while walking towards a brand new customized Ford double-cab parked next to his seven-year-old pickup. The tall chubby billionaire got out, grinning as usual, ruddy face and reddish-blonde hair contrasting with the gray cowboy hat he wore. Perched atop a bald scalp, it matched his upscale western suit and boots.

"Good morning, Jasper."

"Morning, T. Wayford."

"Your mule or mine?"

"You'll get your suit dirty if we take mine. Been a while since it's seen a carwash, and needs vacuuming something fierce."

"Heck with that, it don't matter, let's take yours." T. Wayford walked to the passenger door of his pickup.

Jasper beat dust off the seat with his work gloves before letting his boss in, and drove to the smokehouse. He stabbed a key into the lock and turned it. The deadbolt slid back with a sharp clack.

"Ginny and her friend Blane want to spend the weekend. Do some horseback riding."

Shit! Jasper screamed in his mind while opening the door.

"Are you telling me I'm getting kicked out of my house this weekend?"

"Well not unless you want to," laughed T. Wayford.

"Do I really have a choice?"

"They can stay in the spare bedroom, you don't have to leave. That's why Red only wanted one bathroom and insisted on it being in the hall when I had the place built, so guests wouldn't have any excuse to go in his bedroom."

He couldn't believe T. Wayford was going to allow his daughter and some dude to sleep in the same bed. The shock obviously showed on his face because the big man scowled at him while saying, "Blane's a girl."

"Oh." Not only had the name thrown him, Jasper didn't figure Ginny had any chums that didn't piss standing up, she was such a bitch.

T. Wayford inspected the bacon. "This batch is darn near ready. You and the boys keep a few pounds for yourselves and put the rest on the truck Friday. How much beef can I expect by then?"

"Got six halves that'll have hung two weeks tomorrow."

"Tomorrow's Thursday, think you can get them all chopped in a day?"

"We'll stay after it till we get 'er did."

"Good. Let's have a look at them . . . ."

After reading the tags on every carcass, T. Wayford turned to him and tilted his hat back. "I see you'll have another four ready by next Friday."

"That's right." Jasper pulled the labels from the half-sections of Angus prepared for processing.

"What about the pork?"

"Got about two hundred pounds each of ribs, chops, and ground."

"Send it along, but keep a few racks of ribs for you and the boys. And siphon off five pounds of the ground for yourself. I know you like to make your own sausage."

Jasper grinned. "Much obliged. Wish you'd try some. You might just move me up in the world—have me supplying your greasy spoons with some good sausage for a change."

T. Wayford let go a belly laugh. "What, and fire ol' Ben Bishop?"

"Well, he's getting on up there in years. You're going to have to replace him sooner or later."

"That nigger'll outlive us all." T. Wayford said the term with affection, often calling Ben that to his face. The black octogenarian called the tycoon Honky Boss in return. "You wouldn't know what to do with yourself living in the city. Besides, even if it's as good as I've heard tell, you don't make the right type."

"Sad but true." Ben Bishop had been making smoked sausage, Chorizo, and hot links for T. Wayford since the latter ventured into the food business back in the eighties. Though he'd made his initial fortune in oil, T. Wayford's restaurants were his passion and Ben Bishop's fabulous meat wares could be found nowhere else. None of the outlets opened before five in the afternoon so they didn't serve breakfast sausage, the only kind Jasper knew how to make.

They drove to the finishing stalls so T. Wayford could see how the steers fared, then he wanted to have a look at the hogs being fattened for slaughter. Lunchtime arrived and they motored to the bunkhouse.

T. Wayford settled at one end of the table and he took the other. Tray and Useless sat across from each other on the benches while Dree served lunch—fried chicken, mashed potatoes, gravy, hot rolls, corn on the cob, and salad.

"Good chicken, Dree," said T. Wayford, gripping a thigh with a large bite missing. "What's for dessert?"

"Apple pie and ice cream."

"Well I'd better save room for some then, hadn't I."

Jasper bit into a breast. A scrumptious mix of crunchy breading, tender white meat, and chicken fat exploded in his mouth. While savoring the flavor, he noticed Useless and Tray obviously found it delectable as well. They were face-over-plate, chomping away like a couple of hogs.

Dree seated himself on the bench a couple of feet from Useless. "How's Ginny doing, T.W.?"

T. Wayford had a mouthful but answered anyway. "Funny you should ask. She and a girlfriend are going to spend the weekend out here, and I want you boys to behave yourselves."

Though Dree managed to keep a straight face, Useless and Tray looked as if they might upchuck. Thankfully, T. Wayford was too preoccupied with his grub to notice. An awkward moment later Tray, obviously trying to hide his anguish over such unwelcome tidings, grinned at the billionaire, the lower rim of his moustache grease-soaked from the chicken. "Dang it, we never get to have no fun."

"Jasper, lock ol' Tray up in the smokehouse for the duration of Ginny's visit. I don't need a horny cowpuncher chasing my little girl around all weekend."

"Will do," he obliged with a wink towards Tray.

Tray placed a chicken bone on the edge of his plate and picked up his corn on the cob. "How about I just chase the friend and leave Ginny alone?"

Now T. Wayford was grinning. "What if her friend's ugly?"

"In that case just go ahead and lock me in the smokehouse."

Everyone laughed and Useless said, "Did you know your ranch is haunted, T.W.?"

"Haunted?"

"Sure is. Got a ghost running around the Double Cross."

Jasper reached for his iced tea. "What Useless is talking about is a flash of white he and I saw night before last."

"A flash of white?"

"Mm hmm. Something white just appeared then disappeared twice out back by the elm trees."

"Yeah," said Useless, "and the boss has been hearing an invisible woman crying for help."

T. Wayford frowned. "Where abouts, Jasper?"

"The first time she seemed to be hollering from behind some sunflowers on Willis's ranch. I climbed over the fence and looked all over but there was nobody there. The next time I heard her I was at the slaughterhouse. I think someone's pulling a practical joke, but the boys here assure me it's not them."

"Well I'll be. Talk to Willis about it?"

"No."

"Hmm." T. Wayford wiped chicken grease off his hands with a cloth napkin sporting The Double Cross insignia stitched on each corner, reached into his coat, and brought out a cell phone. "I'll give him a call right now . . . ."

Like the boys, Jasper kept eating while T. Wayford asked his cousin if he'd been hearing cries for help, or seeing flashes of white, or witnessing anything else out of the ordinary.

"All right. Talk atcha later, Willis." T. Wayford slipped the phone into his coat and went back to work on his chicken. "Willis hasn't heard or seen anything. Whichever one of you is pulling pranks, make sure you're not shirking your chores while you're doing it."

Dree and Tray protested their innocence and the matter was dropped.

Jasper looked at Useless. "After lunch, you and Tray go ahead and quarter the six beef halves that don't have tags. We'll slice 'em up tomorrow."

"What do you want me to do, Boss?" said Dree.

"Clean the ranch house for Ginny and her friend. We'll need you tomorrow, or I'd let you do it then."

The big blonde heaved a frustrated sigh.

"A woman's work is never done," razzed Tray. "The price you pay for being born purty."

Useless snorted while buttering an ear of corn. "Hell if I was purty like Thor I'd rent my dick out at ten bucks a minute instead of doing housework. When's Drake due back, Boss?"

"Some time today."

"I thought there was a warm body missing," said T. Wayford. "Where is that cowboy anyway?"

"He had to go to Dallas for his dad's funeral."

"Oh . . ." he raised his brows. "Sorry to hear it. Sad state of affairs for ol' Drake."

After lunch Jasper saw T. Wayford off and checked on a Duroc sow that had dropped a dozen piglets three days ago. Two of the little porkers were runts who hadn't shown any interest in latching onto a tit. Expecting to find both dead, he was pleasantly surprised to see their butts sticking out alongside their larger siblings' as poor mama had her nipples ravaged. Relieved he didn't have to climb in the pen to remove their corpses, he headed for the ranch house to update his bookwork while Dree spruced up the place. He kept the ranch log on a spread sheet in his computer. Shortly after four he turned from his desk when he heard a knock on the front door, which soon sprang open.

"Anybody home?" Drake Jensen took off his hat while stepping into the living room.

Jasper saved his work and rose to greet him.

The rangy cowpuncher's naturally sad brown eyes reflected the struggle to overcome a passage through one of life's dark valleys. His mouth looked grim amidst a salt-and-pepper beard that made him appear older than his thirty-seven years. "Hello, Boss."

"Welcome back." He gave Drake a hug. "Sure sorry for your loss."

"I know . . . sad as it was, it was good to see the family again."

"Well I see you developed a thing for men while you were away," said Dree, walking in as they parted.

Drake cracked a grin and held out his arms. "Come here, you."

Dree obliged. "You gonna be okay?"

"Yeah . . ." he patted Dree on the back. "Life goes on."

Jasper gave the bereaved cowboy a close going over. Having lost his own father, he knew full well how bad it hurt. Drake seemed to be holding up to it as well as could be expected, at least on the surface. "Well let's all have a cup of coffee, what do you say?"

"While you're away from your desk I'll take the opportunity to polish it and mop the living room floor, Boss. Then I'll be done."

"Naw, they're fine. You're done now."

Dree smiled appreciatively. "Well don't expect me to argue with you on that."

"Boss got you doing his dirty work again?"

"Doesn't he always . . .?"

Jasper started a pot of coffee and joined the two hands at the table. "Had a couple of unusual happenings while you were away. I understand you thought you were hearing things?"

Drake frowned at him. "Who told you that?"

"Tray."

"I don't remember telling him that."

"Well he told me you did."

"Huh." It was an expression rather than a question. Drake used it a lot.

"Well, were you hearing things or not?"

"Yeah. Just don't remember telling anybody about it."

"Well tell *me* about it."

"I was working on that fucked up section of fence you'd told me to mend, when I could have sworn I heard a woman holler for help. I looked all around trying to find her but never did see anybody, so figured I had to be hearing things. You know, now that I think about it I did tell Tray. What's the unusual things that happened to you?"

Jasper folded his hands on the table. "Same damn thing. I was finishing up your repair, and just like you, couldn't find a soul. Then it happened again at the slaughterhouse."

"Don't forget the flash of white," said Dree.

"Flash of white?"

He told him about the aberration.

"Huh. What do you think it was, Boss?"

"Don't know."

"You think it's connected to the cry for help?"

"Don't know that either. But if someone's pulling a joke on us—and that's what I think's going on—you can bet they're connected."

Drake leaned his chair back a mite and sighed. "Well I never saw anything but I did hear the cry, and since you heard it too I couldn't have been hearing things. This flash of white of yours, what did it look like?"

"Picture staring at an empty clothesline. All of a sudden a white sheet's hanging on it and before you can blink it's gone. Best I can describe it."

"Huh."

The coffee maker gurgled as a rich aroma wafted from the half-filled pot. Dree took note of the progress. "I'll have to take a rain check on the coffee, Boss. Just remembered I promised Useless and Tray chili for supper and it takes a couple of hours to make, so I'd better get after it."

A big grin jumped on Drake's face. "Got me looking forward to chow time, hoss."

"Glad to hear it," quipped Dree, grabbing his hat from the cabinet as he made for the backdoor.

Jasper resumed the conversation. "If it's a practical joke, how are they doing it you reckon? I looked all over for a tape recorder or walkie talkie but couldn't find one."

"I don't think it's a joke, Boss. I think it's for real, now that I know for sure I wasn't just hearing things."

A shiver went through him at that notion. The worried look Drake had taken on made him decide to change the subject. "Butchering tomorrow."

"Hogs or steers?"

"Steers."

"Am I butchering too?"

"Yeah, and I'm going to let Dree help. I know he doesn't do a bang up job of it yet, but anything he messes up we'll eat. I think he'll be fine with a little practice."

Drake nodded. "A feller can't learn without doing."

"That's a fact."

"Useless and Tray will give him hell though if he screws up like he did the last time you let him try his hand at it."

Jasper blew out a weary sigh. "Speaking of hell. T. Wayford was by this morning and I've got some real bad news. Ginny and a girlfriend are spending the weekend."

"Oh no . . .!" Drake reared back, features contorting into a dire grimace.

"Afraid so."

"I knew I should have stayed in Dallas till Monday."

"This too shall pass." Noticing the coffee maker had quit

gurgling, Jasper got up and poured them each a cup. When he sat back down, Drake fished a package of Winston's from the pocket of his blue jean shirt.

"Let me bum one of those . . ." Jasper reached across the table.

"Thought you only smoked cigars, and only at night since you quit cigarettes."

"That's the rule I laid out for myself, but you know the old saying. Rules are made to be broken."

Drake laughed and handed him one.

Jasper lit the cigarette and exhaled. "Besides, it's not that far till night time . . . ."

* * * *

Drake left at suppertime and Jasper dined alone as he usually did in the evenings, opting for his own catfish instead of Dree's chili. Gazing through a kitchen window with Lone Star and cigar in hand, he tried to think of an excuse to leave the ranch for the weekend so he wouldn't have to put up with Ginny Cross. A heavy sigh emerged. Even if he had a reason, he couldn't leave the boys at her mercy for that long a time. They'd never forgive him. He started to turn from the window but stopped when something white appeared between two elms and suddenly vanished.

Jasper tore out the door and made for the trees.

"Help me!"

It came from the direction of the ranch house behind him. Banger started barking. Jasper turned back and hurried to the dog, now snarling towards the front porch, canines fully exposed. By the illumination of the safety light, perched high on a telephone pole near the house, Jasper could see the hair on Banger's back standing on end.

"Easy boy . . ." he patted the dog's head.

The hound finally hushed, but kept leering at the porch. Though draped in shadows created by the light beaming down on the roof, Jasper could clearly see there was nobody there. He kept petting Banger, watching and listening. Ten uneventful minutes later he went back inside.

4

Mid-afternoon Friday they'd scarcely finished loading a refrigeration truck with processed beef and pork for transport to Fort Worth when a pink Corvette Stingray pulled up to the slaughterhouse. Jasper winced. *Why the hell did Ginny drive to the slaughterhouse instead of stopping at the ranch house?*

It was going to be a long weekend, he could already tell.

She got out from behind the wheel and a blonde woman exited from the passenger's side. A tall beauty with strawberry blonde hair and light-brown eyes that were sexier than hell but always threatening, Ginny had a perfect figure which she dressed to show off. Her designer western shirt, exposing just enough cleavage to force a man's eyes to her large breasts, clung to a narrow waist, accentuating very shapely hips. If they'd been painted on, her jeans couldn't have fit any tighter. "Jasper, get one of your cowboys to unload our things this instant! Why weren't you at the ranch house? You knew we were coming!"

He'd known her since she was a twelve-year-old kid, having met her, T. Wayford, and Red King at a National Finals Rodeo he'd snagged second place in two years before Diablo Toro busted up his knee. Though pushing thirty now, she hadn't grown up a damn bit. "We had things to do. Now drive on back to the house and I'll be there directly to unload your luggage."

"What a bitch," said Tray under his breath, just loud enough the other hands could hear.

"She is for a fact." Jasper headed towards Ginny, standing with hands on hips as if she hadn't heard a word he'd said to her. "You just gonna stand there or do what I told you? If you want help unloading, you'd best drive on back to the house, I'm sure not going to lug it from here."

Ginny shot him a harsh sneer, then turned to her friend. "Come on, Blane." Within seconds she peeled out, leaving a cloud of dust to settle on him and the others.

He signaled the driver to take off, got in his pickup, and drove to the ranch house. Ginny and her friend had already gone inside, leaving the trunk of her car open. Jasper grabbed three pink suitcases and carried them to the front porch, wondering why she'd packed so many clothes just to spend a weekend horseback riding. Before he could set the luggage down to open the door, it swung inward and Ginny waved him in as if *he* was the visitor.

"You want these in the bedroom I take it."

"Please," she said with a sarcastic smile.

Once relieved of his burden, he took off his hat and went back to the living room.

Ginny honed in on him with a gaze reminiscent of an avaricious bird of prey eyeing a soon-to-be-eaten target. "Jasper Miller, meet Blane Weathers."

The attractive blonde had kind blue eyes that were polar opposites of Ginny's predatory orbs. Their builds were similar but Blane was a few inches shorter and not quite as well favored as her snotty friend. A tight fitting blouse went all the way up to the base of her throat, revealing no skin. Hat held against his chest, he gave her a nod. "Hi there."

"Hello. I've been informed you're quite a cook. Looking

forward to dinner."

Her accent wasn't Texan. He started to ask where she was from but Ginny spoke.

"I bragged on your steaks and promised you'd grill us one tonight."

She had a lot of nerve making promises for him, and her brag was bullshit. Ginny Cross didn't dole out compliments without an ulterior motive. The snot box obviously had something up her sleeve and that didn't bode well at all. "Dree's a hell of a cook, Blane. You might want to eat with the boys over at the bunkhouse."

"Not a chance," Ginny spouted firmly.

"Dree, that's an unusual name."

"He's the hunk I told you about."

"And he can cook too?" laughed Blane. "Is he single?"

"All these cowboys are. I think they're all queer—especially Jasper." She stuck her tongue out at him.

Keenly aware Ginny was hoping to get him riled, he ignored the remark and childish action.

"I had the biggest crush on him when I was a teenager but he never even noticed I was alive. That's why I think he's queer. Made Daddy have him chaperon me one day and I tried every trick in the book but he never gave me a tumble."

"Quit talking about me like I'm not here." He turned to Blane. "She never had a crush on me. And if she'd really wanted a tumble, I'd still be locked up in the state pen for molesting a minor."

Ginny's arrogant facade shifted into an expression he'd never seen her wear before. She looked vulnerable. "Do you really mean that?"

Ignoring her question he started for the door. "I've got work to do. I'll start supper at six."

* * * *

Jasper saddled up his paint gelding he called No Name after the song *Horse With No Name* by America, and headed westward in search of Drake, Useless, and Tray. They'd resumed branding cattle after helping him load the refrigeration truck. Fifteen minutes later he found Useless working the fire while Drake and Tray roped the calves.

"You boys doing okay?"

Useless nodded. "Just fine, Boss. Figured you'd be entertaining the ladies."

"Now that's what I call a good time, getting ball-busted by Ginny Cross," said Tray, dismounting his horse and wrestling a calf to the ground he had roped around the neck. Holding a glowing branding iron forged into the Double Cross emblem—two X's in a forty-five degree slant—Useless stabbed the flank. The smell of burnt hair accompanied the sound of sizzling flesh and a protesting bovine.

"Thought I'd give you boys a hand."

"No need." Tray liberated the calf and the young Angus scurried away with a fearful moo. "There's only a handful left."

Drake galloped up with a young bull in tow, dismounted, and forced his quarry onto its side. "Still got your cojones, Boss?"

"So far, so good, but Ginny's just getting warmed up."

Useless applied the brand. "Sad a looker like that has to be such a bitch."

"It is for a fact."

As the calf scampered off with a smoking haunch, Drake shoved his hat back and wiped his brow. "Remember telling us this morning you heard the cry for help again last night?"

"Yeah," Jasper answered warily.

"Well I heard it again a little while ago. Tray heard her too."

"Yeah," said Tray. "Spooky as hell. We couldn't find *no*-body."

"Somebody's yanking us, but damned if I can figure out how. Where did y'all hear it?"

"Come on and I'll show you."

"Lead the way . . . ."

Tray halted near an oak and pointed at the tree. "Came from there."

"Funny ain't it? Always seems to be something to hide behind every time."

"I'm telling you, Boss, I think we might really be dealing with a ghost."

"No we're not." Jasper dismounted and commanded No Name to stand still.

"Well how do you explain it then?"

"We're dealing with a slick practical joker, Tray, not a ghost." He examined the ground around the tree, hoping to find evidence of a buried sound-transmitting device, but the soil hadn't been disturbed. Confused as hell at how the prankster was pulling it off, he climbed back on his saddle. "Well if you boys don't need me, guess I'll see if Dree wants help rustling up the grub."

Tray's walrus grin appeared. "Anything to keep away from Hurricane Ginny, huh?"

"Something like that . . . ."

Dree didn't need help, but since he had forty-five minutes to kill before starting supper and didn't want to spend it around the berating Ginny, Jasper decided to loiter in the bunkhouse kitchen. To his dismay, mere seconds after he made the decision she and Blane walked in.

"Dree, this is my friend Blane Weathers. I can't remember

your last name if I ever knew it." Ginny almost sounded polite.

"Gillis." Dree aimed a charming smile at Blane, who was blatantly eyeballing him, obviously enthralled.

She acquired a flirtatious grin. "Pleased to meet you. So what are you making?"

"Pork chop stew, a Gillis original."

"That big hunk of meat you're chopping isn't a pork chop," snapped Ginny, voice regaining its customary snotty edge.

"No, it's pork shoulder."

"Then why don't you call it shoulder stew since that's what it really is?"

"Because pork chop stew sounds more appetizing than shoulder stew. Has a better nuance to it, don't you think?"

A cruel laugh erupted from the bitch. "Nuance? You're not a gourmet chef, dufus. You cook for cowboys who can't even spell the word. What are you, all looks and no brains? Well I guess you'd have to be, wouldn't you. Otherwise you wouldn't be stuck on a ranch feeding a bunch of hick losers."

Jasper wanted to slap her but opted for a more diplomatic course of action. "You're speaking out of school, Ginny. Ol' Dree damn sure is a gourmet chef, but he just happens to like ranching too."

"I wouldn't know since I've never tasted his cooking."

"And with that attitude you never will." He forced himself to remain calm, feeling bad for Dree, who chopped away in silence, a red tint on his temples revealing the big blonde felt angry or intimidated, or both.

"Suits me. Get one of your cowboys to saddle us up two horses and be quick about it. We want to do a little riding before dinner."

Fighting an irresistible urge to bend the arrogant bitch over his knee and spank the hell out of her, Jasper took a deep breath and held it several seconds before callously blowing it out. "The boys are busy, I'll do it. Follow me."

Clearly taken aback by her friend's rude behavior, Blane meekly raised a hand and bobbled her fingers to gesture goodbye, but Dree kept his eyes on the meat, a closed-mouth smile conveying his relief at the prospect of being rescued from Ginny.

Twenty minutes later Jasper had the women aboard two gentle mounts. "I'll wait till you're done before I start supper so your steaks will be fresh. Bring the horses back here and tie their reins to the hitching post. I'll have one of the boys take care of them before calling it a day."

"Thanks," said Blane. Ginny showed her appreciation by goosing her horse and galloping away.

* * * *

It was almost sunset so the girls couldn't be much longer. Jasper placed three thick T-bones on a cutting board to let them breathe, and twisted the cap off a Lone Star, irritated because over two hours had passed since the time he'd plainly stated supper would commence. Before he downed his first swallow the snooty wench pranced through the backdoor with Blane in tow.

Ginny eyed his beer. "I see you still drink cow piss."

"You wouldn't hold it against me would you?"

Blane laughed but Ginny gave her a sharp look. "Have you ever tasted Lone Star beer, Blane? I tell you, it really does taste like cow piss."

He winked at Blane. "As only Ginny would know. Never tasted cow piss myself."

She giggled and cut her eyes to Ginny. "Neither have I."

Ignoring his comeback, the stuck-up heir to T. Wayford's billions took note of the steaks. "Unless you're planning on eating two of those, you'd better put one back. One is more than Blane and I will be able to eat together. And no potatoes for us, we're low carbing."

"Low carbing," he muttered with annoyance while removing a beautifully marbled cut of beef that had almost enough tenderloin to be deemed a porterhouse.

Blane eyed the two remaining. "Those look scrumptious."

"Daddy's Angus always does. Come on, let's get washed up."

He gave Blane's butt a good going over as she followed Ginny into the hall. Though not as shapely as Ginny's faultless ass, The Man Upstairs had done a very good job on it. Thinking how the good Lord had definitely blessed her with a far superior personality to the bitch's, he pulled a head of lettuce and two bell peppers from the icebox to hack up for a salad.

When they returned, Ginny put a bottle of wine in the freezer compartment of the fridge.

"What the hell are you doing?" He pointed his knife at the icebox while saying it.

"Needs to chill a little. Meant to put it in the fridge when we first got here but forgot."

"Well don't leave it too long, the bottle will break if it freezes."

"I know that, smart ass! About ten minutes in the freezer will chill it just enough."

He sliced an onion in half and started dicing it.

"Can I help with anything?" asked Blane sweetly.

"No, but thanks for offering."

She sat down at the table. Ginny joined her and they started jabbering girl talk like they were alone. He let his mind wander back to the cry for help. It had to be someone messing with them but how were they doing it, and why were they doing it? After awhile his thoughts drifted to the state inspector's visit. In order for T. Wayford to legally serve them in his restaurants every steer and hog had to be inspected before being slaughtered, and again after they were halved and hung. Two hogs were due to meet their fate on Monday and he hoped the inspector would be on time for a change. The punctual examiner he'd dealt with since the Red King era retired three months ago, and only twice had his replacement not shown up late. On his last visit he'd kept them waiting almost three hours.

The timer dinged. He put their steak on the grill and set the dial.

"Don't suppose you have any wine glasses do you?" Ginny haughtily quizzed.

"Wine glasses? How about jelly glasses."

She perused his cabinets. "Good grief, Jasper. Besides coffee cups all I see is jelly glasses. God you're an uncultured dweeb, aren't you." Selecting two, she set them on the table, took the wine from the freezer, and thrust it towards him, demanding he open it.

"Well since you asked so nicely . . ." he took the bottle from her and unscrewed the cap. "Good thing this is a twist off because I don't have a cork screw."

Ginny took it from him, filled the glasses, and screwed the cap back on. "Now I'll put it where you keep your cow piss."

Blane took a sip of wine and smiled. "That steak smells wonderful."

"Wait till you taste it. Nobody can cook a steak like Jasper Miller."

"Angus is pretty hard to beat," he said, wondering what Ginny expected from him in return for the fictitious praise. She'd only eaten his cooking one time, years ago when he'd grilled a bunch of steaks and burgers for a fourth of July barbecue.

"Do you have other breeds too?"

"The Double Cross raises Angus exclusively," Ginny butted in before he could answer.

He winked at Blane. "Well now that's not altogether true. We raise hogs too."

Ginny sneered at him. "You know I meant beef."

Facing the grill again, he turned up his Lone Star.

"What type of hogs do you raise, Jasper?" asked Blane.

"Duroc and Blue Butt."

"I'm not familiar with those but I've heard of Hampshire."

"Durocs are red pigs. Blue Butts are pinkish white-haired pigs with a slight skin discoloration around their butts that's grayish-blue. That's why they're called Blue Butts. And you say you've heard of Hampshire? The original Blue Butts on this ranch were Hampshire and Yorkshire crosses. The Hampshire is a black pig with a band of white across the shoulders. Yorkshire's are white. Blue Butts aren't a true breed, just a cross between a black hog and a white hog. If you cross a Hampshire with a Chester White, for instance, you'll also get Blue Butts."

"I didn't know that." Ginny's tone conveyed interest instead of sarcasm, a rarity.

"What happens if you cross a Duroc with a Blue Butt, Jasper?" Blane inquired further.

"Most of the babies will look like Durocs or Blue Butts as if the two hadn't been crossed. But every now and then you get a light brown pig, and sometimes they'll have dark spots. A few of them come out looking almost like a leopard. All the hogs we have now are crosses from the original two herds, even though most of them look like pure Duroc or Blue Butt."

"I did know that," shot Ginny, sounding high and mighty like usual.

"Well, I didn't. Thanks for sharing that."

He set the table, put the steak on a platter, placed it beside a large bowl of salad, and cut off a third for each of them. Then he put his own meat on the grill.

"Oh you weren't kidding, Ginny. This is delicious."

Feeling pretty immodest over Blane's remark, he chuckled inside. Truth was he'd never eaten a better steak than one he'd cooked himself. Quality meat grilled over the right amount of heat for the exact length of time its thickness caller for never failed, and no beef tasted better than properly fed Angus.

"Told you, didn't I," said Ginny.

Her tenor made him wonder if the previous compliments were sincere. That sure as hell would be a first. What she'd tasted that fourth of July had been grilled over mesquite coals in a barbecue pit, giving the meat a far superior flavor than the electric grill could. It surprised him she didn't say something about the difference.

The girls finished eating by the time the last ding sounded for his T-bone. They refilled their glasses and went to the living room, leaving him to eat his supper in relative peace and quiet. He almost had the first bite to his mouth when Ginny hollered, "Come show us how to work your stereo!" Wedge of steak still impaled on the fork, he lowered it to his plate.

Five minutes later The Judds blared down the hall.

Sitting with his back to the kitchen door, he raised the fork again but a muscle tightened up, shooting a tingling irritation up the back of his neck. He slapped the spot and rubbed it until the sensation dissipated. Afterwards he rolled his head and turned it side to side to loosen the sinew and prevent a recurrence. In mid motion he abruptly froze. From the corner of his eye he saw a woman standing outside the window, dressed in white with a veil covering her face. Before he could get up from the chair she was gone. He bolted through the backdoor as fast as his knee would allow, but to no avail. She was nowhere to be found.

When he first heard the cry at the fence he'd felt concern for the safety of an unknown woman. The cries at the slaughterhouse had irritated him. Last night's white-flash and subsequent plea had mystified him. But now he was flat out scared.

Banger started howling.

Jasper forced himself to go around the house, fearing Tray's ghost talk might be right after all. When he got to the front porch he heard only the muffled noise of music playing in the living room—Banger hushed upon seeing him. He patted the hound's head, traversed the other side of the house, and went back to the kitchen door. Scanning the entire perimeter illuminated by the safety light, he couldn't spot anything out of the ordinary. Finally he gave up and went back inside.

Appetite stolen by the vanishing woman, he shoved his plate in the fridge without bothering to cover it. Then he dumped the girl's leftovers onto the steak platter and ambled through the living room to give them to Banger. Ginny waved at him from the couch. Hollering loud enough to be heard above the blasting Judds, she demanded he join them. Ignoring her, he went outside and gave the hound his treat. When he came back through she bellowed the command again.

He scowled at her and turned the volume down. "This is as loud as you get. You're liable to blow my speakers."

She pouted up. "Party pooper! Come join us. You're the closest thing to a man we have to talk to even if you *are* queer."

Listening to music was the last thing he wanted to do at the moment, but if he told them why he'd have two hysterical women on his hands. Stalling for time he said, "Let me get my beer and a smoke first."

Back in the kitchen he grabbed his beer and fired up a cigar but went outside instead of returning to the living room. He headed for the bunkhouse, two hundred feet away, to see if any of the boys had spotted the veiled woman.

None of them had seen or heard anything.

Useless looked up at him from an overstuffed armchair facing the TV. "Still think someone's yanking us?"

"Uh-uh. That woman didn't look like she was pulling a prank."

"What *did* she look like, Boss?" asked Tray.

"Like I said, she had a veil over her face and was wearing some sort of white garb."

"Like a wedding dress?"

"Yeah, I reckon."

"Was she a white woman?"

"Far as I could tell."

"Could she have been an Indian?"

"Couldn't say. I only saw her for a second. Why, Tray?"

"You know them old stories about Indian burial grounds being disturbed, causing the dead to come back and all that? Maybe this land was once an Indian cemetery and we've done something to piss off their spirits."

Drake coughed out a nervous laugh and brought the recliner he'd been lounging in upright. "Let's not get carried away."

"Maybe it's ol' mother nature come to haunt us," said Useless, wearing one of his obnoxious grins.

Jasper flicked his cigar ash into the fireplace. "Whatever she is, she can come and go quicker than anything I've ever seen."

Dree eyed him from the couch. "If it is someone messing

with you, maybe they're projecting a hologram like they use at Disney Land. It would explain your flash of white and how the woman disappeared so fast. But I don't know if it's possible to beam one from such a great distance the equipment can't be seen."

"Sure don't seem possible to me . . ." Tray downed the last of a Coors and crumpled the can. "I think we're dealing with a real ghost, Boss."

The door burst open, startling everyone. But instead of the apparition in white, Ginny and Blane stepped in.

Features blazing with fury, Ginny leered at him. "Thought you were going to join us!"

"I was. Just had to line the boys out on a few things first." He made a face, hoping the crew could tell from his expression he didn't want Ginny and Blane to know what they'd been talking about.

A sly grin telecasted Useless caught on. "Sure, Boss, be glad to do the shopping tomorrow."

"Uh . . . real good. I need storm supplies." Jasper fished out his wallet and handed him a fifty. Now he didn't even have a supply run to use as an excuse to get away from Ginny for awhile. Useless had outsmarted him and he couldn't do a thing about it.

Blane squinted at him. "Storm supplies?"

"Beer," said Tray with a wink.

She giggled. "I've never heard beer called that before."

"Told you they were queer," Ginny snidely interjected.

Tray started moving his eyebrows up and down. "Come on into the bedroom with me and I'll show you how queer I am."

"Ha! In your dreams, shit face!" Ginny glared at him with the condescension of a queen, insulted by a flirtatious remark from the court jester. "You couldn't handle a real woman like me and you know it."

"Wanna bet? Truth is you can't handle a real man like me."

Hands flying to hips, she snapped her head his way. "Are you just going to stand there, Jasper? You can't let him talk to me like that!"

He blew out a bitter sigh. "You started it."

"Damn right she did."

"That's enough, Tray," he warned, still looking at Ginny. "And you back off too."

Outrage and indignance exploded on her face. "You don't tell me what to do, Jasper Miller! You may be in charge of these losers but you're damn sure not in charge of me!"

"I'm in charge of this ranch which means I'm in charge of you as long as you're on it."

"We'll see about that! What till I see Daddy and tell him how you treated me!"

"Call him. No need to wait."

She glowered at him but didn't accept his invitation.

"Here, let me get him for you . . ." he stepped to the wall phone, picked up the receiver, and started dialing.

"Come on, Blane, let's go back to the ranch house." She shot him one last look of contempt while crossing the room. "My daddy's ranch house!"

Jasper hung up the phone when she pulled the front door open. A high-pitched scream pierced his eardrums as she slammed it shut from the inside. In the blink of an eye Ginny was in his arms hyperventilating, clutching him so tight he could barely breathe. While trying to compose himself he noticed every face in the room had the same look of shock. It took quite an effort to pry her loose. "Tell me what you saw."

Though she tried to answer, only violent gasps came out of her mouth as she struggled for breath.

"You saw a woman, didn't you—a woman dressed in white with a veil."

A vigorous nod assured she had.

Dree ran out the door. Tray and Drake bounded outside right behind him. Useless, who'd been relaxing barefoot, hurriedly yanked his boots on and joined the chase. Jasper didn't bother. He knew they weren't going to find her.

Confusion and alarm radiated from Blane's fear-widened eyes. "Jasper, what's going on?"

"Ginny saw a woman. The same woman I saw earlier. That's the real reason I came over here—to see if any of the boys saw her." He grabbed Ginny's hands, trying to calm her. "Where was she?"

Still gulping air, Ginny managed to get out, "At . . . the . . . door."

He turned to Blane. "I saw her standing at a kitchen window. A second later she flat out disappeared."

Slack-jawed, perplexity riveted to her face, she mumbled, "I don't understand."

"Neither do I . . . ."

Ten minutes later the boys came back. As he figured, none of them saw a thing. He had Ginny calmed down and sitting on the couch with a glass of water. Blane sat beside her with one of Tray's Coors. Noticing him eyeing the beer Jasper said, "Took the liberty of telling her she could have one. Hope you don't mind."

"That's okay, Boss."

Blane looked up at Tray and smiled. "Thank you."

A clap of thunder rattled the walls as a hard rain started falling.

Useless gawked at him. "Boss, I was just outside and there wasn't a cloud in the sky."

"He's right." Drake scratched nervously at his beard. "The sky was full of stars."

Jasper took a deep breath and exhaled a ragged sigh. "Not

that unusual for a storm to come up fast around here."

Another thunderclap roared, leaving everyone silent, listening to the pounding rain . . . .

5

The three of them were drenched by the time they reached the kitchen door. Jasper had waited almost an hour, but the rain showed no signs of letting up, so it had boiled down to either braving the weather or sleep in the bunkhouse. The prospect of the trouble that would cause wasn't worth staying dry over. While trying to wait out the storm, he'd told Ginny and Blane everything that had happened since Drake first heard someone cry for help.

The girls went to the spare bedroom and he changed clothes in his.

Entering the living room, he saw they'd apparently decided to dress for bed. They were in robes and house shoes, occupying the chairs on either side of the fireplace. Each held a jelly glass filled with wine. He started a fire and went to the kitchen for a beer and cigar. Gazing cautiously at the exterior walls, relieved to see nothing but rain through the windowpanes, he returned to the living room and plopped down on the couch.

Ginny set her glass on the floor and swept her wet hair back with both hands. The motion made her robe part dramatically above her breasts, showing a goodly amount of bulging mammary flesh, which bobbled enough to reveal she planned to sleep topless. The pink terrycloth came together again as she lowered her arms while exhaling a sigh. "That rain's just not going to stop, is it."

"Not any time soon, doesn't look like." He glanced towards the window, trying to forget seeing the upper portion of Ginny's fabulous tits. She'd turned him on and that pissed him off. The pane was vibrating from the stormy onslaught.

"I like this rugged fireplace," said Blane. "Makes me feel like I'm back in the old west."

"Is that a fact." He smiled at her while saying it.

"Mm hmm." She got up and stood with her back to the flames. Her sash had loosened and the robe's edges were barely lapped. When she put her hands behind her butt to warm them they raked against her hips, causing the entire robe to gap open just a crack, divulging she wore nothing beneath it. Catching him looking, she glanced down and immediately rectified the situation, face knotting with angry surprise.

He quickly focused his attention on the gun cabinet.

"You're not thinking of using one of those, are you?" Ginny asked.

"Against a ghost?" He tried to sound humorous but the tone came out serious, like such a prospect would be futile.

"I don't believe in ghosts," said Blane.

Her voice sounded normal so he let his gaze return her direction, hoping she realized he'd merely been caught by surprise and hadn't meant to stare. "I don't either. At least I didn't before tonight."

She'd relaxed but seemed to be pondering something. "The rain started shortly after Ginny saw the woman. Maybe the atmospheric conditions were just right to produce an optical illusion."

Ginny gave her a firm look. "That was no damn illusion."

He nodded in agreement. "If you'd seen her, you wouldn't

think it was either, believe me."

"Well it couldn't have been a ghost because there's no such thing. So if it wasn't an optical illusion it had to have been a real woman you guys saw."

Thinking that over, he took a drag from his cigar and exhaled. "If she is a real woman, she's the fastest human alive."

Blane cut her eyes to Ginny. "Tell me what she looked like again."

"As I told you before, she was wearing a white veil and a white flowing dress that had a light sheen to it. I couldn't make out her features."

"What color was her hair?"

"I don't know. The veil was attached to some sort of headpiece, kind of like a nun wears."

"Could she have been a nun?"

"No, it wasn't a nun's habit."

"More like a wedding veil," said Jasper.

Ginny mulled that over a few seconds. "Yeah, that's what it was. She appeared to be dressed like a bride."

"I wish you hadn't slammed the door so I could have gotten a look at her."

"Instinct took over, Blane, I had no choice. It scared the living shit out of me. She just appeared out of thin air."

"I heard that . . ." he turned up his beer and swallowed. "Seeing her vanish at the window was about the scariest thing I've ever seen in my life."

After protesting again that it had to be a real woman rather than a ghost, Blane started for the kitchen. "I'm going to get some more wine. Want me to fill you up while I'm at it?"

Holding up a half full glass Ginny said, "No, I'm fine."

He downed the last of his Lone Star, rose to his feet, and set the bottle on his desk. "You can bring me another round of cow piss if you don't mind."

Blane giggled at his lame remark and headed for the kitchen. He watched her leave the room, relieved she wasn't holding a grudge over him getting an accidental peek at a half inch sliver of her body.

"Look over here," Ginny whispered.

Turning her way, he received an electrifying jolt. She'd pulled her left tit out with her right hand and was aiming the nipple towards him. "Bet you'd like to suck on this. Huh, cowboy."

Staring speechlessly, he couldn't take his eyes off the wondrous breast and erect nipple. The sight of her long pink fingernails almost cutting into the delicate flesh overwhelmed him. Ginny was a bitch by every definition of the word but he couldn't force his eyes away from her spellbinding display. She gave him a seductive smile and shoved the big boob back inside her robe an instant before Blane returned.

"I tried to open it for you but couldn't."

"Thanks." He took the beer from Blane, twisted off the cap, and downed a third of it, still looking at Ginny, who was staring at him. For the first time since meeting Ginny Cross he found himself wishing something he'd have bet any amount of money would never cross his mind: he'd give anything to be alone with her. From his peripheral vision he saw Blane starting to notice their mutual eyeballing. Lowering the bottle from his lips, he pried his eyes off the gorgeous spoiled bitch and looked towards her friend. "Best cow piss I ever tasted."

She sat down and jerked her head towards Ginny when the latter said, "I can think of something that would taste much better."

Her voice was lusty and she hadn't quit ogling him.

An edgy laugh rose from Blane. "Did I miss something?"

"No." Ginny smiled knowingly and raised her glass.

He turned towards the window. "The rain's letting up a little."

"I wonder if something else isn't up just a little."

Ginny's statement embarrassed him and he wished she'd shut up about it.

Blane cleared her throat. "Okay, guys, I must have missed something. Do you two want to be alone?"

"Me and Jasper?" the cock-teasing bitch snickered. "Now why would I want to be alone with a queer cowboy?"

"Don't make me pull a Tray on you." He immediately regretted the knee-jerk response. It had just popped out.

"Are you making the same offer he did?"

When she'd given him the show he'd wanted nothing more than to throw caution to the wind and ravish her, but those crass subliminal remarks of hers had extinguished the fire, forcing him back to reality. Screwing Ginny would bring nothing but trouble, maybe even wind up costing him his job. "I wouldn't call what Tray said an offer. Sounded more like a threat to me."

"Offer, threat, who cares? Are you interested in me or not?"

"Doesn't matter. You're the daughter of my boss—his only child, the apple of his eye—so we'd best nip this in the bud right now."

"Daddy will never know. Like I'd tell him anyway. He'd have a cow."

He shot her a sarcastic grin. "Until I do or say something that pisses you off and you decide the best way to get even is make out like I forced myself on you."

"I won't tell Daddy, you've got my word on it."

Blane giggled. "Ginny, you're throwing yourself at him. Have you no shame?"

"Like I told you, I threw myself at him when I was a kid.

He's the one I want, and I'll keep after his queer ass until I get him." Though speaking to Blane, she was giving him the unblinking ravenous stare that he hated. The gleam in her eyes didn't reflect unrequited love, but a shameless greedy desire to possess.

"Quit talking about me like I'm not here and stop staring at me, dammit." His words had no affect. Ginny continued scrutinizing him as if he were merely a piece of jewelry in a display case. Seeing her naked boob had weakened his resolve and she damn well knew it. But unbeknownst to her he'd gotten over it in a hurry. He wondered what had prompted her to spew that bullshit about him being the one she wanted.

Thunder rolled and the storm regained its momentum.

"Help me!" It came from the front yard.

Jasper flew out the door and immediately got drenched by the downpour. But he hardly noticed the wet bombardment because this time he saw her. She was standing about twenty feet on the other side of Banger's house, holding her hands out towards him, waiting for him to come to her. The dog barked and howled from inside his shelter, either not wanting to get wet, or too scared to come outside.

Cautiously, he moved towards her as she cried out again.

Arms beckoning for him, she stood that way until he almost got within reach of her. Then she vanished. Grisly amazement drenched him like the cold rain. She had to be a ghost, logic defied any other explanation. Sensing something at his back, he spun on his heels, heart pounding with fear. It was only Blane. Blonde hair drooping down the sides of her face in limp wet tangles, soaked robe clinging to her full figure, she wore an astonished expression of incomprehension that exhibited what he felt.

"Did you see her?!" Ginny yelled from the porch, its roof protecting her from the deluge.

"Yes!" Blane cried through a torrent of raindrops assaulting her face.

He put his hand on her back, signaling her to go inside, and they returned to the house.

Making their way to the spare bedroom so Blane could change into something dry, the terrified girls caterwauled about the woman in white. Ginny had seen her too and also saw her vanish. Deciding to mimic them, he dug his house shoes and bathrobe from the closet. They never came out of there except when he went to visit his mother or sister. Leaving his wet jeans and shirt on the bedroom floor atop the ones he'd stripped out of earlier, he went to the bathroom to pee but suddenly felt an urgent need to take a dump as well. Ten minutes later he went back to the living room to find his unwanted houseguests passing a bottle of tequila back and forth, using wine as a chaser.

"Let me have some of that." He took the bottle from Blane and downed two big swallows before handing it back. "Cuervo Gold, damn good tequila. Glad you brought it."

"We didn't bring it, it's yours."

He frowned at Ginny, who'd spoken. "I don't have any tequila here."

"Well we found it in the guest room just now."

"It was in the chest of drawers," said Blane, who'd wrapped herself in a patchwork quilt. "Hope you don't mind, I found this in one of the drawers too. My robe was soaked and it looked so warm and comfortable."

"Must have belonged to Red." He was referring to the tequila rather than the quilt, which he recognized as his old boss's.

"Red?"

"The man who lived in this house before me." He made for the couch and flung himself on it lengthwise. "What I wouldn't give for a smoke."

Blane handed Ginny the Cuervo, set her wine on the floor, and rose to her feet. "I'll get your cigars."

"No, I mean a cigarette."

"Oh." She sat back down, holding the quilt together with her left hand.

In a few moments he started feeling the tequila. He drank so much beer on a regular basis that it took ten or more to bring him to the other side of sobriety, but that wasn't the case with hard liquor. He closed his eyes and listened to the girls gab about the ghost woman, wishing he had a cigarette. Blane asked Ginny if he'd fallen asleep.

"Nope," he said, lids still sealed. "Wide awake."

"Would you like another drink?"

"Sure." He opened his eyes and started to get up but Blane had crossed the room, one hand holding Cuervo Gold, the other keeping the quilt closed. She offered the tequila and as he sat up to take it, the bottle slipped. Trying to catch it, he fell forward, accidentally pushing his face towards her midsection. She instinctively grabbed for the falling jug with both hands and the quilt parted. Jasper managed to catch the hooch before it hit the hardwood floor but his face smashed against her bare crotch, and Blane's hands wound up on top of his head.

"Oh shit!" she howled.

"Sorry, it was an accident . . .!" he pulled away from her, getting an extreme close up of black pubic hair as he reared back, clutching the tequila. Blane obviously wasn't a natural blonde.

Face as red as an apple, she hastily pulled the quilt back together.

"What are y'all doing over there?" wailed Ginny with an accusing tone.

"Nothing. Jasper just had an accident that's all."

He took a long draw from the bottle, carefully handed it to Blane, and she made her way back to the chair. The sudden rain, Ginny's breast exhibition, the disappearing woman, and Blane's twat had turned this into a stormy, scary, erotic night. Thinking of the poor gal's mortified expression, which must have mirrored his own after being eyeball to pubs with her pussy, he couldn't keep from laughing. Soon Blane got to giggling about the mishap too. Before long Ginny was chortling along with them.

The laughter finally died down and his thoughts swam around the woman in white. "I wonder what happened to her."

Ginny let out a tipsy guffaw. "Well hell, Jasper, she vanished, that's what happened."

"No, I don't mean that. I wonder how she died."

"I think she's a spirit," Blane opined after a moment's silence. "I don't think anyone can come back as a ghost after they die."

"Spirit, ghost, same difference," said Ginny.

"No, it's not the same. A spirit has always been a spirit just as a human has always been a human. But a ghost would be a human that has died and somehow became reanimated in a spiritual state. I don't believe that's possible."

Jasper frowned. "Why would a spirit cry out for help? Wouldn't a spirit be like an angel or some other form of supernatural being, be invulnerable and all that?"

"I don't know, but I firmly believe we saw a spirit not a ghost."

Ginny blew out a sigh. "Well I think she's a ghost."

"Me too," he agreed.

Blane took a shot of tequila and burped. "Like it really matters either way."

The fire was dying down so he threw some more wood on

the flame, taking the opportunity to take another shot of Cuervo while near the bottle. Then he went to the kitchen for his cigars, though he wanted a cigarette far more than a Swisher Sweet. For several minutes he stared through the backdoor window, smoking while pondering the mysterious veiled woman, halfway expecting her to appear on the back porch.

"Ugh, I've overdone it, Blane," said Ginny when he returned to the living room. She had a nauseous look on her face. "Time for me to go night-night. Goodnight, queer cowboy, see you tomorrow."

Blane, who didn't look so swift either, left the tequila on the floor and followed her into the hall. He picked up the liquor and wobbled towards the couch, knowing he was going to hate himself in the morning . . . .

6

Jasper woke up on the couch with a bitter tequila aftertaste lodged in the back of his throat. He grunted loudly while forcing himself to his feet. Reeling with dizziness, his head hurt and he couldn't focus his eyes. His stomach seemed to be rotating like the drum of a cement mixer and he remembered he'd never eaten supper. Nausea rose from the aching pit of his gut and he barely made it to the bathroom in time to empty its contents in the toilet. With nothing left to puke, dry heaves commenced and he kept retching for what seemed like forever. When he finally managed to quit belching air, he rose unsteadily from the commode he'd been hugging, tossed the robe, and got in the shower.

The hot stream felt like a million needle pricks on his shivering skin. Gritting his teeth, he washed quickly, hurriedly shut off the tormenting surge, and went to the lavatory to brush his teeth and shave. No sooner had he finished toweling the residual shaving cream from his face when a gas pocket formed in his belly, forcing him back to the toilet. This time he sat down on it. With a violent burst his bowels voided. The gross sounds of escaping gas and runny excrement splashing into the water seemed to put an exclamation mark on last night's foolishness. He shouldn't have drank so much tequila anyway, but especially not on an empty stomach. Knowing aspirins wouldn't stay down, he couldn't do a thing to suppress the agony pounding his temples.

Last night the Cuervo Gold had provided a security barrier—dulling his wits so he didn't have to deal with the ambiguous emotions arising from Ginny's come-on and the rude awakening that the woman in white had to be a ghost. But the shield had evaporated, leaving behind a throbbing head that still had to face the realities of both.

Passing the spare bedroom, he wondered if Ginny and Blane would want breakfast. He knew they wouldn't if they felt half as bad as he did. Besides, anything he fixed would most likely be cold by the time they woke up. The mere thought of food made him nauseous, so he decided they could drive to town and eat if they woke up hungry. He made coffee and sat down at the table, cradling his aching head in his hands, awaiting the morning's caffeine fix.

After getting coffee'd up he made a fresh pot for the sleeping women, grabbed his hat, and headed out the front door to face the day. Below a bright cloudless sky lay muddy ground and soaked pastures. All the low areas looked like miniature ponds and Ginny's Corvette sat right in the middle of one. Banger had his head pressed against the door of his perpetual feeder, enjoying an early morning snack. He thought about how much smarter dogs were than men. They never woke up with a hangover. Sliding behind the wheel, he cranked the engine and drove off, heading for the pig pens.

They rotated Saturday feedings and though he didn't have to, he knew taking his turn slopping the hogs kept the boys' morale up. The smell of manure greeted him when he got out of his pickup. Unlike swill-fed swine, properly nourished hogs discharged wastes that gave off a barnyard smell rather than a sewage stench. Pigs fed swill—the technical term for human-food leftovers—had the smelliest crap of any form of livestock. Illegal without a permit, it had to be re-cooked and there were limitations to what could be used. Pigs on the Double Cross were fed a mixture of hog finisher and corn if they were mature, and pure pig starter from weaning to fifty pounds.

He pulled up to the feed shack and killed the engine. Twenty minutes later, pickup laden with five-gallon buckets brimming with swine nourishment, he commenced dispensing breakfast to a large heard of squealing Durocs and Blue Butts. Watching them stab their snouts into the feed troughs made him queasy. A quarter-ton sow raised her head with an open mouthful of mush and the sight almost made him start puking again. Then a boar savored a stream of piss from a gilt in heat, nostrils twitching with eagerness as the urine poured over them. He wretched and coughed up a wad of phlegm, cursing himself for being so stupid last night. By the time he got all the ravenous pork appetites satisfied and headed for the smokehouse, Jasper wished he'd never even heard of Cuervo Gold.

Useless waved at him when he got there, motioning for him to roll the window down. "No need getting out, Boss. Just got through checking the hams. I'm fixing to head to town for the supply run."

Jasper leaned his head out the window. "All right, but get the boys to round up four steers for finishing before you go."

"Gotcha. How'd the evening go with Ginny and Blane?"

He told him about the woman. Useless turned another shade of pale upon hearing he now believed her to be a ghost.

"Never thought I'd hear you say that."

"If you've got a better explanation, I'd love to hear it."

"Can't say as I do. You look a little puny this morning, Boss. Not coming down with a cold from braving the rain last night are you?"

Jasper wiped his mouth with the back of his wrist. "I'm hung-over as hell."

"Thought you never got hangovers."

"Don't from beer, unless I drink a whole case. The girls found some tequila that Red must have stashed way back when."

Useless grinned. "Sounds like a party."

"No. We were just shook up after seeing the woman."

"Hell, you should have gotten ol' Ginny so drunk she couldn't remember anything, and cut you off a piece. "

"That's the only way I'd ever cut off a piece from Ginny—if I was damn sure she'd never remember it. She tries to boss me around enough without me giving her blackmail ammunition. Can't you just hear her? *I'll tell my daddy what you did to me if you don't do just like I say!*"

"Hey that's a pretty good Ginny imitation. Sounded almost just like her."

He shot him a lazy smile along with the finger.

"Up yours too, Boss," chuckled Useless, flipping him off.

"Well I'd best get to it."

"Hope you get to feeling better."

"That makes two of us . . . ."

Jasper set out for the barn to check the hay supply. Passing the ranch house along the way, he didn't see Ginny's Stingray which brightened his mood considerably. He hoped she'd left for good and hadn't merely taken Blane to town for breakfast. The thought of her cutting the weekend short brought such relief he almost forgot about the hangover. After inventorying the alfalfa he drove to the corn silo. Besides being mixed with hog feed the corn also served to fatten beef. Once confined to the finishing stalls, steers subsisted solely on alfalfa and grain. The chore of bagging up fifty-pound sacks for the feed shack and barn alternated. He never messed with sacking corn, but checked the silo regularly to make certain some thief hadn't snuck onto the ranch and helped himself to a dump truck full. It hadn't happened on his watch but Red got pilfered twice. The venerable old cowboy had told him, "The one thing you never do is take anything for granted in the ranching business—what with the worry of thieves, storms, varmints, plagues, or a shiftless hand walking out on you. So always be prepared for the worst and keep your hands happy but busy."

He'd followed that advice and taken it a step further. During his first year as foreman, Jasper noticed things seemed to move more efficiently when they were shorthanded. His work ethic wouldn't permit him to bark out orders and merely supervise their completion like his old boss had done. Unfortunately his willingness to continue getting his gloves dirty after being placed in charge had been exploited by several of the punchers working on the Double Cross in those days—always asking for assistance they didn't need instead of pulling their own weight.

So one day, after firing two cowboys he'd repeatedly caught goofing off, he reassessed the situation and came up with an idea. Useless, Tray, and Drake never goldbricked, taking great pride in their work as had a puncher named Clyde, who'd done all the cooking and helped out in between preparing meals. With their hearty approval he'd successfully petitioned T. Wayford for higher wages in exchange for less overhead by cutting the crew down to the four reliable hands. Like him, each could do the work of two men when situations called for it, and got paid accordingly. Everything went smooth as silk until Clyde got afflicted with severe arthritis and had to give up ranching. Thereafter, numerous cooks either quit on him or got fired for being lax about chores that took them out of the kitchen. Then Dree came along and solidified that position. While the big blonde didn't have Clyde's cow-punching talent, he worked his ass off and had superior culinary abilities.

Silo found to be unscathed, Jasper drove to the entrance of the ranch, passing over a cattle guard laying beneath a bricked archway with a sign hanging from the center of the arc. Fancy-twists of metal letters spelled out *The Double Cross* with the same motif as the branding iron perched on either side of the name. Turning right, he coasted for thirty feet along the shoulder of a two lane highway, and stopped at the mailbox. It contained a letter for Useless, a post card for Dree, several pieces of junk mail, and an electric bill addressed to him.

The bill wasn't for the ranch, T. Wayford covered those expenses. It belonged to his mother, a lifelong housewife who'd been allotted only eight hundred dollars a month social security after his dad died. Jasper had tried to get her to accept a sizable chunk of his pay since he lived rent free with no utility burdens of his own, but the proud woman wouldn't hear of it. He'd insisted on helping out in some way after learning his sister Jasmine had been shouldering all her bills and property tax, though his brother-in-law actually earned the *In God We Trust*. "We make well over three times the money you do, Jasper," she'd said rather smugly after begrudgingly turning the light bill over to him. "We'll take care of Mother."

He drove to the ranch house for lunch and whooped with joy at still not seeing a pink hotrod parked out front. The girls most likely would have returned by now if they'd merely left for breakfast. Ginny had apparently gone home. Not having to feed her and Blane meant he could take his chow with the boys, so he made for the bunkhouse.

Dree served burritos, nachos, Spanish rice, refried beans, and guacamole. Jasper had worked up a modest appetite and the grub went a long way towards relieving the hangover. With a small meal in his stomach—a fraction of the amount he'd normally eat—he almost felt normal. "You boys playing cards tonight?"

Tray swallowed a bite and shook his head. "Not me. Figure on heading to town for some pune-tang instead of letting you hard dicks bluff me out of my pay."

"Me too," said Drake.

"What about you, Dree?"

"I'll stay and play if you want, Boss."

"Likewise," spouted Useless before downing a gulp of iced tea.

"Don't stay on my account."

The pale cowboy grinned. "Not going to entertain the ladies again?"

"Ladies done left."

"Thank God." Dree clapped his hands while saying it.

Jasper nodded. "Amen to that. So we playing then?"

"Bring your money but don't plan on leaving with it."

"Figure I'll be leaving with most of yours, Useless."

"Highly unlikely." The cotton top scooped some guacamole onto a nacho. "Did you tell the boys about seeing the ghost last night?"

"First I've seen them today." He looked around the table. "Heard her cry out like she always does, and almost got right up to her before she vanished right before my eyes. The girls saw it too."

"Huh," said Drake. "Did it scare you?"

"Hell yeah it scared me."

Tray lowered his tea and burped. "Scares me just hearing about it. I'm not sure I want to work on a haunted ranch."

"You're not threatening to quit on me are you?"

"No, Boss. At least not yet. But you've got to admit this is some weird shit we've got going down here. So far she's been harmless, but what happens if we start dying off one by one from her sucking the life force out of us or something like that."

"Saw a movie like that," Dree said dramatically, pretending to be terrified. "This beautiful alien woman hypnotized men and did that very thing—sucked the life force right out of them." He let that dangle a couple of seconds, then relaxed his face. "But all our gal wants is help, at least that's what she keeps saying. I don't think she's dangerous and ghosts are nothing but myth. God may be testing us with an angel to see how we react. He works in mysterious ways, as the old saying goes. If we can figure out how to help her, maybe she'll quit appearing. Could be she's supposed to make us think she's caught between our world and the spirit realm, and needs our help to get to the other side."

Useless cackled at the notion. "What the hell do a bunch of cowpunchers like us know about getting a ghost across the river Jordan?"

"Nothing. But there must be something we can do or she wouldn't be haunting us, now would she."

"Or maybe she's wrong. She thinks we can help her but we can't."

The possibility seemed to worry Tray momentarily. Then his expression shifted from concern to mirth as he cut his eyes to Dree and winked. "And what keeps her from sucking the life force out of us when she finds out we can't?"

"Not a thing," teased Dree. "So I suggest we find out how to help her."

"Now just how do you propose we do that?"

"Simple, Tray. Next time she appears and asks for help, just ask her how we can."

Jasper shrugged his shoulders. "She doesn't hang around

long enough to do that."

"Seems to me her visitations are getting longer each time." Dree bit off a healthy chunk of burrito and smiled while chewing.

"Not to change the subject, but here's your change, Boss." Useless stood up, dug some cash from his pants, and handed it to him before sitting back down. "I left the beer on your back porch."

"Why didn't you put it in the icebox?"

"Door was locked."

"Hmm. The girls must have locked up when they left. Did y'all get the steers rounded up?"

"Not yet," said Drake. "Tray and I had to fix a gate this morning. Figure on doing that first thing after lunch."

"All right. Well as much as I like sitting around telling ghost stories with you boys, we've got work to do and we'd best get to it."

"Did you check the mail?"

"Oh, thanks for reminding me, Useless. You got a letter as a matter of fact, it's in my truck. Dree, there was a post card for you."

"Anything for me?" asked Tray.

"Nope. Nothing for you and Drake."

Tray sighed. "I guess Angelina Jolie just ain't gonna write me back."

"Hell if I couldn't do better than that, believe I'd quit." Jasper got up from the table. Leaving the boys laughing at his remark, he went outside to get the mail. When he came back they were arguing over who was prettier, Angelina Jolie or Jennifer Aniston. Doling out the letter and postcard he quipped, "Who did Brad Pitt leave for who? That ought to settle it . . . ."

* * * *

Jasper's heart fell when he got to the ranch house after calling it a day. The damn pink Corvette had returned, so his Saturday night plans were shot to hell. He headed for the bunkhouse to tell Dree he wouldn't be able to make the poker game because the girls had come back. Ginny might want to play and that would be a disaster just waiting to happen . . . .

She was sitting at his kitchen table drinking champagne when he unlocked the backdoor and stepped into the kitchen carrying the case of Lone Star Useless had deposited on the porch. A low-cut blouse barely covering her nipples pulled his eyes from several partially emptied cartons of Chinese takeout. Forcing himself to quit ogling her chest, he tossed his hat on the cabinet. "I see I won't have to cook for the two of you tonight."

"Oh there's no longer two of us. I took Blane home. It's just you and me tonight, cowboy. Thought you might enjoy eating Chinese for a change of pace. I was going to wait on you but got too hungry."

Eyeballing the narrow vessel she had her lithe fingers wrapped around he said, "Where'd you get the glass?"

"Brought it from home. Brought you one too. It's chilling in the fridge."

"Don't want no champagne, but I will clean up those leftovers. Been a small forever since I've had Chinese food. How long have you had a key to the ranch house?"

"I don't have a key to this place."

"Then how'd you get in?"

"The front door was unlocked, silly."

"Figured you gals locked up when you left."

"Nope." She raised the gleaming champagne glass and took a sip.

"Then who locked the backdoor?"

"I don't know but we didn't do it."

Except when being away overnight he never secured the house and had no recollection of locking the kitchen door that morning. Apparently the hangover that had mercifully dissipated was responsible for his absentminded action. He stashed the warm beer in the bottom of the fridge and grabbed a cold one sitting next to Ginny's champagne and extra glass. Then he pulled a fork from the silverware drawer and sat down at the table.

Last night's breast episode came to mind as he ate—how Ginny had doused his extreme arousal with her sharp tongue, snapping him back to his senses and the cold hard fact she was nothing but trouble. Without doubt she planned to sleep with him. Without doubt he couldn't allow it, not if he wanted to keep his sanity for long. And without doubt a sure fire knock-down drag-out fight would commence the minute she tried to seduce him and discovered he wouldn't give in. It was best to get things like this over with in a hurry. Looking down at the leftovers, he dunked an egg roll in a carton of sweet-and-sour sauce. "I appreciate the grub and hope you're enjoying your champagne, but we're not going to sleep together, Ginny. Just so you know."

"Oh really?"

"Really."

"Look me in the eye and tell me that, cowboy." She issued the challenge with a sultry tone.

Jasper looked up to see she'd unbuttoned her blouse and was cupping a breast in each hand, repeatedly squeezing them with her sexy fingers as if trying to make them squirt milk at him. Jeans immediately feeling too tight at the crotch, his throat turned bone dry. "Ginny, please . . . don't do that."

"Your lips say no, but your eyes are glued to my tits."

They were. He couldn't look away from the mesmerizing scene. Her extraordinary boobs and erect pink nipples held him spellbound.

"Now I'm going to your bedroom and get naked, and you're going to be a good little cowboy and follow suit. By the time I'm done with you, you're going to forget all about every woman you've ever known . . . ."

* * * *

Screwing Ginny Cross was unlike anything he'd ever experienced because he'd never deflowered a virgin before. He held her as she sobbed into his shoulder. Seeing her devoid of pride, completely exposed, crying from the pain he'd inflicted, made him feel dirty with guilt. "Why didn't you tell me? I never would have touched you if I'd known."

"I know."

"Oh hell, I've really done it this time . . . damn."

"It's okay," she sniffled out.

He heaved an exasperated sigh. "How did you manage to stay a virgin all this time?"

She didn't answer for several minutes. By the time she did, the tears had stopped. "You stole my heart the day I met you. After that day we spent together in Dallas, when I saw I couldn't get you to want me, I cried all night long. I've had boyfriends, almost went all the way several times, but just couldn't because I knew if I did I'd be nothing but a cheap whore because I didn't love them, I loved you. I tried to get over you—tried so hard not to love you—that's why I quit coming out here with Daddy so often. But I had to see you once in a while or I'd have gone crazy."

"Then why did you come out here with Blane?"

"To find out once and for all whether I had a chance with

you. I planned that stunt I pulled last night with my boob. Blane knew all about it. Her job was to see if you wanted me or not after I did it."

That blew his mind and he made a face to show it. "You couldn't tell?"

"Of course I could tell it turned you on," she giggled. "It had to, otherwise you'd really have to be queer. I needed to know if it was me or only my boob that was turning you on. We were going to dress in robes before the night was over and Blane was going to accidentally expose herself so we could judge if it was really me you wanted or just any hot woman. Serendipity stepped in. We didn't have to wait until late in the evening to change, the rain forced that. But before Blane could do her act the ghost showed up and she got her robe wet. When she had to change a second time we had a problem. She didn't have another robe to pop open so you could have a peep show. But we found the quilt and she was able to accomplish the feat."

"So I didn't see her body by accident?"

"No. The original plan was for her to be standing by the fireplace, ask you something that would make you look at her, thinking she was unaware her robe had gapped open. Then we were going to compare your reaction to her with your reaction to me. We both made sure you noticed we weren't wearing bras beneath our robes. That was stage one—who would you stare at the most. It was hilarious watching you try not to look. Stage two of course was my stunt. Stage three was Blane's." She exhaled a breath and snuggled closer. "It was a three stage strip plan."

He wedged his brows and grunted. "I don't see how you could tell anything from my reaction."

"Are you serious? You were so hot for me when I pulled out my boob I thought you were going to cream your jeans on the spot. But I could tell you were embarrassed when you saw Blane's bod."

If he'd known Blane had exposed herself on purpose it would have turned him on as much as Ginny's tit show. But he'd let her think what she wanted. "So what happens now?"

Moist lips spreading with a sexy smile, she started messaging his groin. "Well, for one thing, I've always been told the first time hurts but it feels real good after that. I experienced the pain, now I want the pleasure . . . ."

7

Morning and evening feedings were the only chores to be performed on Sundays and Jasper didn't participate in that rotation. Barring any ranch emergencies, as long as Ginny's car remained parked out front the boys wouldn't be bothering him, so they'd been able to spend the whole day in bed.

"I need to go here pretty quick," she said, nuzzling the side of his neck while he lay stretched out on his back. "I wish I didn't have to work tomorrow."

A shocked laugh escaped him, sounding nowhere near as incredulous as he felt. "You have a job? Hell I thought you spent all your time finding ways to spend your daddy's money."

"Hardly, but if he had his way that's the way it would be all right. He can't understand why I want to work in the first place, but what really bothers him is I won't work for him."

"Why not?"

"Because I don't believe in nepotism . . ." she rolled over on her back and sighed. "I bet you think he bought my car, don't you."

"You mean to tell me he didn't?"

"Nope."

He leaned up on his elbow. "What is it you do anyway?'

"I'm chief decorator for the biggest interior design

company in The Metroplex."

"Is that right. Well I'm impressed." Surprised as hell was more like it.

"You should be, only the upper echelon can afford our services."

"So why do want to waste your time on an old cowpuncher like me? I could never fit into that world."

She turned her face towards him. "No one's saying you have to."

"So you're just using me for sex?"

"Hell no! I want to marry you, Jasper."

Despite seeing she was serious, he couldn't help laughing at the crazy notion. "That'll never happen. T. Wayford would fire me on the spot the second I asked him for your hand."

"Daddy doesn't own me. And so what if he fires you? It's not like this is the only job in the world you can do is it?"

"Pretty much is, I'm afraid."

"Bullshit. Do you realize how many areas you could branch into with your skills and experience? You can run a ranch. Why not run your own instead of somebody else's? Or open your own butcher shop or even a restaurant and become one of Daddy's competitors. Wouldn't that be a hoot?"

He laughed again. "Ol' Dree and I could sure make a restaurant fly. At least as far as the food quality's concerned."

"You said that in jest, but the truth is you could, and you wouldn't need Dree to do it. I'll never forget watching you somehow stay on those bulls as if you were defying gravity. That incredible competitive instinct didn't go away when you got hurt, Jasper. It's still inside you—you just need to wake it back up. "

Stewing on that he decided to confide a secret ambition he'd long ago accepted would never come to fruition. "You know what I'd really like to do?"

"What?"

"Start my own sausage company." He sat up and crossed his legs.

She did likewise, breasts jiggling sensuously in the process. "You mean like smoked sausage?"

"No, breakfast sausage. My grandma came up with a dandy recipe. I tweaked it just a little and made it taste even better. I bet it would sell if I could get it marketed, but the only thing I know about such things is that it would take a hell of a lot more cash than I'd ever be able to raise."

"Have you talked to Daddy about it? He could give you the backing you need."

"I teased him about replacing Ben Bishop."

Her jaw dropped. "Are you telling me your sausage is better than what Ben makes for Daddy?"

"Ben doesn't make breakfast sausage. T. Wayford doesn't serve breakfast in any of his joints anyway. But you can ask the boys how good it is. They love my sausage. Haven't been able to get your daddy to try it yet."

"Let me talk to him. I'll get him to."

Eyeing her reddish blonde crotch, saturated with his semen, he thought about what happened yesterday after she'd left the kitchen. He'd sat there for a few minutes trying to resist the urge to follow her to his bedroom. Despite knowing he was probably making the biggest mistake of his life, temptation had gotten the better of him and he'd found her lying naked across his bed. Feverish with lust, he'd hastily stripped, dug a rubber from his chest of drawers, and went to her.

"Nothing's gonna come between your dick and my pussy!" she'd angrily declared while yanking it from his hand. "I'm clean as a whistle and you don't have to worry about knocking me up, because I've been on the pill since my teens."

Too overcome with passion to resist, he'd lowered himself between her spread legs, almost losing control, her snatch had felt so tight. Then she'd screamed "Oh it hurts! It hurts! But don't you dare stop!" and he'd ejaculated immediately, filled with shame to discover he was her first lover. It amazed him how quickly she'd acclimated. The second interlude had ended with her convulsing in the throes of a fiery orgasm and she hadn't failed to climax since. Ginny's pussy had loosened only a little after being invaded for the first time, and was by far the best he'd ever pounded.

"Hello! Up here!"

Jerking his eyes to hers, he blew out a sigh. "Sorry, got lost in thought."

"You were staring at my cunt so I don't have to ask what you were thinking about. Stop feeling guilty for taking my cherry, I wanted you to. Anyway, like I said, I'll talk to Daddy and convince him to try your sausage."

"Shouldn't you try it first?"

"Do you have some?"

"Sure do . . ." he reached out and groped her exquisite firm tits, grinning as her nipples hardened against his palms. "Would have made some for breakfast if you hadn't insisted on cereal so we could get back to bed."

Ginny's face ignited with lust as if she were a sex-starved nymphomaniac about to receive a hard dick for the first time in years. "Make love to me again, then fix me some."

* * * *

Jasper fried up a dozen sausage patties and used three for egg sandwiches which composed his supper. Ginny allowed herself only one patty, but declared it was the best breakfast sausage she'd ever eaten. He put the remaining eight in a baggie for her to take to T. Wayford. "You'd better hit the road if you want to get home before ten."

She gave him a long wet smooch. "Hate it I have to leave. I'll come back as soon as I get off work next Friday, and I'll call you every day."

"Nope. I don't like talking on the phone unless I have to."

"I didn't mean to make small talk, silly."

"I'm not into phone sex."

Ginny protested vehemently but he refused to budge. "Don't call me unless you've got something important to say like T. Wayford loves my sausage or you can't make it Friday. Otherwise I'll hang up on you."

* * * *

The state inspector said he'd be there by eight but hadn't shown until forty minutes after. They spent that Monday morning slaughtering, gutting, skinning, halving, washing, then storing the hog carcasses. By the time the inspector finished his final examination it was well past lunchtime. After chow Jasper salted the hides he'd stretched out on the ground to dry before they could be soaked in a solution of borax and water for a few days. When they were ready he'd scrape off the fat before having them delivered to Fort Worth, whereupon they'd be further processed and stained to become customized pigskin footwear alongside similarly treated cowhide from the Double Cross.

Except for bowels and bones, they employed every part of the hog. Jasper confiscated the heads, using the jowls for tamale meat, the brains for cat food, and the ears for Banger to chew on. The feet, considered a delicacy by many Texans, were stored and shipped with the beef and pork to T.

Wayford's restaurants to be pickled and served. He couldn't muster up the nerve to try pig's feet so he had no way of knowing how T. Wayford's faired against his competitors. All the organs were salvaged. When the next refrigeration truck arrived they'd be shipped off to a warehouse in Dallas for various uses which Jasper had little knowledge of, and no inclination to learn.

After tending to the hides he went inside the slaughterhouse and picked the skulls clean of meat, having already removed the brains before eating lunch. Then he tossed them into an incinerator located behind the building. A five hundred gallon butane tank fueled the burner, which worked similar to a crematorium, turning even bone to ash. Checking the gauge and finding the tank to be at seventy percent, he spun the incinerator's timer dial to automatic, pushed the start button, and headed for his pickup. Before he got to it the woman cried out from somewhere behind him. He turned and saw a flash of white disappear to the right of the smokehouse. For a few chilling seconds he waited to see if she'd cry out or manifest her presence again, but she did neither.

Until after sunset.

This time he happened to be standing on the back porch. The woman in white stood about thirty feet from him, arms extended, repeatedly saying, "Help me!" Instead of going towards her he merely watched, hoping she'd stay long enough for him to discern what her face looked like beneath the veil. Instinctively he felt she might not disappear so quickly if he didn't approach her. At least half a minute went by before she vanished, and during that time he'd confirmed two things by the appearance of her outstretched hands, the only parts of her anatomy not covered in what looked to be some sort of wedding apparel—her race and age.

The ghostly figure was, or at least used to be, a young white woman.

Though she'd manifested well within the area illuminated by the safety light, she seemed to give off a glow of her own like a low watt light bulb shaped into a Christmas ornament. Her last words before disappearing confused him. She'd lowered her hands and looked down while saying, "I am the body and I need help."

Three Lone Stars later Jasper still pondered the statement.

The phone rang.

"Hello?"

"Howdy, Jasper, T. Wayford here. Ginny gave me some of your sausage and I've got to tell you it's dang good."

"Thanks." He'd have been surprised if the billionaire hadn't liked it since everyone who'd ever tasted it did.

"She wants me to help you market it but I told her I needed you running the Double Cross." His employer's tone sounded patronizing.

"Hell that's just a pipe dream I've had since my rodeo days ended. I never gave any serious thought to pursuing it for real."

"Well she thinks you should and she's right. I know the food industry and if that wasn't just a lucky batch, you've got the touch. Can you make it taste the same every time?"

A rush of feral excitement washed over him. "Are you serious, T. Wayford?"

"Hell yeah I'm serious. At least if that wasn't just a lucky batch I am."

"No, it wasn't luck. Turns out the same every time."

"Glad to hear it. Next time you make up a batch siphon me off a few pounds. I want to have some restaurant consultants and food experts taste it and see what they think. If they think it'll sell, you and me just might start us up a sausage

partnership."

T. Wayford liked to joke around but he'd never known him to be cruel. It figured to be the real deal but he wanted reassurance. "You're not just funning me, are you?"

"I'm as serious as a hog at meal time."

He hadn't felt such extreme elation since first staying on a bull the full eight seconds. Before he could say how much he appreciated the opportunity T. Wayford spoke again.

"I was only foolin' around about telling Ginny I couldn't cut you loose as foreman. Who can you train to take over the ranch, assuming this is a go, and how long will you need to train them?"

Pulse elevating, he swallowed a joyful lump down a throat gone dry with euphoria. "Any of the boys except Dree, and it wouldn't take more than a month I reckon. But I can pull double duty if you're serious. The secret's in the seasoning—and that's got to stay my secret—but I can ratio a package per pound mix. Add the seasoning to the right amount of quality pork and anybody that's strong enough to stir raw ground meat thoroughly can make it."

"Is that right?"

"Yep."

A hearty laugh rang out. *"You're thinking too small, Jasper. I got where I am by thinking big. If this is a go, you'll have to live near the plant. I'll need you close by so you can keep an eye on the quality. You may go long spells without having to do anything more than give it a test-taste regularly, but you've got to be on hand since it's your baby. When Ginny started in on me I figured she was up to something because she wouldn't leave till I tried some. Figured she might have laced it with Tabasco peppers and wanted a good laugh at her old man. She messes with me like that. But I finally gave in, and I've got to tell you it's the tastiest breakfast sausage I've ever bit into."*

He grinned at the notion of Ginny pulling such a stunt. And if the sausage panned out T. Wayford wouldn't frown on them getting hitched because his daughter would be marrying a successful businessman rather than a lowly cowpoke. "I'm surprised she got it to you so quick. She must have dropped it off last night, huh?"

"Nope, brought it to me today just after breakfast."

"Bet that made her late for work."

"Late for work? What work?"

"You know, her interior design job."

"Job . . .?" T. Wayford bellowed a loud guffaw. *"Ginny doesn't have a job. Shit, I've been trying to get that girl interested in something besides piling up bills for me to pay ever since she finished college."*

His brows shot up. "Hell you say!"

"Hell I don't."

Learning Ginny had lied to him vacuumed away all elation he'd felt over the sausage. "She told me she worked for a big time interior design company and bought her Stingray with her own money."

More cackles erupted. *"You've got to watch my Ginny, she can convince you the moon is blue. Hell I've bought every car she's ever owned. That girl's never earned a nickel."*

Drawing in a deep breath, he held it for an angry moment before exhaling. "I guess you never tried to get her to go to work for you either, like she said."

"Now that time she was telling you the truth. Gotta run. I'll be out there this Thursday, think you can have me a batch to take back with me?"

"I'll have you some ready."

"Great. See you Thursday . . . ."

The excitement over the possibility of becoming a sausage

mogul tried to resurface, but the disappointment he felt over Ginny lying to him hindered it. He thought about her being a virgin and realized she was bound to have lied about that too. Though she'd felt tighter the first time than the others, she could have been merely squeezing her pussy. Some women were talented that way. The squeals of pain would be easy to fake. Virgin or no, he couldn't countenance the thought of having a liar for a wife. Not that it mattered because she'd probably lied about wanting to marry him in the first place. He thought of what she'd said to Blane, claiming she'd thrown herself at him when he'd chaperoned her in Dallas. Try as he might, he couldn't conjure up a single memory remotely suggesting she'd done anything of the sort. What had he gotten himself into?

I knew I never should have messed with that bitch . . . .

* * * *

Bawling since George Strait crooned about breaking his leg, Jasper downed the last of his beer, turned off *Amarillo By Morning*, and went to bed. A ghost appeared to be haunting him and a spoiled rich bitch was taunting him.

Fuck 'em both . . . he turned over on his side and tried to cheer up by summoning a daydream of becoming a sausage baron.

8

Unlike beef, pork didn't need to age for two weeks. Twenty-four hours allowed enough time for rigor mortis to come and go. After that, everything but the hams and bacon could be cooked up and served. In the slaughterhouse with Useless and Drake, butchering the two hogs they'd dressed out yesterday, Jasper pondered the new opportunity T. Wayford offered. He decided not to say anything about the sausage until the experts gave their judgment. Instead, he told them about seeing the ghost again.

"Wonder what she meant by *I am the body?"* said Useless, slicing a thick slab of pork belly from a halved carcass.

"Beats me."

Drake chuckled. "Maybe she meant she has the best body on earth. Is she built?"

"Couldn't tell. Her clothes are real loose. But she has pretty hands and she's a white woman, or was once upon a time."

"Huh. So she's not an Indian. That blows ol' Tray's theory about an Indian burial ground then."

"Reckon it does."

Useless muttered the phrase while separating the last portion of boneless meat from the bottom of a rib section. He carried the ribs to the meat saw, ripped the baby backs and spareribs free, then cut the meaty portion of loin across the grain of sawn-through spine into large restaurant quality chops. That accomplished, he switched off the machine and turned towards him. "You know what, Boss? If ol' Thor's right about her being an angel, then maybe she means The Body of Christ. At least that's all I can come up with by her saying *I am the body*."

"Body of Christ?"

"Yeah. Haven't you ever heard that expression?"

"It's a metaphor for The Church," said Dree, entering the room.

Drake cocked his head with a frown. "Meta-what? Boy, where the hell did you learn that word?"

"At college, you stupid hick. Actually I think I learned it back in high school, which you probably didn't make it through a year of."

Puffing out his chest in an exaggerated gesture of pride, Drake retaliated with, "I'll have you know I finished the tenth grade, thank you very much."

Useless grinned. "Yeah, you're a real scholar."

Drake ignored the wise crack and aimed a taunting smirk at Dree. "But whose stupid? A man who didn't finish high school and wound up working as a cowhand because of limited career choices, or a man with a college degree cooking for such a man?"

"Me, I'm the stupid one." Dree patted his breastbone as he spoke.

"There you go."

"But let me ask you this. Who's really stupid—the man who cooks for such a man, or the man who insults the cook who has the power to slip all kinds of no-no's into such a man's food?"

Drake raised his hands in surrender. "You got me, hotshot. You're the smart one. Please don't put laxatives in my beans. I know Monte Walsh is one of your favorite movies."

That got everyone to laughing.

After they all sobered, Useless looked his way. "What do you think she meant, Boss?"

"Couldn't say. By the way, Dree, she didn't just say she was the body. Her exact words were *I am the body and I need help*."

The big blonde tilted his head contemplatively. "If she's not some apparition of the devil, then her saying that could be a reference to The Body of Christ, all right, because it sure needs a lot of help. The visible church is so worldly it hurts."

"What do you mean visible church?" asked Drake. "Makes it sound like there must be an invisible church too."

"In a manner of speaking. Everyone who truly believes in Jesus Christ is part of His body which is The Church, and in that sense, you can't see the whole church, only God can. But not everyone who says they believe really does. Anyway, all the people that call themselves Christian comprise the visible church. And if she means The Body of Christ, then she's definitely angelic rather than demonic."

Jasper wondered how Dree knew so much about the subject. "I thought angels were macho."

"I would imagine they can take any form they like. But The Body of Christ is also called The Bride of Christ, and a bride is always feminine."

"Except when two faggots marry."

Dree sneered at Useless. "Does your brain ever come out of the gutter?"

"Nope, that's where it lives. It's nice and cozy there."

Shaking his head with a weary grin, Dree turned to him. "Anyway, it's distinctly possible that's what's going on, Boss."

"How could we help The Church?"

"Search me. But if she *is* an angel you can bet she'll

eventually clue you in on it."

"Wonder why she spoke to you?" Drake queried.

"Probably because he's in charge of the ranch," answered Dree. "Angels were created in rank and file, and they respect the order of authority among humans, the ones God ordained that is."

Jasper grabbed a section of shoulder and started hacking off pieces for the meat grinder. "How do you know so much about this?"

"Studied a little theology in school."

"Well Drake heard her first."

"Yeah, but you're obviously the one she's interested in. And I'll remind you, Boss, you're the one that saw her first. Anyway, I came down here because I've got a roast in the oven for supper, leaving me about an hour of free time. Just checking to see if I could help out."

"You sure can. Finish cutting this shoulder and grind it for Ben Bishop's sausage. I'll get started on the hams." Jasper stepped back to allow him access.

Tray walked in.

"How's the corral repair coming along?"

"Got 'er did, Boss."

"Good." He pointed to a section of hog laying a couple of feet from what he'd assigned to Dree. "Strip the meat off that shoulder over there and grind it up."

Eyeballing Dree through a squint, Tray said, "What are you doing here? Hope supper's not gonna be late."

"Supper's in the oven, roasting as we speak."

"What is it?"

"Beef tenderloin roast."

Tray smacked his lips and started stroking his chin. "Now that's what I call a man. You're all right, Dree."

"Boss saw the ghost again," said Useless. "And she talked to him too . . . ."

After Tray got caught up on the latest ghost news, Useless asked his opinion on whether or not her mysterious statement could have meant The Body of Christ. The handlebars of his moustache dimpled inward as he puckered up while thinking it over. "I don't see how a woman can claim to be The Body of Christ, so my vote is she didn't mean that. Maybe she's the Virgin Mary. A lot of people claim to have seen her."

Jasper felt a stab of indignation over Ginny when Tray said virgin.

Dree heaved a sigh. "There's all kinds of problems with the idea of Mary being the Immaculate Conception but I won't delve into that. I personally don't believe she's appeared to anyone. And by that I don't mean people haven't thought they've seen her, just that what they saw was probably a demon pretending to be her."

Useless tore off a section of butcher paper and started wrapping loin chops. "Why would a demon pretend to be Mary?"

"To get the focus off Christ were it belongs."

"Well I just don't see how we can help her no matter what she is."

"I'll say it one more time, Useless, all we have to do is ask her." Dree looked his way. "What do you think, Boss? It can't hurt to ask."

"Nope, sure can't. If she ever sticks around long enough to ask her, I will . . . ."

* * * *

The week went by uneventfully and he neither saw nor heard the ghost. T. Wayford now possessed three pounds of his sausage which he'd picked up yesterday. With Friday's chores behind him, Jasper geared up for Ginny's arrival. He decided against confronting her over lying about her career, opting instead to trip her up by constantly asking about it. He was standing on the porch puffing on a stogie when the pink Corvette drove up.

"Hey, darlin'!" she shouted while getting out of the car. She had on jeans and an unrevealing button-up pink shirt that wasn't tucked in.

"Hey."

"I missed you so much . . .!" she ran up and threw herself against him. The smell of her sensual perfume mixing with Swisher Sweet smoke made for an odd scent.

Cigar clinched between his teeth, he hugged her back, halfheartedly. "How was work?"

"Oh it was hell week, let me tell ya."

"Rough one, huh?"

"Oh man, don't get me started. It would bore you to death."

He eased back to look her in the eye. "No, I want to hear all about it."

"Aren't you going to kiss me?"

Tossing his cigar in the barrel, he gave her a closed-mouth smooch. She tried to pry his lips apart with her own but he broke away.

Her sexy countenance flashed with angst. "Is something wrong?"

"Just tired. Had a hell of a week myself . . ." he guided her into the house.

"Okay, I must have done something to piss you off. Are you mad because I didn't call, even though you told me not to?"

"No. Wasn't expecting you to."

"Then what's wrong?"

"Nothing."

She studied him for a few seconds. "Gave Daddy your

sausage and he loved it." The words came out terse and even.

"Yeah, he took three pounds with him yesterday so he can have some experts check it out." He tried to sound light-hearted, hoping to convince her he wasn't mad.

"Your sausage is going to make you a millionaire." Her exhilarated tone and now relaxed attitude conveyed his effort succeeded.

The prospect thrilled him, but he wasn't about to count his chickens before they hatched and set himself up for a horrible disappointment if T. Wayford's advisors didn't give him a thumbs up. "Let's hope you're right."

"This is going down, Jasper. Daddy having it taste-tested is a mere formality. Before long you won't have the excuse of being a cowhand to prevent you from asking him for my hand. Just the thought of it is making me wet." Her eyes glazed over with a bedroom stare and she started unbuttoning her shirt. "I want you."

He hadn't planned on sleeping with the lying bitch again but she had him at her mercy when the bra came off and hit the living room floor . . . .

They were lying in his bed, exhausted and sated. Jasper leaned up on his side, facing her. "Tell me the truth, Ginny. I really wasn't the first man you screwed, was I."

Expecting her to pitch a hissy fit, cuss him out for daring to call her a liar, his mind reeled when she started crying instead, and sobbed out, "No . . . I lied."

"Why?"

"Because I wanted you to respect me. Wanted you to always remember our first time, and knew you would if you thought you were my first."

Seeing she had the guts to admit she'd lied vaporized his

anger. "You didn't have to do that. There's no way I'll ever forget it, and that would be just as much a fact if I hadn't thought you were a virgin. What else have you lied to me about besides faking all those orgasms?" He knew damn well every one of them had been real but wanted to keep her off guard.

"That's all. Everything else is true. I don't blame you for thinking I faked coming but I didn't."

Resentment rose up again over her not confessing she'd lied about having a job, but he concealed it. "So who was your first?"

Still sobbing, she whimpered, "A lifeguard."

"How old were the two of you?"

"I'm ashamed to say I was only thirteen. He was eighteen."

"Man, he better thank his lucky stars your daddy didn't find out. T. Wayford would've had his ass locked up for life. I knew you were an early bloomer, but thirteen's a damn young age to lose your cherry."

She sniffled and started wiping her eyes. "How old were you the first time?"

"Hmm . . . around twenty-one I guess."

A teary-eyed grin sprouted as she poked him in the ribs. "That's bullshit."

"Maybe I was a little younger than that, but not much."

"Stop teasing me, and tell me. How old were you?"

"Twenty."

"You are such a liar, Jasper Miller."

He gave her a tightlipped smile before saying, "Comes natural to some people."

"Are you referring to me?" she barked indignantly.

"Should I be?"

"I told you why I lied."

Nestled on his side, he put both hands under his face. "Tell me about your job."

"What do you want to know?" Her voice had a nervous edge to it.

"Everything."

She cleared her throat and started rattling on about interior design.

"T. Wayford doesn't know about your job, does he," he interrupted while she was in mid sentence.

The color left her face. "You didn't tell Daddy about my job did you?"

"Sure did."

"Oh no . . .!" she started bawling again.

"Strangest thing. He seems to be under the impression he bought your car."

"Okay, I lied! I don't have a job, and Daddy bought my car."

He rolled over on his back and didn't say a word until she finally stopped weeping. "Why do you make up stories like that? What's the point?"

She got tearful again. "I don't know why I do it. I'll just say whatever sounds the most impressive at the moment . . . I've done it all my life. While I'm saying it, I really believe it, that's the weird part. I'm always sorry afterwards, but too ashamed to admit it. You're the only one that's ever forced me to tell the truth. I really am interested in interior design, though. If a dozen real interior decorators had been there when I lied to you, every one of them would have been convinced I was telling the truth no matter how arduously they grilled me over it. And that holds true for any of my stunts. I never lie about something I know nothing about. I guess it's some sort of wish fulfillment, like wishing you really were the only man to ever make love to me.

"That stuff I told you about Blane and I planning to test you was a lie. But it just suddenly came together in my head how clever we would have been had we planned it. The truth is I was almost as shocked as you when I pulled out my boob. It was purely impulsive. I thought about doing it—didn't think I had the nerve—had to prove to myself I did—next thing I know, to my amazement I'm actually doing it."

He sat up, tossed his legs over the edge of the bed, and rested his elbows on his knees. "You're a complicated little bitch, aren't you."

Ginny pulled the top sheet from the covers and wrapped herself in it while rising to her feet. Then she stepped in front of him, looking like a Greek Goddess with disheveled hair and a wrinkled robe. "Please don't hold it against me, Jasper. I've told you the total truth. I love you. I was never lying about that."

"How would I ever know?"

"You know it's the truth. If it wasn't, why would I be here? I'm Ginny Cross. Any man in Texas that's not queer would give his eye teeth to have me and you damn well know it. If all I wanted was a good time, you think I'd choose a middle-aged ranch foreman who walks with a limp? Hell no. I'd be tooling around Dallas with some cattle baron or oil tycoon who'd be lavishing flowers and gifts on me for the chance of luring me to his bed. I don't want that, Jasper. You're the only man I've ever had real feelings for, and the only one I ever will. Your forcing the truth out of me makes me feel like a new woman—brand new, like I've been washed clean. I can't say I'll never lie to you again because I probably will, it's so ingrained in me. But I promise I'm not lying when I say I love you. Please, you've got to believe me."

He looked at the long fingers with their pink talons clutching the sheet, recalling the wonderment he'd felt seeing them squeeze her tantalizing breasts at the supper table. His gaze wandered to her beautiful face, shrouded by strawberry blonde tresses, falling in sensual disarray down to her pretty shoulders. Her eyes had transformed from the leer of an eagle in search of prey to the helplessness of a sparrow as they pleaded with him to forgive and believe.

Ginny typified the ultimate taker—selfish, spoiled, and vain—a modern day version of a Delilah or Jezebel, refusing to be refused, the world at her feet. A wise man would turn away and fear her as a Medusa, never allowing himself to look at her again lest she turn him to stone. He couldn't do the wise thing, however, because of one irrefutable fact. She had to have a real case for him or she wouldn't be standing there holding a sheet around her voluptuous naked body. What she'd said about being sought after was true, she could have her choice of men. Since he had nothing but himself to offer her she couldn't have had an ulterior motive in seducing him. Whatever lies she'd told him before or would tell him in the future, she'd spoken the truth about how she felt about him.

"I believe you." Jasper hoped he wasn't going to regret saying it.

She dropped the sheet, pushed him onto his back, and covered him with her wondrous torso. "I'm going to make you so happy, darlin'."

"Help me!"

A mere six feet away, with hands stretched towards them, stood the veiled woman in white. His heart pounded as he tried to force his gaping mouth to ask how he could help her, but she disappeared before he could form the words.

"Holy fucking shit . . .!" Ginny rolled off him and shot upright. Breasts heaving, she drew her knees to her chest and wrapped her arms around her shins, shivering like a mass of gelatin freshly dumped onto a plate. "You're gonna have to move away from here! Now she's coming in the house, and who knows what she'll do next?"

He got up and jerked his jeans on, zipping his fly with a shaking hand. His fingers were a little calmer by the time he started pinching the snaps of his shirt together. "She doesn't mean any harm, I'm sure of that, but I wish she'd stay the hell out of my house. That damn near gave me a heart attack."

Still slack-jawed, Ginny nodded. "It scared me so bad I almost peed in your bed."

Someone banged at the door.

"Oh shit, don't let one of those stupid cowboys know we're fucking. If they tell Daddy, he'll kill me."

"Stay here and get dressed, I'll get the door. No one's going to know anything. Besides, I can tell by the sound that knock doesn't belong to any of them."

"Oh my god . . .!" greater alarm flashed across her face. "My shirt and bra are in the living room."

He brought Ginny's garb to her and answered the door. The knocker turned out to be a conservatively dressed young woman with glasses, dark hair neatly packed in a bun, holding a laptop computer with a book stacked on top. Solicitors were as rare as hen's teeth on the ranch and he wondered why this one had come to call so close to nightfall.

"Can I help you?"

"Hi, my name is Lorraine Bradbury. You're Jasper Miller, aren't you?"

"What's left of him."

She gave him an expectant look which took him a few seconds to interpret as her wanting to be asked inside. "Um, won't you come in?"

"Thank you."

Jasper led her into the living room.

"Mind if I sit these on your desk?"

He gestured with a wave of his hand and she set her burden down.

"What can I do for you?"

"Does the name Tulia Barella ring a bell?"

Memories of his late teens awakened in his mind. "Yeah, I went to school with her. We dated a couple of times. What's she to you?"

"My mother."

Eyeballing her closely, he could see a faint resemblance, but Lorraine was more cute than pretty, unlike the lovely Tulia. "I guess she must have married some guy named Bradbury after high school."

"She did. My father died of a heart attack three months ago."

"Sorry to hear that."

"He died right after my mother told him I wasn't his biological daughter. According to her, you're my real father."

Jaw falling with astonishment, he hurled a sour laugh. "Then you're a walking miracle, Miss Bradbury, seeing as how I never had sex with your mother."

"She told me you'd say that." The words came out dryly through a defiant smirk.

He drew a deep breath and slowly exhaled, trying to hold his temper. "I said it because it's true. We only went out twice. The first was a school dance, and the closest thing we came to sex that night was a kiss goodnight when I walked her to her door. The second time we dated I took her to a rodeo and she left with some girlfriends before it was over, so we didn't so much as kiss that time. There's no way you're my daughter."

She turned to his desk, opened her laptop, and switched it on. "I have several interesting photographs to show you. They're rather intimate, and it seems strange to me in light of what you're saying that you and my mother would have so many pictures taken."

Knowing he'd never posed for a photograph with Tulia,

Jasper was curious as hell to see what her daughter had to show him. His visitor soon had the photographs on the screen. There were at least a dozen thumbnails. Lorraine expanded the first one and a picture of him and Tulia leaning their heads together filled the monitor. Satisfied he'd gotten a good look, Lorraine shrank it and pulled up the next one. It portrayed Tulia and him locked in a passionate kiss. The third picture depicted him standing behind Tulia, giving her a fake choke hold. Another showed them in profile, gazing into each other's eyes.

Anger surged through him alongside a current of whopping bafflement as to why Tulia would dump such a load of bullshit on her daughter. They'd never been cross with one another, and had mutually decided to remain merely friends when it became evident romance simply wasn't in the cards. Not wanting to scare the girl, he buried his emotions and calmly said, "Those are fakes. I never took one cotton-pickin' picture with Tulia. I don't know why she told you I was your father or how she had these photographs faked, but it's a crock. That one where we're kissing? I can tell you where she got my part of it. Me and a girl named Celeste had a picture taken just like that. A friend of hers surprised us and snapped it. It wound up in the high school yearbook. I wish I had it here so I could show it to you, but my mother's got all my high school shit stored in her attic."

Expression unwavering, Lorraine picked up the book. "This is my mother's diary. Allow me to read an excerpt written the night of the school dance, the one where you said you only kissed her goodnight:

"Tonight I allowed Jasper Miller, the love of my life, to take my virginity from me. We made love in the back seat of his car after he swore to me that he'd love me forever and ever as I know I shall love him. We plan to marry right after high

school and live the life of nomads following the rodeo circuit. This will upset Mommy and Daddy, but once Jasper establishes himself as a top star, they will understand."

Jasper was stupefied. "I don't know what's going on here but that diary's as much a pile of bullshit as those pictures. Back seat of my car, huh. Hell I picked your mother up in a pickup on both dates. I've never owned a car in my life."

"Want to introduce me to your new friend, Jasper?"

He turned to see Ginny prancing into the room. "This is Lorraine Bradbury. She thinks she's my daughter."

"So I gather. I've been standing in the hall listening the whole time."

The young woman looked at Ginny and gave her a polite hello.

Completely ignoring the greeting, Ginny bore down on the bespectacled girl, eyes in predatory phase, gleaming as if anticipating the taste of fresh prey. "Why are you here instead of your mother? She's the one making the allegation so she should be the one telling Jasper, not you."

"My mother committed suicide the day after my father died."

"Exactly where did this suicide take place?" demanded Ginny unapologetically.

"Fort Worth."

"What date?"

"The seventh of July, this year."

Hands on hips, Ginny stared haughtily down her nose at Lorraine Bradbury. "Okay, little missy, I'll check on that and you'd better not be lying. If that pans out I'll pay for a DNA test to prove Jasper's telling the truth. Meanwhile you leave him the fuck alone. Now take your computer and your diary and get your ass off my daddy's ranch. And don't you dare come back here or I'll have you arrested for trespassing."

Mouth ajar with fear, Lorraine Bradbury quickly grabbed her things and hurried out the door.

Crossing her arms beneath her breasts Ginny hissed, "That little bitch. Wonder what she's up too?"

"I don't know. It's not like I've got any money or anything. But way to go. You really put the fear of God in her."

She smiled. "I *was* good, wasn't I . . . ."

* * * *

To keep the boys from catching on, Ginny did a lot of horseback riding over the weekend. Jasper pretended to be put out over having to lodge and feed her, promising a grateful Dree he'd do his best to keep her away from the bunkhouse. The crew avoided the ranch house like the plague for the full forty-eight hours. He woke up Monday morning with mixed emotions and a sore penis. Tuesday evening he got a call from T. Wayford that sent him into orbit.

9

A week past Thanksgiving snow started falling on the Dallas-Fort Worth Metroplex. Jasper nervously adjusted his tie in front of a mirror on the tenth floor of the Dallas Hilton. Finally getting it right, he strolled across the room to a window and watched the snowflakes lazily flitter downward. Unlike him, they knew exactly where they were headed. The ambivalence he felt almost overwhelmed him. In a short while he'd be signing a contract that would radically change his life, according to T. Wayford. Not only had the billionaire paid for the hotel room, he'd spent over a thousand dollars for a blue western suit with matching cowboy hat and boots for him to wear to the meeting. And he'd done all that after sending a limousine to the Double Cross to transport him to Dallas. It had really impressed the boys, but he'd waved goodbye to them through the back window three days ago with a big lump in his throat. He would have driven his pickup but the way he'd gotten surprised with the news had left him no choice but to leave it on the ranch. Seven weeks after T. Wayford's hotshots advised him to market the sausage, someone had knocked on the ranch house door.

"Jasper Miller?" a Mexican man in a driver's uniform had inquired, extending an envelope for him to take.

"That's me. Something I can do for you?"

"Senor Cross told me to give this to you."

Thoroughly confused, and scratching his head over the matter, he'd opened the envelope to find a letter from T. Wayford.

Howdy Jasper,

Pack a change of clothes and head to Dallas. We got all the kinks worked out and it's time to sign the contract. You told me last week Drake was ready, so give him the key to the ranch house. The man who gave you this letter will be your driver for the next few days. Follow his instructions and don't argue with him. See you when you get to Big D!

-T. W.

"Says you have instructions," Jasper had said to the man, while stuffing the letter back in the envelope. "What are they?"

"I am to drive you to the Hilton Hotel in Dallas."

"Nah, I'll take my pickup, but thanks."

"I'm afraid that is an order from Senor Cross, he told me not to take no for an answer . . . ."

His emotions ran the gamut as he thought about the changes to come. It still hadn't quite sank in that people in Texas and those abiding in the four states bordering it—Louisiana, Oklahoma, Arkansas, and New Mexico—were going to find a new sausage on the shelves of their supermarkets in a matter of weeks. The name would be *Grandma Miller's Superior Sausage*. Within three years it would be distributed nationwide, providing the sausage hit as big as T. Wayford's experts anticipated. In return for handing over his grandmother's recipe, he'd glean fifteen percent of the profits, and according to T. Wayford's advisers, likely be a millionaire inside of twelve months. Though elated at the prospect, a big part of him wanted to stay on the Double Cross and continue living the simple life of a cowboy.

Useless, Drake, and Tray had cut cards to see who'd be

trained as foreman, and lady luck favored Drake with the ace of spades. A few days after he'd started showing Drake the ropes, a young cowpuncher named Billy Culpepper came aboard. Short but tougher than nails, Billy worked hard and all the boys liked him, especially Dree since he finally had seniority over another hand.

The ghost hadn't appeared again since she'd manifested in his bedroom, scaring the daylights out of Ginny and him. Lorraine Bradbury never paid him another visit and he still didn't know what she'd been up to. Ginny had checked on the suicide and found that Tulia Barella Bradbury died on the seventh of July as Lorraine said. The obituary didn't mention the cause of death, only that she'd passed away at her residence in Fort Worth.

Blane got seriously injured in a car wreck while vacationing in Hawaii, and Ginny flew to the island to be by her side. He didn't expect her back for at least a week. As their relationship developed, he'd sadly come to grips with the fact that what he felt for her contained a heap more lust than love. Trying to spare her feelings, he'd used the excuse that their personalities didn't mesh well enough to be a married couple. She'd bawled and squalled over hearing it but hadn't changed her tune one note. Ginny still wanted to be his woman even if he wasn't willing to take her as a wife. No one knew about their torrid affair and they planned to keep it that way. If any of the hands suspected her frequent visits had to do with anything other than horseback riding they'd never said so. Since none of them ever wanted to be around her, it hadn't been hard keeping things clandestine.

A knock on the door signaled the time had come at last. His nerves tensed up when a smiling bell hop stuck his head into the room. "Mister Miller, your limousine is here . . . ."

T. Wayford had chosen a private and very exclusive club as

the location to close the deal. It cost ten thousand dollars a year to be a member but he got in free as the billionaire's guest. They got seated at a large round table covered with crushed velvet. Besides himself, the meeting consisted of T. Wayford, flanked by his two lawyers, Bradley Bushman—the man they had to sign the contract with to get the sausage distributed—and Bushman's attorney. Shortly a pretty blonde, wearing a low-cut maroon outfit that showed miles of leg, strolled up. "What can I bring you gentlemen to drink?"

"Scotch, honey," said T. Wayford, looking his way. "What'll you have, Jasper? The drinks are on me."

It was only two in the afternoon and he seldom drank before suppertime. "I'll just have coffee."

"Coffee? Hell that's no way to celebrate the launching of your new career."

"It's a mite early in the day for me."

The lawyers all ordered coffee too, but Bradley Bushman told the leggy blonde to bring him a Harvey Wallbanger.

A few minutes later everyone had a beverage.

Jasper chuckled inside at how the lawyers contrasted with their clients. *Must be nice to have somebody else do your worrying for you,* he mused. The coffee drinking lawyers were practically grim, while T. Wayford and Bradley Bushman were relaxed and jovial, ready to celebrate closing the deal with food and drink.

For the next several minutes the lawyers took center stage, pointing to the contract as they passed it back and forth, explaining such-and-such compromise had been added as promised, such-and-such addendum had been altered as requested, and an adjustment had been made concerning his share which greatly confused Jasper. Neither T. Wayford nor Bradley Bushman uttered a syllable while this went on. The lawyer closest to T. Wayford sat his briefcase on the table and placed the contract on top of it. It would have been impossible to sign anything on the soft tablecloth. He flipped the contract to the last page, pointed to a spot, and T. Wayford scribbled his signature.

The lawyer then slid the case in front of him. "Jasper, if you'll please sign to the right of where your name is printed."

Lightheaded with disorientation, he gripped the pen firmly and complied, wondering if Dree had experienced such mixed emotions when signing his rookie deal with the Dolphins. Bradley Bushman's attorney received the contract and instructed his client where to commit himself. Bushman did so and the deal was done. Everyone shook hands. The whole scenario was dreamlike. Jasper felt excited, yet apprehensive about how this venture would turn out.

When the waitress returned T. Wayford said, "Allow me to order for you, Jasper, this place has some fine cuisine. My sidekick here will have escargot and—"

"Not on your life, T. Wayford, I'm not eating snails!" The mere thought almost made him gag. "Ma'am, I'd like a steak, medium rare—doesn't matter what kind, so long as it's beef and big—baked potato, and salad."

While everyone else placed their orders, T. Wayford turned to him and grinned. "At least taste one of mine, I bet you'll love it. But enough about snails. How you fixed for capital?"

"I've got about three grand stashed back."

"Well that's good, but I've arranged a fifty thousand dollar advance against your royalties. That was the adjustment the lawyers were just talking about. When they start coming in you'll only get ten percent until the advance is paid back—interest free of course—then once that's been satisfied you'll draw your fifteen. I've also got an apartment set up for you that I paid a twelve month lease for. Like the limo, hotel room, and duds, it's just a bonus from me—no charge. Since you won't have to pay rent, the fifty large should tied you over till the royalties start flowing in." The big billionaire reached inside his coat and produced some keys and a small packet which he handed to him. "Here's the keys to your new apartment and your account information. Give it to Forrest Wills, I wrote his name on it so you won't forget. All you have to do is sign in. I've instructed the bank to take my name off the account when you do. The money's already in there."

Jasper's head spun. He'd been totally uprooted from his old way of life and didn't seem to have any control over his new one. "Exactly where is my new apartment?"

"Arlington. Now I know you're worried I got you something real ostentatious but I took under consideration what a shock all these changes will be to your system. Got you something just above modest. When you're ready for the high life, you'll know it."

"Just above modest, huh." He had no idea what that would mean to T. Wayford but feared it was probably what he'd call ostentatious. "If you don't mind my asking, how much a month does just above modest run?"

T. Wayford let out a nervous laugh. "Now don't you go to worrying about that. I told you it's a bonus, you don't have to pay me back. Shit, Jasper, you're going to make me a lot of money, it's the least I can do."

He gave his benefactor a persistent smile. "How much is just above modest, T. Wayford?"

"Five grand."

"Holy shit! Sixty thousand a year for an apartment?"

Bradley Bushman cackled. "What's the matter with you, boy? If this kind of money scares you, what the hell are you going to do when you're sitting on top of millions, which is sure to happen because you've come up with a superior product, and with T. W. and myself on board, it *can't* fail because we never do."

He sucked in a deep breath and shook his head. "I don't know, Mister Bushman. Everything just seems to be happening so fast."

"Oh hell," laughed Bushman, "you'll get your sea legs, or should I say money legs, in no time. You had to give up your beloved grandma's secret recipe. Now that's bound to have been one hard thing to do. And you're no longer running a ranch, something you've done for so many years it became totally ingrained in your system. You traded in your glad rags for the attire of a successful businessman—the tie feels tight, the tailor made suit feels strange, but in time it'll feel as natural as faded jeans and well-worn boots."

Bushman was damn sure right about the guilt over giving up his grandma's recipe and the way the suit felt. "You talk like you've been there."

"I have, boy. I started with nothing and worked my ass off until I attained the success I felt like all my hard work deserved."

T. Wayford laughed. "When Bradley says he started with nothing, he means a measly half million dollar inheritance."

"Now you didn't have to go and tell that!" Bushman protested jocularly. He was basically a black haired version of T. Wayford, Jasper realized as the two men took pot shots at one another for several minutes, all of it in good fun.

The blonde brought their food. His meal consisted of an eighteen ounce porterhouse, baked potato that had to weigh a pound, gargantuan Caesar salad, and a submarine-shaped loaf of freshly baked bread.

T. Wayford and Bradley Bushman ordered more drinks, and even though the clock had yet to strike three, he decided to have a beer. When he asked for Lone Star he noticed the tycoons stifling a laugh. The lawyers remained stoic.

Explaining they didn't serve Lone Star, the pretty lady tactfully suggested a dark German lager which she promised he'd like. He accepted her challenge and hadn't gotten three bites of tender steak put away before she brought him a frigid pitcher of dark beer with a half-inch of foam on top. She filled a frosty mug and said, "Enjoy your meal, sir."

He took a sip and marveled. "I'll be damned, this *is* good."

"Well she told you so, didn't she?" chuckled Bushman.

Popping a snail from its shell, T. Wayford speared it with his fork and sliced off a chunk. "Now try a bite of this, Jasper."

Before he could protest, it was in his mouth. Not only did the flavor put him off, the texture reminded him of scallops which he shunned for that very reason. He told his boss turned business partner as much, after spitting the gross morsel into his napkin. Anxious to get rid of the aftertaste, he took a big swig of beer . . . .

After the meal everyone shook hands again and one of T. Wayford's lawyers looked his way. "You'll receive your copy of the contract in the mail within a few days, Jasper. At your new address of course."

He felt like a hayseed amongst a bunch of city slickers. It never occurred to him that he should have a copy of the contract, and the fact that it hadn't made him feel like a fool. If the lawyer hadn't told him, he never would have given it a second thought.

Following T. Wayford's lead, he rose from the table, whereupon the billionaire put a hand on his shoulder. "This is one damn good deal I got for you. In some ventures like this the originator of the idea doesn't get as much as five percent."

Jasper raised his brows, dumbfounded that anyone would be willing to sell their invention so cheaply. "I really appreciate everything you've done for me. Let's hope Grandma's recipe knocks 'em dead."

"Oh it will." T. Wayford adjusted his hat and it dawned on Jasper he'd forgotten to take his off after entering the club. "The driver will to take you to your new apartment and I'll give you a call later to make sure you got settled in okay."

Now holding the high-dollar Stetson in his hand he said, "Thanks, T. Wayford, but I need to get back to the ranch and start moving my stuff."

"All your stuff has already been moved, along with your pickup. Dree found a spare set of keys in your desk. Drake started shopping for furniture right after you left, and moved into the ranch house day before yesterday. Now I know this is probably rattling you pretty good, but I forced this clean break to keep you from having any second thoughts. Your cow punching days are over, hoss. The sooner you deal with that fact the better."

Jaw practically hitting the floor, he could only shake his head with wonder, trying to take it all in.

"All the boys are real excited for you and they wanted to help any way they could. You can visit the Double Cross whenever you want, but there's no need to go there today. Settle into your new digs and take it easy for a while. Production will start in a few weeks and though the sausage will be sampled daily, you need to drop by every couple of days or so and give it a fine taste test. Technology's a wonderful thing but can be a nightmare when it fouls up. The spices and pork will be mixed mechanically by computer, and you're the only one that can tell if there's a subtle variation in flavor, indicating a glitch in reading the weight or applying the right amount of seasoning. We can't allow a single errant pound to get shipped to market. That's why I put you in Arlington. Your new apartment's not far from the plant."

Jasper hoped there were no more surprises. His whole world had been turned upside down and everything seemed unreal, like he was lost in a dream. "I still feel guilty as hell, giving away Grandma's recipe."

T. Wayford stuck his thumbs in his pants' pockets, causing the tail of his gray coat to bunch up at his wrists. "Well in a way you didn't. The recipe we're using is a modification of your grandma's. Only you know how you modified it, so technically her recipe is still a secret."

He hadn't thought of it like that. The notion made him feel a little better.

"We've got the production lined out and distribution readied. All that remains is for me to get with the advertising agency and knock the kinks out of that. They hit me with a million approaches, but what I'm seeing is an old woman—your typical grandma type—frying up the sausage for a big family breakfast. While she's cooking she'll give a big spiel about how hard she worked to find just the right recipe. We'll get some young actress who lacks any real talent, make her up, and turn her loose. She'll make a career out of it."

Jasper started scratching his head. "Why not just get an old woman to play Grandma Miller?"

"Because she might go and die on us, and we want consistency. You can't have another grandma replacing the original."

"Oh, well that makes sense."

"And we don't need some young talented star or she'll dump us just as soon as her acting career takes off. Then we have the same problem—replacing grandma, which is a no-no."

He marveled at the man's foresight. "I guess that's why you're so successful, T. Wayford. You're always thinking ahead."

"You don't get anywhere in the business world without thinking ahead, Jasper. Way ahead."

They walked out of the club. The snow had stopped and the ground accumulation was rapidly melting in the fifty degree temperature. His driver opened a back door of the limo and Jasper climbed in, wondering how much T. Wayford was paying for the service.

"Are you ready to see your new apartment, Senor Miller?"

"Um, damned if I could tell you how to get there, I forgot to ask T. Wayford."

"No problem, Senor Miller, I know the way . . . ."

10

Twenty minutes after they reached Arlington the limo driver stopped at the security entrance of an enormous apartment complex and said, "I'm escorting Jasper Miller of apartment one-o-one." The guard asked for a driver's license. Jasper complied and they were allowed to pass. Numerous arrays of two-storey duplexes with balconies and carports were coated with brown stucco, roughed up to give them an adobe look. Four apartments composed each residential block—two duplexes facing opposite directions, separated by fenced in backyards. He spotted his pickup resting in the carport attached to the right side of apartment 101. The dwelling next to his numbered one-oh-two and the carport to its left was empty.

A suitcase and the box his blue cowboy hat came in, which now contained his black Stetson, were all he had to carry. The chauffeur offered to haul them for him but he thankfully refused. Having no idea what proper procedure was, he tipped him twenty dollars.

"You're employer has been most generous, but I appreciate the gratuity. Best of luck to you, Senor Miller."

"Same to you." He turned towards his new residence. A concrete porch about eighteen inches high and ten feet deep, shared by his apartment and 102, ran the length of the duplex, tapering into ramps where each carport began. The porch could also be mounted by two sets of half-moon steps aligned with the front doors, half again as wide. A firewall dividing the two residences supported one end of a concrete beam that stretched beneath the balcony to a pillar standing on the outer edge of the porch, matching similar cylindrical structures on either end. The beam served to support an upper adobe wall that split the balcony in half.

Suitcase dangling from his left hand, Jasper ascended the steps of 101, crossed the porch while shoving the hatbox under his left armpit, unlocked the front door, opened it, and stepped inside. He set his burden down on a six by six checkerboard entry composed of one-foot-square granite tiles alternately colored blue and white. A huge living room lay before him, covered with dark blue carpet, nicely complimenting pale blue walls. His desk and computer were sitting at the back wall. It stretched two thirds the width of the room and stopped to his left at an open dining area where the carpet gave way to grouted squares of stone identical to the entry. His small kitchen table looked extremely out of place in a space constructed to accommodate a small crowd at meal times. Several feet behind it, sliding glass doors, with heavy blue curtains pulled to the sides, gave access to a cement patio.

Looking at the left side of the living room, he spotted his couch and coffee table centered along the shared wall of the duplex with an easy chair setting a few feet from each side. The gun cabinet had been placed at the front corner. Directly across the room from his couch sat his entertainment center, resting to the left of a door inserted into the wall of a stairway, that separated the living room from an area he assumed was a den. A closet loomed behind the door. The stairs started about twenty feet from a large window in the front wall, matching one on the other side of the front door. Both had weighty blue drapes which were parted, allowing sunlight to beam through. He went to the window in front of the stairs and discovered the curtains were powered, operated by a button beneath the windowsill. Jasper opened and closed them a couple of times before further exploring his new abode.

The dining area extended into a kitchen with loads of marble counter space covering highly varnished rosewood cabinets. A dishwasher and trash compacter occupied a section near the sink. Across from those appliances a bar, that had four stools sitting beneath it, stretched between an electric range with a microwave above and a side-by-side refrigerator, boasting a water dispenser on the cooler door. His electric grill and timer sat midway between them. Seeing the contents of the ranch house fridge sitting inside the new icebox made him grin. Whoever transferred them had tried to match the way he kept things. At the end of the room he spied folding doors and a pedal-operated garbage can perched next to a regular door. Ignorant about compacters, he planned to use it for disposing refuse. The folding doors enclosed a pantry, he discovered. All his canned goods, boxes of macaroni-and-cheese, and various bottles of sauce had been stocked within. His spices had made the trip as well, neatly stacked in a built-in bracket with five shelves.

Jasper opened the door by the trash can and saw a washer and dryer, both of which looked brand new. He wondered if they were furnished or T. Wayford bought them. On the ranch he washed his clothes at the bunkhouse because the ranch house—designed by the immanently frugal Red King, who'd thought it would be needless duplication—hadn't been equipped for such. Consequently he had no laundry soap, fabric softeners, stain removers, or anything of the kind since T. Wayford furnished all that for the mutual possession of every cowpuncher on the Double Cross. Yet cabinets above the washer and dryer held boxes and bottles filled with substances to handle every imaginable laundry need.

He walked over to the sliding glass doors and peered through them. A butane-powered barbecue pit sat on the patio, beyond which extended a small backyard with a tall stucco fence dividing his lawn from one belonging to whomever lived behind him. Returning to the entry, he took his black Stetson from the hatbox and hung it next to the holster on his coat rack someone had attached to the wall near the front door. Then he pulled the blue hat off his head, placed it in the box, and carried it upstairs, along with his suitcase.

The stairs ended at an L-shaped hall with a large storeroom facing the landing. He left the suitcase and hatbox there, and went exploring. Running past two spacious bedrooms of identical size, each containing a stately bathroom, the hallway terminated at a locked door with two lengthwise panels of opaque glass. The deadbolt operated solely by key. T. Wayford had given him a ring that contained three, one of which had MAIL stamped on it. Discovering the front door key also fit this lock, he turned the fancy handle, pulled it open, and saw it led to the balcony. Swank wrought iron railing ran along the outer edges while the stucco wall, supported by the concrete beam below, blocked the view of one-o-two's upper deck. Astroturf covered the balcony floor, and atop it sat two outdoor recliners he doubted were complimentary because they didn't appear to have been subjected to the elements for any length of time. The balcony could also be reached through a set of French doors, but closed drapes prevented him from peering through them, and the handles didn't have key slots.

Jasper returned to the stair landing and entered an

immense master bedroom with drawn curtains he suspected hid the French doors. He pulled the drapes and confirmed it. Then he opened another door and found an extraordinarily ornate bathroom. It had fancy his-and-her lavatories, a roomy shower stall composed of dark glass, and an elegant Clawfoot bathtub with silver engravings in black porcelain. Stepping back into the main area, he looked around. His bedroom furniture was even more out of whack with the upscale surroundings than his kitchen table. Someone had made his bed, and the contents of his chest of drawers were undisturbed. He checked the closet to find his clothes hanging within a vast walk-in half the size of the ranch house living room. Still extremely disoriented, he unpacked his suitcase and stowed it, and the hatbox, in the closet.

After exchanging the blue monkey suit and boots for his ranch duds, he went downstairs to finish checking out the so called *just above modest* domicile. Located on the back wall of the area he figured to be a den were two doors. One belonged to a coat closet, the other to the first floor bathroom. A sunken tub big enough for two had a thermometer dial for a sauna, and jets along the sides signified it also served as a whirlpool. Wire racks fastened above the faucet held several small bottles of shampoo and conditioner, along with a stack of tiny bars of soap wrapped in golden paper. Feeling more like a hotel guest than a resident, he made his way to the living room.

Someone had left a city map of Arlington on his desk next to his spare pickup keys and a telephone. A dial tone buzzed in his ear when he lifted the receiver. T. Wayford already had it connected. He hung up the phone and perused the map, looking for a street called Beacon, where the plant was located. Planning on mapping the shortest route there, he chuckled when it dawned on him he not only didn't know what street he now lived on, he'd forgotten the name of the apartments.

A loud click sounded after he closed the front door. It locked automatically. Relieved he hadn't left the keys inside, Jasper walked to the carport and got in his pickup. He explored the entire complex and saw the only way out was through the security gate the limo driver had stopped at when they arrived.

"Water Crest Manor, twenty-five ten Waylon," said the guard when Jasper asked him the name and address of his new home.

"I need to get to Beacon Street. Could you give me the quickest route?"

"Beacon runs parallel to Waylon." He pointed towards the entryway, located about a hundred feet from the security booth. "When you get to the highway turn right, you'll be on Waylon. Turn right again at the first stop sign and you'll intersect with Beacon four blocks down that road . . . ."

Making the first right turn, he saw the name of the apartments brilliantly displayed along the high adobe fence surrounding the complex. Ten minutes later he arrived at the plant. Jasper got out of his pickup and strolled towards a large white building four or five stories high—he couldn't be sure because there were no windows above the second floor.

A pretty brown-haired receptionist with very striking eyes looked up from her desk and gawked at him with surprise when he stepped inside. "May I help you?"

He took off his hat and lowered it to his right thigh. "I'm Jasper Miller."

She launched from the chair with an excited smile and an outstretched hand. "Oh, Mister Miller, it's such an honor to meet you! T. Wayford assures us your sausage is going to be the biggest commodity this plant has ever produced. My name is Peg Drinkwater by the way."

"It's a pleasure." He couldn't understand her reaction since it remained to be seen whether the sausage would sell or flop. The exuberance she displayed increased the pressure he'd been feeling since the limo hauled his ass off the ranch, and also made him a little nervous. She kept pumping his arm until he pulled his hand from hers. Peg Drinkwater appeared to be in her early twenties but was gushing like a giddy adolescent meeting a rock star. "What other commodities does this plant produce?"

"It's being modified to produce nothing but your sausage. We used to make cold cuts here, every kind you can think of, but T. Wayford moved that operation to one of his smaller plants."

The billionaire had to really believe in his sausage to go to that extreme. Hearing he had, rattled him further. He hoped like hell T. Wayford wouldn't wind up regretting the bold move. "I'm supposed to drop in from time to time and test the sausage, make sure everything's up to snuff, and I was just getting my bearings. I'll let you get back to whatever you were doing. See you later, after production starts."

"I'll certainly be looking forward to it, sir."

"Call me Jasper."

That seemed to thrill her.

In spite of the additional stress he now felt over the fate of his sausage, Jasper found himself grinning on the way to his pickup. He'd dealt with rodeo groupies before his career ended, and couldn't help comparing Peg Drinkwater's apparent adulation to that of the young girls who'd thrown themselves at him back in the day. He was about to start his pickup but a thought occurred which prompted him to pull the key from the ignition and go back inside the plant.

She once again hurried to her feet when he walked in.

Holding his hat to his chest he said, "Miss Drinkwater, do you have any plans for the evening?"

Her face turned flush as a big smile appeared. "No, why do you ask?"

"I wonder if you'd mind showing me around Arlington tonight. I just moved here this very day and don't know anything except how to get here from my apartment. I'll buy your supper in return for the favor. Any place you like."

The smile grew brighter. "I'd consider it a privilege, sir."

"I thought we agreed on Jasper. What time do you get off?"

"We knock off at five but I'm working late, everyone else went home half an hour ago. I can leave now if you'd like."

"Tell you what, let me give you my address and you can pick me up, say around seven?"

"Seven is great."

"Do you know where Water Crest Manor apartments are?"

"Mm hmm."

"I'm apartment one-o-one. See you at seven . . . ."

Back at the apartment he tossed his hat, lay down on the couch, and closed his eyes. Normally he didn't take naps but he'd hardly gotten any sleep the night before—tossing and turning, thinking about the contract and the future.

11

A buzzing noise woke him. It came from an intercom perched above the light switch at the front door. Jasper pushed a button centered beneath the speaker and said, "Hello?"

"Mister Miller, a Peg Drinkwater is here to see you. Shall I let her in?"

"Yeah," he yawned out. Stretching his arms along the way, he returned to the couch and put his boots on, still not fully alert. Naps knocked the hell out of him, which was why he seldom took a siesta during daylight. Several minutes went by before the doorbell brought him back to his feet.

A gush of icy air assaulted his face when he opened the door. Peg Drinkwater stood across the threshold clutching a purse with shaking gloved hands—coat and furry hat covered with white flakes. Her bottom lip kept shivering even after it spread with a smile. Jasper looked past her and couldn't see more than a few feet beyond the porch because of heavy snow falling from every which direction. He quickly motioned her inside.

Her perfume pleasured his nose as she hurried past him to get out of the cold. She'd applied it sparingly which he appreciated. He didn't like having his nostrils overwhelmed with a woman's cologne. Ginny had a tendency to wear a tad too much on occasion.

"Brrr! I was afraid I was going to have to pull over and spend the night in my car, the snow's falling so hard. I barely made it."

"When did it start snowing again?"

"About ten minutes before I got here. The temperature dropped thirty degrees when this front hit an hour ago but the weatherman wasn't expecting snow until tomorrow, and there was supposed to be only a thirty percent chance we'd get some then."

"Is that right?"

"Yes, sir."

"Jasper. Don't be yes-siring me."

"Sorry," she giggled.

Another yawn forced itself out. He covered his mouth and realized he needed a shave. "Sorry about that, I just woke up from a nap. Didn't think I'd sleep so long. Make yourself at home. I'll go get cleaned up if you don't mind waiting."

"Not at all." She took off the hat and fluffed her hair. The thick brown mane had glints of gold and curled inward at her shoulders.

"Mi casa su casa. There's beer in the icebox if you don't mind Lone Star."

He went upstairs to his new bedroom. The upscale shower made him feel like someone's guest, as did the slick lavatory he rinsed his razor in while shaving. Catching himself being extra careful so as not to leave a mess, he smeared shaving cream on the mirror and threw his towel on the floor to kill off the lingering sensation of being a visitor. Laughing at the absurdity of his actions, he wiped the mirror with a washrag and hung up the towel.

When he got back to the living room it tickled him to see Peg Drinkwater had taken him up on his offer. "Now there's a sight for sore eyes, a woman who appreciates good beer. Some gals turn up their noses at Lone Star."

A polite smile crossed her face. "Alongside Michelob it's my favorite beer."

"You're pulling my leg."

"Mm mm." As if to accentuate the fact, she brought the bottle to her lips.

It was almost full so she'd obviously only pretended to like Lone Star to impress him. She couldn't have taken more than a sip or two since he'd made the offer before going upstairs. He wished she'd been honest instead of wasting one of his beers. Shit like that really grated on him.

"I'm afraid this is my second one, hope you don't mind."

Learning he'd misjudged her induced a grin, accompanied by an involuntary wink. "Not at all. Let me join you."

She'd chosen to sit in the easy chair closest to the dining area, after depositing her purse and winter garb on the couch. A clinging brown sweater and snug slacks revealed she had a superior build. He hadn't noticed it at the plant because she'd worn a loose-fitting business jacket. Lone Star in one hand, he rolled the chair from his desk with the other, turned it towards her, and sat down. "How much has T. Wayford told you about me?"

"Quite a bit." She took another sip and swallowed. "He called a special meeting just to tell all of us at the plant about you. Besides informing us how you came up with your sausage, he also said you used to be a top rodeo star but had to give it up because a bull hurt your knee. That's how you wound up going to work on his ranch. T. Wayford said you're the best all-around cowboy he's ever seen."

"He exaggerated a mite. I hadn't made it to the top of the rodeo world like he makes it sound. I was on my way there though, I have to say."

Clutching the sweater at a point along her belly, she

yanked it side to side, either to kill an itch or because the garment now felt uncomfortably warm. The action caused her full breasts to shake alluringly. “Do you like the apartment?”

“Yeah, pretty much. T. Wayford rented it for me. I didn’t know I’d been moved from the ranch until he told me earlier today. Come on, I’ll give you the grand tour . . . .”

Jasper showed her all around the first and second floor, and as they descended the stairs he noticed the window was covered with frost. Rubbing out a peephole, he checked the blizzard’s progress. “We might want to postpone my tour of Arlington, Miss Drinkwater. Doesn’t look like that snow’s going to let up.”

“Humph. If you want me to call you by your first name, then you’d better start using mine. Call me Peg. Or Peggy if you’d like.”

“Please tell me it’s Peggy Sue,” he said with a teasing smirk.

She laughed. “As a matter of fact it is. Peggy Sue Drinkwater.”

The warm chortle surprised him more than discovering she hadn’t lied about liking Lone Star. Endearingly down home, it didn’t fit with his first impression of her—a rather prudish city girl, hoping to make it big in the business world. “Buddy Holly would be proud. You probably don’t know who that is but he had a hit called—”

“*Peggy Sue*, I know. His band was called The Crickets. I love all those stars of the fifties. Dion and The Belmonts, Little Richard, Jerry Lee Lewis, Richie Valens, Del Shannon, The Everly Brothers, Leslie Gore, Connie Francis, Brenda Lee, Elvis of course—”

“Hey, I’m impressed,” he interrupted, fearing she might spend the rest of the evening rattling off names if he didn’t. They were now back in the living room.

“My mother made CD copies of my grandfather’s entire

record collection, which included all the hits of the fifties and sixties. That's what I grew up listening to."

That really amazed him. "Well your grandfather has good taste. The musicians of my generation can't touch what came out in the fifties and sixties. It must have been great growing up in the golden age of rock and roll."

Her pretty face crinkled with a frown. "I figured you for a country freak as far as music's concerned."

"Oh I like country too, but I love rock."

Still squinting at him, Peggy Sue reacquainted herself with the easy chair she'd sat on earlier. "I would have sized you up as a diehard George Strait fan."

"And you'd have been right." He grinned and winked while saying it. "He's my favorite country singer."

"*Amarillo By Morning* must have a special meaning to you, with you once riding the rodeo and all. Especially where he mentions breaking his leg."

T. Wayford couldn't have told her about his deep affinity with the classic because the billionaire didn't know about it. Her perception blew his mind. The woman sitting before him bore little resemblance to the nervously-excited girl he'd met at the plant. Her demeanor reflected the maturity of a woman much older than what her young face projected. His gaze settled on her beautiful eyes.

They suddenly flared with concern. "I'm sorry, did I offend you?"

"Oh no. Didn't mean to stare, it's just that . . . well you're right as a matter of fact. Sometimes late at night, when I get to feeling sorry for myself, I play that song and bawl like a titty baby."

The arresting orbs relaxed as sympathy replaced unease. "It's important to let off emotional steam from time to time. I would imagine it's very therapeutic for you. Knowing you excelled at it, yet having to walk away from the rodeo had to be awfully hard to take. Switching from riding bulls to raising them must have created at least a modicum of conflict, if only on a subconscious level. Internalizing something like that is unhealthy."

"You're pretty smart." He spoke it through a nervous smile. Jasper didn't like talking about his knee and couldn't believe he'd just confessed something to her he'd never told anybody. No one knew about his occasional pity parties except The Man Upstairs. "I bet you went to college, didn't you."

Peggy Sue released a second hearty laugh. "Yes I did."

"Thought so. Graduated top of your class no doubt."

"Actually I graduated third highest."

"How may students, five?"

"No, just three."

He snickered and took a pull from his bottle. "Never went to college myself. Figured I didn't need any more education past high school since the rodeo was always going to be my life. Man did I have a rude awakening."

"Actually you were right. You didn't need college. It wouldn't have helped you get to where you are. You're about to become a millionaire according to those in the know. Not every college grad accomplishes that. I certainly haven't, though I hope to someday."

"How long you been out of school? A year? Two?"

"I graduated from Texas seven years ago."

"You're yankin' my chain!"

"No, I'm serious."

That put her closer to thirty than twenty as he'd previously thought. And graduating third at the University of Texas meant she really had a lot going for her. "Why are you working as a receptionist?"

Her features contorted as if she'd just been insulted. "Who

said I was a receptionist?"

"Nobody, I just assumed you were, with your desk being so close to the front door. Like it was your job to receive people."

"It might interest you to know that T. Wayford chose me to oversee your sausage. I pull down a six figure salary per annum as one of his three vice presidents. Receptionist indeed."

He scratched at his right temple. "So you just happened to be at the receptionist's desk when I met you?"

"No, it's my desk, but like I told you, the plant is being modified to produce your sausage. All the offices are being remodeled as well. It's the only place for me to work at the present time."

"Six figures huh . . .?" he glanced around. "This apartment is way out of my league, but it must seem pretty mediocre to you, I guess."

"Not at all, I really like this apartment." A reprimanding squint accompanied the statement, making him take note of her irises. Their hue now puzzled him.

"What color are your eyes?"

"Hazel green. May I have another beer?"

"Sure, have as many as you want." He took her empty to the kitchen, dropped it in his new trash can, twisted the top off a cold Lone Star, and brought it to her.

"Thanks." She took a light pull and cleared her throat. "Why did you ask me that?"

"About your eye color?"

"Yeah."

"They look green now but I could have sworn they were brown."

"Oh that," she snickered. "One color dominates the other on occasion. I have no idea why."

"Excuse me a minute." He searched the kitchen for cigars.

If he'd left any at the ranch that's where they'd have been found. Coming up empty he ransacked his desk, hoping one of the boys might have stashed them there. They hadn't. Nervous about the meeting, he'd forgotten to take his Swisher Sweets from the Hilton.

"What are you looking for?"

"Cigars. Whoever brought my stuff from the ranch apparently didn't find any laying around."

"About to have a nick fit?"

"Something like that."

She went to the couch and picked up her purse. "I don't have any cigars but I do have some Marlboro lights if you're interested."

Jasper beamed. "My hero! Hell I only smoke cigars because I still haven't gotten over cigarettes. I quit a year ago."

Giggling, she handed him a white-filtered Marlboro and a gold lighter.

He lit up and inhaled deeply. Even though it was a low tar version of the brand he'd given up, a butt had never tasted so good. Peggy Sue Drinkwater was full of surprises. Savoring the addictive pollutant, he exhaled slowly and handed the lighter back. "You must not smoke much, or you're just being polite, not lighting up by now."

"I smoke three cigarettes a day. One after each meal. I never allow myself more than three."

His brows shot up. "Hell if I could hold 'em down to three a day I wouldn't even consider myself a smoker. I was up to nearly three packs a day when I quit."

She placed the Marlboros and lighter on the kitchen table, then closed her purse. "That's a new pack. Only one was missing before I gave you that one, so there's eighteen left. Knock yourself out."

The ashtray, along with the salt and pepper shakers, had

been placed on the table like he'd kept them at the Double Cross. He thumped an ash into it and looked towards the sliding glass doors. "I guess I'd better rustle us up some grub because I don't think we'll make it to a restaurant. The snow hasn't let up a lick."

"You're right, but why don't you let me cook for us?" She headed for the kitchen and he followed.

"The picking's might be a little slim for you, Peggy Sue. But you're welcome to check things out and give 'er a try if you'd like. Here's the pantry, and of course you know where the icebox is."

"Icebox," she said deliberately through a reflective smile. "I couldn't believe you said that earlier. My mom calls them iceboxes."

The statement, coupled with the look on her face, stirred him. He could tell the term impacted something deeper within her than a fondness for the nickname. It seemed as if they'd always known each other. A spark of guilt flared inside over Ginny. Something special appeared to be developing between him and Peggy Sue.

She opened the pantry doors and gripped her waist while giving the contents a thorough going over. Then she checked out the refrigerator. "Hmm . . . I need two sauce pans, one no smaller than three quarts, and a colander. I'll also require a twelve-inch skillet, cutting board, good sharp knife, a mixer, and two large bowls. Have we got all that?"

"If all my stuff made it from the ranch we do."

Together they scoured the kitchen and rounded up everything she needed.

"So what are we having?"

Pulling sweater sleeves up to her elbows, she frowned reprovingly. "Get out of the kitchen. When dinner's ready you'll know what we're having."

He grinned. "Can I at least sit at the table?"

"You can sit at the table, but the kitchen is off limits until I'm through."

"What am I supposed to do about beer?"

"Okay, I'll make an exception for that. You may come into the kitchen to fetch beer, then out you go."

Chuckling, he sat down at the table and squashed out his cigarette.

Peggy Sue took a white package from the freezer, choosing to do something with ground beef that came from a Double Cross steer. She placed it in the microwave and punched some numbers. With the meat thawing, she set water to boil in the three-quart sauce pan, salted it vigorously, and diced a large onion. When the water started boiling she opened a box of macaroni and cheese, emptied the pasta into the billowing steam, then went to the fridge for milk and butter. By the time the macaroni and cheese was done, the meat had thawed. She dumped it in the skillet, browned it slightly, added the onion, and let it simmer while she pierced two cans of chicken broth with a church key, emptying each into the other sauce pan. Then, using an electric can opener mounted beneath an upper cabinet, she opened two cans of cream of mushroom soup, stirred their contents into the beef, and commenced peeling potatoes. He didn't know he had a garbage disposal until she ground the skins down the sink before cutting the spuds into small chunks and tossing them in the chicken broth. Wielding the knife like a pro, she transformed a head of lettuce, two tomatoes, and a handful of radishes into a salad.

* * * *

Jasper pushed his empty plate back and looked across the table at Peggy Sue. "I never would have thought of having mashed potatoes with macaroni and cheese."

"Too much starch I know, but sometimes I like to live dangerously."

"Well it works. That was good chow."

"Thank you." She slipped a cigarette from her pack and lit up.

"Thought you only smoked three cigarettes a day."

She blew out a stream of smoke. "I do, this is my third one."

"Oh that's right, one after each meal."

"That's the way I do it."

Watching her inhale again, he slid the ashtray to her, wishing he had such discipline.

"So you really thought my eyes were brown at first?" she said while exhaling.

"Yeah, seemed like they were."

"Do you like my eyes?"

The question caught him off guard, embarrassing him, and he didn't know what to say. They were gorgeous but for some reason he couldn't tell her that. Maybe because of loyalty to Ginny, he didn't know. Though he'd never marry the spoiled bitch, he had feelings for her that went at least a little beyond lust.

"I've embarrassed you, I'm sorry." She flicked an ash and took another drag.

He started to spout a white lie and claim she hadn't, but thought better of it. "Kind of amazes me, you sensing that."

She smiled knowingly. "You're one of those people who what you see is what you get. You wear your heart on your sleeve—it's impossible for me not to sense your emotions. But you never answered my question. Do you like my eyes?"

"I love your eyes . . ." he looked away and took a big guilt-driven pull from his bottle. He could smell the smoke of her exhalation and knew she was staring at him.

"Is there a certain someone in your life, a significant other?"

Breathing out a sigh, he turned back towards her. "To tell you the truth, I'm not sure. How about yourself?"

"No one at the moment." She glanced towards the patio. "There must be a foot of snow on the ground and it's still falling hard."

"Yeah. Looks like you're stuck here for the night."

"Poor me." She again brought the cigarette to her lips.

The way she said it aroused him. Worried she might pick up on that too, he changed the subject. "Hate I didn't get to see the highlights of Arlington. You *will* show me around some time, won't you?"

"Of course . . ." she put out her cigarette, which was only half smoked.

He watched the action with admiration. "And you'll really be able to stay out of that pack until after breakfast tomorrow?"

"Yep. Won't be a problem for me in the least."

"That's really something. I don't think I've ever heard of anyone being able to do that before."

"Audrey Hepburn never smoked more than six cigarettes a day. At least that's what the actress that played her in the movie said."

"Well that's not as severe as three, but still way fewer than I could muster. Much easier for me to just quit than cut down."

A wry grin crossed her face. "Doesn't look to me like you've quit. Looks to me like that's exactly what you've done—just cut down. This isn't the first time you've had a cigarette since you quit, is it."

"No. There's been a handful of times I fell off the wagon, but it was always somebody else that had the cigarettes, I haven't bought any since I quit. My rule is no nicotine till the work day's done, then I can have as many cigars as I want before bedtime."

"You're showing a lot of discipline there, going all day without nicotine. I bet you can condition yourself to smoke like I do if you give it a try."

"Uh-uh, because I don't usually drink beer till the work day's done, and when I'm drinking beer I'm craving a smoke the whole time."

"I only crave a cigarette after a meal."

"Wish I could say that."

"Excuse me, I need to visit the little girls room."

He eyed her butt as the beautiful brunette strolled across the living room. She was about Blane's height but her build came much closer to rivaling Ginny's. The pleasure he derived from the view made him feel guilty over the strawberry blonde again. As Peggy Sue disappeared on the other side of the stairs, making for the first floor bathroom, his thoughts went back to the day the woman in white had manifested just a few feet from his bed, turning Ginny hysterical and almost giving him a heart attack. Wondering why she hadn't appeared after that, he gazed at the sliding glass doors. Would he see her standing on the other side of them at some point, or was she bound to the Double Cross? For several minutes he gazed at the falling snow, pondering the question.

"What are you so deep in thought about?" Peggy Sue asked while reentering the dining area.

Watching her sit down at the table, he answered with a question. "Do you believe in the paranormal?"

"Paranormal? Such as?"

"An apparition asking for help." He didn't want to say ghost.

She grinned. "I can tell by the look on your face that you

do. Why don't you tell me about it?"

He laid everything out, including a brief bio of each of the boys and their opinions on the matter. Peggy Sue listened attentively, raising her brows several times, but in amazement rather than disbelief.

"How many people actually saw her?"

"Me, T. Wayford's daughter Ginny, and her friend. Useless saw the flash of white but only that one time I told you about."

"But all the cowhands heard her ask for help, right?"

"No. Useless never heard her speak and Dree never saw or heard anything."

"Which of them is the most honest?"

"They're all good eggs. Not a liar in the bunch."

She got up and started gathering the supper dishes. "But if you had to choose one, who would it be?"

"Dree, I guess."

"And he never saw or heard anything?"

"That's right."

"How well do you know Ginny Cross . . .?" she headed for the sink. "No disrespect to T. Wayford but she has a reputation for being a pathological liar. From what you've told me, she could have been lying about seeing the woman at the bunkhouse since no one else saw her at the door."

He heaved a bitter sigh. "I can sure vouch for Ginny being a liar all right."

"Which means she may be lying about seeing the woman."

"No, she saw her. If you'd been there you'd know it to be a fact too, the way she screamed when she opened that door."

Peggy Sue put the plates in the dishwasher, stowed her tasty concoction in the fridge, and started rinsing the pans. "What do you know about Ginny's friend?"

"Not much. I only saw her that one day."

After loading the cookware she searched the cabinets until

finding some dishwasher soap, which hadn't come from the ranch house as it didn't have a dishwasher like the bunkhouse. She pushed a button and the appliance sprang to life. "I think it's a hoax and Ginny's behind it. I can't explain how she's doing it, but obviously she'd need help pulling it off. The ghostly woman is just an image someone's projecting, some type of hologram. That's why she always disappears before you get too close to her. If you got close enough to touch her, it would be just like stepping in front of a film projector. Your hand would intercept the image."

The only time he'd ever seen the veiled woman indoors Ginny was there. Peggy Sue might be right, but he couldn't figure Ginny's motive. "If it is a hoax and she's behind it, what would be her point?"

"What's the point of the geeks who come up with computer viruses?" she asked on the way back to the table. "Just something to do that's mean and wasteful. That's the true nature of a lot more people than any of us want to believe. They do mean things without provocation. They do it just because they can. I've only seen Ginny a few times and we've never interacted beyond being introduced to each other, but from what I've heard she's not only a liar but a spoiled narcissistic bitch as well. Who knows what people like that are capable of? Mean people do mean things without motivation."

"Motivation," he mumbled sourly. "Ginny doesn't need any motivation to whip out a lie, but she's a great actress if she's behind the ghost. The last time I saw the woman in white Ginny was with me. It scared her worse than me and I damn near had a heart attack over it."

A skeptical smile developed after a moment's deliberation. "Have you ever seen the woman when you weren't on the ranch?"

"No."

"Ever heard any cries for help away from the ranch?"

"Never."

"Ever seen any flashes of white?"

"Nope."

"So I could be right. If I am, whatever paraphernalia she's using must be stored on the ranch somewhere, unless she has an accomplice who's doing everything from a van or truck."

He shook his head. "It would be awfully hard for a vehicle to get anywhere near the places I've heard or seen the woman without me or one of the boys noticing it. And I've only been away from the ranch for a few days, less than a week. I last saw her a good while before I left, so just because I haven't seen her away from the ranch doesn't mean I won't."

"If I'm right you won't see her here in Arlington until Ginny finds out where you live. She doesn't know yet, does she? I mean even you didn't know until today."

"Unless her daddy told her, she doesn't. Last time I talked to her I was still on the ranch. She's in Hawaii. Blane, her friend I told you about, got banged up in a car wreck. That's why Ginny flew over there."

That seemed to surprise her. "She flew all the way to Hawaii to sit with an injured friend?"

"Mm hmm . . ." he went to the fridge for a fresh Lone Star.

"Me too please."

Back at the table he set an open beer in front of her and helped himself to a cigarette.

"Do you really want that or is it just force of habit?"

"Oh I really want it." He lit up and exhaled.

A compassionate smile briefly appeared, ending when she turned up her beer.

"I'll take the couch, you can have my bed."

"Very chivalrous of you but I wouldn't dream of it. I'll sleep on the couch."

"Nope. You get the bed, end of story."

She glanced at her watch. "Well I hope you're not intimating that the evening is drawing to a close. It's a quarter to ten—still early, at least to me."

"Not at all. I just wanted to get the sleeping arrangements understood and out of the way."

"Very well done . . ." she tilted her bottle towards him.

He raised his in salute. "Thank you."

The phone started ringing. Jasper went to his desk and answered it to find T. Wayford on the other end of the line.

"Just wanted to make sure you got settled in all right. Were all your things stored the same way you had them at the ranch? I gave explicit orders to make a note of where you kept everything and have it just how you left it."

"They did a good job. I don't suppose you know which one of the boys did it, do you?"

T. Wayford laughed. *"Wasn't any of the boys, just the movers. Is your pickup all right? Didn't see any new scratches or dings on it, did you?"*

"Nope. Fit as a fiddle, just like I left it. Drove to the plant and met Peggy Sue Drinkwater."

"Great. She's in charge of production. I hope the two of you hit it off."

"Oh yeah. She was going to show me around town but we got snowed in, so she cooked supper for us here at the apartment. She's still here as a matter of fact."

"Well she'd best stay there. There's a traveler's warning in effect. No one's supposed to drive if they can help it. This snow storm stretches from Abilene to Texarkana and isn't expected to let up before two a.m. Now you behave yourself and don't go to molesting one of my employees."

Jasper chuckled. "Oh you're no fun."

"I know, just an old prude like Ginny's always saying. So

what do you think of the apartment?"

"It's great, but I wish you hadn't gone to all that expense."

"Glad to do it, Jasper. I wouldn't be where I am now without a little help in the beginning, so you might say I'm just returning the favor, paying for my financial raising so to speak. Remember, I wasn't born with a silver spoon in my mouth like my cousin Willis."

"I really appreciate it."

"I know you do. Well I'll let you get back to visiting with Peg. Tell her I said howdy."

"Will do . . . ."

"T. Wayford says howdy, *Peg,"* he said on his way back to the table.

She smiled. "Yeah, he calls me Peg."

"Well I call you Peggy Sue. You don't mind do you?"

"Not at all."

He took a long pull of Lone Star and suffered through a silent burp. "Good. And you can call me Jasper."

"I think we've already covered that. You're not getting drunk are you?"

"On beer? Hell no. It takes hard liquor to mess up this cowboy. I'm just in a good mood that's all. I tossed and turned all night last night, worrying about signing the contract, thinking about whether the changes in my life are going to suit me or ruin me, wondering about what ol' Grandma would think of me giving away her recipe if she was still alive. Anyway, now it's a done deal and there's no point in worrying about it. Plus I met a real pretty lady and as it turns out she'll be in charge of making sure my sausage gets done right. T. Wayford Cross doesn't suffer fools gladly, so I know she has to know her stuff or he wouldn't have put her in charge. Besides, I've talked to her enough to know she's got brains as well as beauty."

Peggy Sue had smiled with sealed lips while listening to him. Now puckering them around the tip of her bottle, she partook of its contents. A glint of concern appeared in her eyes as she swallowed, and the corners of her mouth turned down slightly afterwards. The expression made it look like she was hiding something. "I'm flattered you think so highly of me. I hope I don't disappoint you."

"I hope you don't either. But I don't mean it the way you do."

Her brows rose. "Well in what way do you mean?"

"I'd hate to find out you're a liar."

"Oh, well if that's all you're worried about as far as me disappointing you, then you have no worries at all. If there's a more honest woman on this planet than me I'd sure like to meet her."

He studied her for a few seconds. "Is that a fact."

"It is."

"Well time will tell, won't it."

Recoiling slightly, she let a moment of silence roll by. "Integrity's real important to you, isn't it."

"Sure is . . ." he stubbed out his smoke.

"Well it is to me too. And you're right, time will tell. And in time you'll learn that that unless I'm obviously joking, I never prevaricate about anything."

"Let's hope so."

She cocked her Lone Star towards him. "Bank on it."

Women were sure funny creatures. He'd never come across one that had the capacity for being totally honest. Even his grandma, the most sincere woman he'd ever known, had embellished the truth from time to time when she had a hankering to tell some tall tale. Peggy Sue came off like a truthful woman but so did Ginny, despite being such a bitch. If T. Wayford hadn't unwittingly exposed her as being a liar he'd have never known it. Would the same thing eventually happen with Peggy Sue? He took in her bulging breasts. The brown-haired beauty didn't have it in her to pull one out and taunt him just for kicks, so maybe she was above viewing the truth as a plaything as well.

"What are you thinking about?"

Quickly redirecting his eyes he said, "Um, just this, that, and the other."

"This, that, and the other, huh."

The look on her face mortified him. She knew he'd been looking at her tits. Embarrassed as hell, he got up and went to his desk for a deck of cards. Finding them right away, he pretended to keep searching, buying enough time to let the awkward moment pass. Back in the dining area, he dug all the change from his pocket, laid it on the table, sat down, and started shuffling cards. "Thought we might enjoy a few rounds of penny-anti poker. You know how to play?"

She grinned. "For a minute there I thought you were planning on strip poker."

"Now why would you think that?" he said nervously, knowing damn well it had to be a reference to him ogling her boobs.

Thankfully, she merely shrugged while saying, "The only poker I know how to play is blackjack and seven card stud."

They spent the rest of the evening gambling in the two modes she understood. Peggy Sue had the devil's luck at blackjack but sucked at seven card stud, lacking any form of poker face. Nonetheless he saw to it she won most of those hands as well, often folding when she raised, even though he could easily tell she was bluffing. She had to work in the morning so he called it quits at midnight, resisting a strong urge to try for a goodnight kiss.

Stretched out on the couch, unable to quit thinking about

her and all the sudden changes in his life, he had a hard time falling asleep. It had been a helluva day . . . .

12

Blue walls greeted his eyes when he cracked them open. Not realizing where he was at first, Jasper eased himself into a sitting position on the couch. His first night in the new apartment had been spent in a deep, recuperative slumber. He slipped out from under the quilt he'd used for covers and put his pants on. Leaving his shirt and boots behind, he went upstairs—mad at himself for not thinking to bring his toothbrush and toothpaste downstairs before turning in, sorry he didn't have a spare for Peggy Sue to use. Now he'd have to creep through the bedroom and try not to wake her in the process of fetching them. Quietly easing the door open, disappointment tugged at him when he saw the bed was made. He went to the French doors and opened the drapes. Though the skies were still overcast, it wasn't snowing and he didn't see any tire tracks on the lane leading to the security booth. Evidently Peggy Sue had walked quite a distance through the blizzard last night since she obviously hadn't parked at his apartment. That explained why she'd been shivering so bad. At some point this morning she'd made the trek again, heading the opposite direction. He hated she'd left before he could tell her goodbye.

Neither his toothbrush nor toothpaste could be found in the bathroom. *I could have sworn I brought them in here yesterday, dammit.* They weren't in his suitcase either. Like his cigars, he'd apparently left them at the hotel. He couldn't stand having his habitual morning routine interrupted—wash the body, brush the teeth, shave the face, in that exact order. Still aggravated, he stripped and returned to the bathroom. After a shower and shave he stepped back into his jeans, grabbed a fresh shirt and hooded winter coat from the closet, and went downstairs. While putting his boots on he thought about how hard it was going to be navigating through that snow to get to a store for dental supplies.

His teeth starting gnashing from the bitter cold only seconds after the automatic lock clicked behind him. The balcony doubled as a roof but hadn't prevented the angling storm from depositing several inches of snow on the porch. When he stepped off it his legs sank into the freezing whiteness almost to his knees. He'd missed the steps. Marveling that Peggy Sue had braved it, he wasn't about to try driving through that deep mess. No longer worried about brushing his teeth, he hurried back to his warm apartment.

He opened the door and almost had a stroke when a terrified shriek raped his ears. Peggy Sue stood like a statue with wet hair, a towel wrapped around her torso, hands pressed over her heart as if to keep it beating after the shock. "My gosh, Jasper, you scared me to death!"

"You didn't exactly extend my life expectancy none either," he growled, slamming the door closed. "I thought you'd left. Why didn't you bathe upstairs?"

"I wanted to use the whirlpool and your bedroom bath doesn't have one. I was on my way to the kitchen to get a glass of milk and spend a few more minutes luxuriating. By the way, I borrowed your toothbrush, hope you don't mind. I'll just slip back into the bathroom and get dressed . . . ."

As she walked away he couldn't help but stare. The towel

barely covered her enticing ass, affording him a view of the entire length of her gorgeous legs. He feasted his eyes until she closed the bathroom door behind her, then headed for the kitchen to make coffee, tossing his coat on the desk along the way.

By the time Peggy Sue came strolling in, wearing clothes with her hair now wrapped in the towel, the pot was almost full.

"Do you have a blow dryer?"

"Never had the need for one, sorry." He fetched two cups from an upper cabinet. "I take mine black. You?"

"Oh I have to have cream and sugar."

He pointing towards his unmarked canisters, sitting a couple of feet to the right of the sink. "Sugar's in the second largest one, milk's in the icebox, and I'm off to brush my teeth."

"Hope you don't mind me borrowing your toothbrush. It really grosses some people out."

"And I'm one of those people . . . ."

Eyeing the secondhand on his watch, Jasper held the bristles under the faucet for two minutes, hoping the scalding water might sterilize them. The thought of swapping spit with Peggy Sue in a kiss greatly appealed to him, but having her germs on his toothbrush was revolting. Trying to put the disgusting thought out of his mind, he applied toothpaste and tended to his teeth.

When he got back to the kitchen Peggy Sue was pacing the floor, talking to someone on her cell phone. "That bad, huh. Okay, let your crew know the plant will be closed for the day . . . Very good. See you tomorrow morning, hopefully." She turned off the cell and stashed it in her purse, resting on the table beside her coffee. "That was Steve, the construction foreman. He said Beacon Street has been blocked off because of the snow so there's no way anyone can get to the plant. Looks like I'm off for the day."

"I hope you don't have cooties," he said with a wink.

She grinned. "As a matter of fact I do. It really bothers you that I used your toothbrush, doesn't it."

"Reckon I'll live."

"So what are we having for breakfast? Some of your famous sausage I hope. I'm dying to try it."

"You haven't tasted it yet?"

"No, we won't be able to start making it until the plant's finished. To hear T. Wayford talk it's almost an emotional experience to eat it. I'm exaggerating, but only a little. Your recipe is being jealously guarded and the seasonings are going to be mixed in bulk form in Dallas before being shipped to us. The mix will go through four stages with none of the departments knowing exactly what they're adding to it, as each will be receiving their quota premixed. All of us at the plant are eagerly awaiting our first taste."

That made him feel both proud and pressured. "Well you're in luck because it just so happens I have a batch on hand. I'll fry us a few patties. How do you like your eggs?"

"Sunnyside up."

"You mean over easy, I take it."

"Mm mm, I mean sunnyside up." She sat down and raised her cup for a sip. "And I'll take two."

"Grody . . ." he made a face while grabbing a tube of canned biscuits from the fridge. Once he had them in the oven he started frying the sausage and three plats of store-bought hash browns. Before long the mouthwatering aroma of sizzling pork and browning taters permeated the air.

Accompanied by two sausage patties and a square of hash browns, the practically raw yolks of Peggy Sue's eggs were a grotesque sight. He placed a couple of golden biscuits on a saucer and carried her breakfast to the table. Then he fetched butter and jelly from the icebox before sitting down to scrambled eggs and double portions of everything else he'd given her. "Hope you like Grandma Miller's Superior Sausage."

Watching her take the first bite of what she'd hopefully be supervising the production of for years to come, he awaited her reaction.

"Mmm, T. Wayford certainly wasn't embellishing."

"So you like it then?"

"Oh yeah." She consumed another section of the patty and started on her eggs. Partially raw white, mixed with the barely cooked yoke, wiggled like a wad of slime as she forked it between her lips. "Good eggs too."

Wincing, he shook his head and sliced a biscuit in half.

Peggy Sue surprised him again by eating everything on her plate. Most women didn't do such things, thinking it to be unladylike. He asked if she'd like for him to cook her some more.

"Oh no, I couldn't possibly eat another bite, I made a pig of myself as it is. Jasper, that's the best sausage I've ever eaten. There's no way it's not going to be a hit."

"Glad you like it. Let's hope a lot of consumers feel the same."

"Oh they will, there's no doubt." She fetched a cigarette and lit up.

Though he badly coveted one of her cancer sticks, his no nicotine during the workday rule had to be enforced. When she inhaled her first puff, he stared longingly.

Exhaling through a grin she said, "So who's stopping you? Have one."

"Can't. Not during the work day."

"Work day? I don't see you doing any work. Have one. It'll

only kill ya."

He blew out a sigh and reached for the pack. "I'm getting weak willed now that I'm no longer a cowpoke."

"Oh you'll never quit being a cowpoke. You can take the cowboy off the ranch, but you can't take the cowboy out of the man."

Staring at the forbidden white stick, he struggled against an irresistible urge to light it. "Where you from anyway?"

"I was born in Brownwood but grew up in Austin. That's where I graduated high school and later college."

"So you're pure Texan like me, huh."

"Mm hmm. Where were you born?"

"Waco."

She smiled. "So you're the Waco Kid, who would have guessed? Is that where you grew up as well?"

"Yep."

"Have any siblings?"

"A younger sister, that's it."

"What's her name?"

"Jasmine. She's fourteen months younger than me. How about yourself?"

"Two brothers and two sisters . . ." she took a drag.

"Where abouts do you fit in that brood?"

"Right in the middle," she said while exhaling. "I got stuck between an older brother and sister, and a younger brother and sister. Do your parents still live in Waco?"

"Mom does. My dad passed away several years ago. How about you?"

"Both still live in Austin. Must be hard losing a parent."

He nodded. "One of the most painful experiences in life. What does your daddy do?"

"He's a dentist. My mom's his hygienist. How about yours?"

"Mom was a housewife, Dad was a carpenter and part time

rodeo clown."

That seemed to mildly impress her. "Rodeo clowns have a dangerous job, getting those bulls to chase them after the rider falls off. Did he ever get hurt?"

"Only once. Cracked his ribs when a bull hit the barrel before he could duck inside. The rim slammed into his chest as it was tipping over. He said it was the most painful thing he'd ever experienced. It happened when I was ten. Years later I got thrown from a bronc and landed on my side. It bruised my ribs real bad and I found out he wasn't exaggerating. You don't want to catch a cold with banged up ribs. A cough hurts like hell. I'll take any other injury. I was able to keep my knee immobile, but you can't stop breathing until your ribs heal."

She made a hurtful face. "I'll take your word for it. Sounds horrible."

"It is."

Stubbing out her cigarette, she looked towards the patio. "I wonder how I'm going to get home. If that snow doesn't melt you'll be stuck with me all day."

"Poor me," he said, mocking her statement of last night.

Lips spreading with a grin, she continued gazing at the sliding glass doors.

He slid the unlit Marlboro light back into her pack, rose from the table, and put the butter and jelly back in the fridge, noticing a scarcity of brown bottles in the process. "How well do you know this part of town?"

"Well enough. Why?"

"Is there a store within walking distance?"

"There's a Seven-Eleven about half a mile away, that would be the closest store, and there's a supermarket about a quarter mile further than the Seven-Eleven. What do you need?"

"Beer and cigars. Won't need them until this evening but that blizzard's liable kick back up, so now would be the smart time for me to make the trip."

Pulling the towel from her head she said, "If you'll wait till my hair dries I'll go with you."

"Think you can find that particular Seven-Eleven in the phone book?"

"I already know where it is, silly. We don't need the address."

"Call and make sure they're open. I'd hate to freeze my ass off getting there, only to find it closed due to the storm."

* * * *

They hiked to the security booth, having to march like Russian soldiers because of the deep snow. Jasper intended to duck beneath the railroad crossing type barricade and continue on, but the guard waved for him to stop while sliding a window open. "I need some identification and your apartment number, or the name of who you were visiting before I can let you pass."

"You're kidding." Jasper's words produced vapor thicker than cigarette smoke.

"No, sir. I'll have no choice but to summon the police if you don't comply."

He had to take off his gloves to get the license out of his wallet. Handing it over he said, "My name's Jasper Miller and I just moved in yesterday."

"What's your apartment number?"

"One-o-one."

The attendant returned his license, turned to a computer, and typed a few licks. "Here it is. Jasper Miller, one-o-one. Have a nice day, Mister Miller."

"How cold is it out here, you have any idea?"

Glancing to his right, apparently checking a wall

thermometer, the guy said, "Eighteen degrees."

"Have you seen any traffic on the highway?"

"A few vehicles, not too many. No one has driven in or out of here this morning though."

"Okay, thanks."

The man wasted no time closing the window.

Jasper turned to Peggy Sue. The frigid air had rendered her cheeks a bright crimson. "Are you sure you want to do this? You already told me all I have to do is turn left at the entrance and I won't be able to miss it. Why don't you go back to the apartment?"

She grinned and shook her head. "I love the snow and this will be like an adventure. Come on, let's get going . . . ."

Traffic had kept the snow shallow on the highway and it was packed down along the tire trails. He ventured to the nearest one. "This will be a lot easier than I thought." After taking a few steps his feet slid out from under him and he landed on his butt.

Laughing, Peggy Sue carefully walked over to help him up. "We'd do better to stay on the sidewalk even though the snow's so deep. There shouldn't be any ice beneath it. When cars drive over the snow it melts then freezes."

He dusted his rear and started backtracking. "You talked me into it . . . ."

The hood kept his ears relatively comfortable but the leather work gloves were meant to protect rather than warm. He hadn't been able to find a pair lined with rabbit fur he used on the ranch during icy weather. By the time they got to the store his hands were frozen, even though he'd kept them in his coat pockets most of the way. With a shivering voice he told her was going to the restroom to thaw them out.

The hot water stung his fingers, made so brittle by the cold they felt like even a slight bump would shatter them. But he kept flexing the protesting digits and eventually relieving warmth returned. Hot air from an automatic hand dryer made them feel even better. For good measure he warmed his gloves beneath it as well before leaving the men's room.

Locating the beer section, he grabbed a case of Lone Star and went to the counter. "I need a pack of Marlboro lights and two ten-packs of Swisher Sweets."

The clerk worked the cash register, dug out the tobacco products, and put them in a small bag. Peggy Sue stood nearby, sipping hot chocolate.

"Did you add her cocoa?"

"I already paid for it and this—" she held up a toothbrush. "In case I have to stay the night again."

"I like a woman that thinks ahead." Jasper dug out the exact sum and handed it to the clerk. Peggy Sue took a final drink from her cup and disposed of it. He winked at her while putting his gloves on. "You carry the bag."

She dropped her toothbrush in it and pouted. "I don't know, it looks sort of heavy."

"Would you rather carry the beer?"

"No. I'll tote the heavy bag."

"Yeah, it's heavy all right. Might weigh as much as eight ounces . . . ."

Fingers frigid as popsicles, arms fatigued from lugging the Lone Star, bad knee burning with pain, the security booth was a mighty welcome sight. The crossbar rose and the guard cracked his window open enough to be heard. "Pass on, Mister Miller, I remember you." Jasper was relieved to hear it. He'd dreaded having to dig out his license again.

They trudged about a city block further and finally got back inside his blissfully warm apartment. He tucked the beer in the fridge and immediately warmed his hands in a hot stream at the sink. Then he put a three pound sirloin in the basin to thaw under cool water. That would be their supper. The leftovers of Peggy Sue's beef and soup creation would serve for lunch.

She gave him a sheepish smile as he draped his coat on the back of a kitchen chair and plopped down in it to relieve the pressure on his knee. "Um, I wonder if I might be permitted the use of your washer and dryer. I'd like to wash my clothes if you don't mind."

He fired one back at her. "What'll you do in the mean time, run around naked?"

"I'm sure you have a robe, don't you?"

"Mm hmm."

"Well may a borrow it or will that gross you out like my using your toothbrush?"

"Hmm, I don't know. I'm pretty picky about people wearing my robe."

"Oh are you now? Well then I'll just luxuriate in your hot tub during the interim because I'll need another bath before putting on clean clothes, but you'll have to hide your eyes each time I load the washer. My sweater and pants have to be washed separately, and I'd also like to launder my underwear."

* * * *

Peggy Sue lounged on one end of the couch wearing his bathrobe, while her underwear undulated in soupy suds in the washing machine. She'd taken her bath but this time hadn't gotten her hair wet. He sat on the other side, trying to catch the weather on TV. Either Water Crest Manor furnished an extensive cable package or T. Wayford had purchased it for him. The weather channel hadn't gotten around to the Dallas area so he flipped around the dial while periodically checking it. In the process he came across several TV preachers trying to drum up money. Every one of them looked like they'd come off the same assembly line with their phony smiles, high-dollar suits, gaudy rings, and hair carefully sprayed into place. Stomach already soured by the scripture-twisting money grubbers, it turned another notch when a weather warning crawled across the screen. Another round of heavy snowfall was expected and more roads were being blocked off due to accidents.

He got up and ambled around the living room. "I'm surprised this apartment doesn't have a fireplace."

"That's what it is!" exclaimed Peggy Sue. "I've been wondering what was missing in this huge room. I thought it just needed more furniture but you're right. What's missing is a fireplace."

"Do you have one?"

"Mm hmm."

"I had one at the ranch. It's going to take some getting used to, doing without a cheery hearth."

A thoughtful smile crossed her face. "There's a lot of things that are going to take some getting used to. You've had a whole new life thrust upon you."

"Yeah," he sighed. "And I'm not sure it's gonna suit me."

"You don't like change, do you."

"Nope. I like things nice and simple and predictable."

"To each his own. I love new challenges. I hate it when things get too simple and predictable."

He grinned. "Am I a new challenge?"

"You're my new boss in a manner of speaking. Even though I work for T. Wayford, you're the one that's got to be satisfied with what my people produce. So yeah, in a way you're a new challenge."

"I guess that means you like me then, since you like new challenges."

Instead of reacting humorously to the facetious pop-off, Peggy Sue soberly gazed at him for a long silent moment, apparently weighing her words before responding. "I would have liked you regardless of the situation. You're a real man. There're not too many of them roaming the planet anymore. You, my friend, are part of an endangered species."

"How would you know if I'm a real man or not, you just met me?" He said it drolly but her words had hit him where he lived. He'd never been paid a bigger compliment.

"Anyone that spends more than a minute with you knows it. You've got this air about you that screams it."

"Is that a fact."

"Mm hmm."

"You need to tell my sister that, she can't see this so called air."

"What sister does?" she giggled. "When people grow up they never see their siblings as having really grown up too. They remember too many of the stupid things they saw them do and say when they were kids. It's impossible for one sibling to be totally objective of another. Since she's younger than you, I'm betting you pushed her around and bullied her a lot when you were kids, and she'll never totally forget that."

"You must be clairvoyant. I was about the meanest older brother a little girl could have. At least up until I got to my mid teens."

"Um no, it's not clairvoyance but experience. I have an older brother. So what does your sister think about your grandmother's sausage being marketed?"

He drew in a deep breath. "Haven't told her yet . . . or my mom. They still think I'm working on the Double Cross. It's going to piss them off because they'll see me as a traitor. Grandma was real adamant about her recipe being kept within the family."

"Excuse me? You modified it, so what we'll be producing will be the sole result of *your* recipe and you can tell them that. You won't be lying. And after all, you're honoring your grandmother by calling it Grandma Miller's Superior Sausage."

That thought had never occurred to him. Between Peggy Sue and T. Wayford he might actually get past the sense of feeling like Judas. "The part of wanting to honor Grandma is true enough. Of course it was T. Wayford that came up with the name."

"Was Miller really her surname or was she your maternal grandmother?"

"Yeah, she went by Miller. My dad was her only child."

"How did she come up with her recipe?"

Reflecting on precious memories of holidays past, a sentimental warmness enveloped him. "My grandparent's lived on the outskirts of Woodway, Texas, a small town near Waco. Every May they'd buy a baby pig from this friend of theirs that raised them. Each following November, a couple of weeks before Thanksgiving, they'd have it butchered and process their own hams and bacon. We always had ham and turkey on Thanksgiving and Christmas. The hams, of course, would be from the pig they'd bought the May before. They had the butcher grind up the rest of the meat for my grandma to use for sausage. Each new batch tasted a little bit better than the one before, and finally one holiday season it tasted so good she never altered it. I always loved helping her make it and she passed on the recipe to me. Even though it tasted so good I never understood why she quit experimenting with it, since she'd never failed to make it a little tastier each time. So one day I just started doing what she used to do, try to improve it. It wasn't long till I came up with the recipe you'll be using at the plant. I didn't stop there, but every variation I tried was inferior to that one particular mix, so I finally quit messing with it, figuring that was about as good a sausage as I was ever going to be able to come up with."

Looking a little misty eyed, she donned a tender smile. "That's a wonderful story, Jasper. And I certainly can't see how your recipe could be improved."

"Well I can't top it, that's for sure . . . ."

* * * *

Peggy Sue sat at the kitchen table wearing freshly laundered clothes, smoking her after dinner cigarette. Sitting across from her, he worked on a Lone Star and Swisher Sweet, forcing himself to stay out of her Marlboro's. The white pile on the patio had deepened with another snow blitz.

"When I asked if there was someone special in your life you said you weren't sure. Can I be nosy and ask who this woman is you're not sure about?"

"No need in dredging that up." He smiled to take the edge off his words.

"Okay, if you don't want to tell me, that's fine. But would you at least enlighten me as to why you're not sure?"

"Why I'm not sure . . ." he turned up his beer and downed a mouthful. "Let's just say I'm afraid my attraction towards her might not go much beyond lust. That's about as plain as I can put it."

Her face dropped. The statement obviously bothered her. "But you are sure you're attracted?"

"Yep."

She brought the cigarette to her lips, took a puff, and exhaled. "And how does she feel about you?"

"Says she's in love with me, but who knows."

"Doesn't sound like you put much stock in her word."

"I don't. I know she wants me but I'm not so sure it's not just a physical thing on her end too."

"We're talking about Ginny Cross, aren't we?"

Dumbstruck with astonishment, he gaped at her. "Yeah, but how did you know that?"

"I didn't. It was just an educated guess."

"Well what steered you in that direction? I sure don't remember saying anything that would have clued you in, so what did?"

"The way you'd said she was a liar. Whoever the woman was, you obviously weren't sure she'd told you the truth about being in love. And you said Ginny was with you the last time you saw the ghost so I had a hunch it was her. She's very beautiful and strikes me as the type that would say anything to get what she wants, so I can see how you'd find it hard to resist her, liar though she is."

"You're something else, you know that?"

"Just woman's intuition that's all." She said it with a faint smile but her eyes looked somber. "So Ginny told you she was in love with you."

"Yep."

"How long have the two of you known each other?"

"Since she was a kid."

"I see . . ." she took a drag and expelled the smoke languidly. "Well for once I can believe Ginny's telling the truth. I bet she is in love with you."

He puffed on the stogie, wishing it was one of Peggy Sue's Marlboros. "I don't think Ginny knows her own mind."

"Her mother dying when she was only three must have affected her very deeply." She stabbed out her cigarette, leaving over half of it un-smoked. "Of course that's no excuse for her rude behavior. That was brought on by T. Wayford."

"Yeah, he sure spoiled her all right. By the way, he doesn't know anything about this and I want it kept that way, understand?"

"I figured as much, and don't worry, your secret's safe with me. Wonder why he never married again? In the seven years I've known him he hasn't even gone out on a date to my knowledge. Have you ever heard of him seeing anyone?"

"Nope, and I've known him for seventeen, though I didn't really get to know him until I went to work for him fifteen years ago. I think his ambition somehow became his mate along the way. I don't know that there's any room for a woman in his life. Or it may be that he's so doggone rich he can't bring himself to trust one out of fear she'd only be marrying him for his money."

Her lips pursed with a reflective pout for several moments before parting for a nip of beer. She seemed to relish Lone Star almost as much as he did. "I've seen pictures of his wife and it might be he's never met anyone as beautiful. Ginny favors her a lot."

"She does for a fact." Imbibing a swig, he muffled a burp and wiped his mouth. "How did she die anyway? I asked my old boss Red King and he told me if T. Wayford wanted me to know his personal affairs he'd be the one to tell me, otherwise it was none of my business. He warned me T. Wayford was real sensitive about the subject so I never asked him or Ginny. Useless said he heard she died in a car wreck."

"She did."

"T. Wayford tell you that?"

"No, Ralph Pope did."

"Who's Ralph Pope?"

"One of the other two vice presidents. He's in charge of T. Wayford's oil and gas interests. He's the big fish of the three of us."

"So you're not the big fish of the three vice presidents, huh.

Are you the second biggest?"

"Mm mm. I'm just a minnow compared to Pope and Bristol."

"Bristol?"

"Tommy Bristol. He takes care of T. Wayford's financial investments, local and abroad. My job until recently has been to oversee his commercial food production so he can concentrate on his first love—his restaurants. But my role became specialized when a certain cowboy came up with this real scrumptious breakfast sausage."

Grinning over the compliment he said, "So who's in charge of the other food production now that you're stuck with me?"

"That's still in the works, several people are being considered."

"Will they become a vice president too?"

"No, and it won't be just one person. Four will be chosen and they'll be an extension of me so to speak. I'll be the one they report to, and I'll be accountable to T. Wayford for their productivity or lack thereof."

"Do you have any say as to who gets picked?"

"I handed T. Wayford a list of qualified candidates and now it's out of my hands."

He glanced towards the sliding glass doors. The frozen whiteness lying beyond them made the warm apartment feel cozy, but it would have felt much more so with comforting flames dancing in a fireplace. "How did you hook up with T. Wayford?"

"I was fresh out of college and looking for work, so I answered an ad for a marketing assistant at Cross Enterprises. I was still living in Austin and the position was in Dallas but the ad promised quick advancement and an exciting career for the proper applicant. I was intrigued enough to drive to Dallas and check it out, because who hasn't heard of T.

Wayford Cross? I got hired over hundreds of other applicants, and worked my way to where I am now."

Jasper whistled through his teeth to show how impressed he was. "So you beat out hundreds of other people, huh. Way to go."

"Sounds like I'm bragging, sorry."

"Not at all. Funny, we're a lot alike. When my rodeo career went bust Red King hired me on at the Double Cross, so both of us have worked for T. Wayford all our working lives."

"Uh-uh," she objected. "You were in the rodeo so you had another job before going to work for T. Wayford."

"Oh I never considered the rodeo work . . ." he butted the cigar. "I'll say this though. If you've got to work for somebody, he's the man. They don't come any better than Theodore Wayford Cross."

"This is true."

"I always thought he ought to run for governor or even president. That hoss knows how to get things done—done quick, and done right. His foresight is amazing."

She nodded. "He's been approached to run for governor several times but insists he has no interest in politics. And you're right. He has incredible foresight and business instincts. If he were to lay out a hundred business proposals, you can bet at least ninety-five would be tremendous successes."

"You can for a fact. And he'd find a way to make those other five succeed in the end." He looked down at his beer and mumbled, "Let's hope his instincts are right on the sausage."

"They are."

"Ah, I don't know. It's going to bum me out big time if the sausage bombs."

"It's going to exceed expectations, Jasper. Quit being such a worry wart."

“Let’s change the subject. You up for another round of cards?”

“Sure. Provided you’ll quit letting me win at seven card stud.”

He had to laugh. Her intuitiveness blew his mind.

Once again they turned in at midnight, but she’d insisted on playing spades after he kept shellacking her at poker, keeping his word to stay competitive. Peggy Sue had waxed his ass ninety percent of the time after the transition.

13

Jasper woke up at nine, once again not sure where he was at first. A surprise awaited him when he stepped into the kitchen. Peggy Sue had made coffee and left a note explaining the arctic storm expired some time during the night and she'd gone home. She thanked him for a wonderful time and looked forward to showing him around Arlington in the near future. She'd also written down the numbers for her home, cell, and work phones, as well as her email address. He peeked through the curtains of the patio doors to see the snow rapidly melting under a clear blue sky. Turning back towards the table, he noticed she'd left her cigarettes for him. Her thoughtfulness made him smile but he resisted the urge to light up.

* * * *

With the map of Arlington sitting beside him on the passenger seat, Jasper navigated his way to the bank. There were still patches of snow on the ground but the temperature had risen to almost sixty degrees. He stopped at a toll block, pulled a ticket from the slot, and the barrier slowly rose, permitting access to the subterranean parking area of the bank. He parked and found an elevator. Once inside he pushed L for Lobby and soon found himself on the first floor.

Carrying the packet T. Wayford had given him at the club, he walked up to a teller. "I'm Jasper Miller. I've been instructed by T. Wayford Cross to ask for Forrest Wills."

The young lady picked up a telephone and punched some numbers. "Please tell Mister Wills that Jasper Miller is here to see him."

Before long a statuesque brunette wearing a professional smile rounded the corner carrying a folder. "Could I see your driver's license and social security card please?"

He slipped the credentials out of his wallet and handed them to her, noticing the folder was labeled *Cross/Miller.*

Satisfied he wasn't an imposter, she gave them back. "Come with me please."

She led him to an office with glass walls. A tall bald man rose from his desk and stuck out his hand. "I'm Forrest Wills. It's a pleasure to meet you, Jasper."

While he shook hands with Wills the woman put the folder on his desk.

"Please have a seat."

"T. Wayford told me to ask for you. He gave me this—" he handed Wills the sealed packet and sat down on a chair cattycorner to the desk.

The banker tore it open, unfolded a piece of paper within, and chuckled while reading it. "T. Wayford informs me in this little note that your sausage can make my hair grow back."

Jasper couldn't hold back a laugh.

Still grinning, Wills pulled a pristine sheet from the *Cross/Miller* folder, situated it where Jasper could read it, and pointed to a spot near the bottom of the page. "Just sign your name here and the account is yours."

His new address was printed below the line where he scrawled his signature.

Wills handed him a business card. "Hope you'll always do

your banking with us, Jasper. If you ever need anything just ask for me. T. Wayford speaks very highly of you. Can't wait to try your sausage when it comes out."

"Glad to hear it. I hope you and a whole lot of other people like it."

"T. Wayford sure thinks we will."

"Come with me, Mister Miller," said the smiling brunette, "and we'll get you fixed up with a debit card, get your checks ordered, validate your parking, and all that good stuff. . . ."

* * * *

It was almost six o'clock. He'd left the bank a quarter after four planning to return to his apartment. But seeing a sign over an entrance ramp for Interstate Twenty West beckoning drivers to Weatherford forty miles away, he hadn't been able to resist taking it. The Double Cross lay an hour's drive northwest of the city. Though he'd only been gone a few days, it seemed like months. He wanted to see the boys and fill them in on all that had happened since the limo carried him away from the ranch. A sentimental lump formed in his throat as he banged over the cattle guard at the entrance gate.

Banger stood up and surprised him by excitedly wagging his tail as he got out of the pickup. "I'll be doggone if you didn't miss me, boy." The front door opened while he was petting Red's old hound, and out stepped Drake Jensen.

"Well look what the cat dragged up. How the hell are you, Boss?"

"I ain't your boss no more, Drake. You're the big chief now."

The new foreman walked over and gave him a hug, followed by a wily smile. "So how did it go, are you lighting your cigars with twenty dollar bills yet?"

"Not yet," he laughed. "Are the boys in the bunkhouse?"

"Yeah. I was just about to mosey over there for some grub. Hungry?"

"As a horse."

Useless jumped out of his chair when they entered the living room. "Well if it ain't the sausage king of the west come a-slummin'. Damn if you ain't a sight for sore eyes. I swear, seems like you've already been gone a year."

"I know . . ." Jasper accepted the cotton top's embrace.

"Howdy, Boss," said Tray, latching on to him as soon as he turned Useless loose.

"Like I told Drake, he's the head honcho now, I'm just a civilian."

Dree hurried in from the kitchen. "Jasper Miller!"

Before he could blink the big blonde had him in a death grip. "What's for supper, Dree?"

"Chili and cornbread."

"Sounds great . . ." he broke free and patted Dree on the back. "Got enough to share some with a loafing cowboy?"

"You bet."

"Howdy, Mister Miller."

Jasper turned to see Billy Culpepper walking up from the hall. "It's Jasper, Billy, not Mister Miller . . . ."

Over a steaming bowl of chili, which he was letting cool down, he filled the boys in on the contract, the apartment, T. Wayford's huge advance, and his new acquaintance Peggy Sue Drinkwater.

Tray gave him a walrus grin. "You mean to tell me you were snowbound with a solid nine and didn't so much as kiss her? What the hell's the matter with you, Boss?"

"She's not the type you move in on fast, Tray. With a gal like that you have to bide your time—wine and dine her, the whole nine yards."

Drake cocked his head. "So she'll be in charge of your

sausage?"

"Yep."

"Huh. Sounds like she'll be in charge of your other sausage too, soon enough."

Everyone laughed.

"It's so exciting to witness a dream turning into reality," spoke Dree jubilantly. "So exactly when will we see your sausage in the stores?"

"In a few weeks. There's not an exact start date." He looked around at the friendly faces at the table. "I miss this place already."

"You're moving on up," said Useless. "Reckon you'll forget all about your cowboy days soon enough."

"You know that's a lie as much as I do."

Useless grinned. "Reckon I do."

"So tell me, Boss—" Dree grabbed a handful of cherry tomatoes from a communal platter also laden with jalapeños and green onions "—when the money starts pouring in what are you going to do with it?"

"Hell I don't know. Buy a lot of Lone Star beer I reckon."

That brought a chuckle from the boys, then Tray quipped, "Well if it becomes too much of a burden, feel free to throw some my way. I'd love to help you deal with it."

"Reckon you would, you old horse thief. So tell me, if I did do that, what would you do with it?"

A bewildered smile edged its way across Tray's face. "Buy a lot of Coors, I reckon."

"Boy," said Useless, "great minds sure think alike, don't they?"

When the new round of laughter died down Dree looked at him soberly. "Have you seen the vanishing woman since you left?"

"Nope. How about y'all?"

"Nary a thing," said Drake. "Billy, here, still thinks we're pulling his leg about it."

Jasper glanced at the new hand. "Don't know what it is or why it happened, but it's true enough."

Billy shook his head with a smile and went back to work on his chili.

"I told Peggy Sue about it and you know what she thinks? That it's a hoax and Ginny's behind it all."

"Ginny . . .?" Useless arched his white brows. "Now why would she think that?"

"Because Ginny's the type that would do something like that just for kicks."

"Ginny's not smart enough to pull off something like that."

"Peggy Sue thinks she has an accomplice who's helping her do it."

"What? She thinks one of us is in on it too?"

"No, Useless. Told her I was confident that if it was a hoax, it wasn't anyone on the Double Cross behind it. She said the woman always disappears before I can touch her because if she didn't, I'd see her on my hand which would prove her image is somehow being projected."

Useless gave that some thought, then reached for the cornbread. "All I can say is that must be one hell of a projector, being able to do that without a viewing screen and from so far away the damn machine can't be seen. Nah, I don't buy it."

Tray and Drake echoed the same sentiments.

The room got quiet as everyone tended to their grub. He noticed Billy Culpepper attacking his as if the young puncher hadn't eaten for days. But hunger wasn't the reason. Dree had created a gastronomic masterpiece so delicious Jasper couldn't quit chowing down until his overstuffed belly forced him to relinquish the spoon. Now he knew why Useless, Tray, and

Drake were always begging for chili and cornbread for supper. They were pacing themselves, so as to prolong their enjoyment. He wished he'd done the same. "Dree, that was the finest damn chili I ever ate, beats mine all to hell. I'd have eaten over here every time you made it if I'd known it was this dandy."

Smiling like a boy eyeballing his brand new bike on Christmas morning, Dree swung a fist into the air as if he were a victorious boxer who'd just knocked out an opponent. "Wow! I know you wouldn't say that if you didn't mean it, so I finally found something I can cook better than the master. Means the world to me, Boss, thanks for saying it."

"Jasper, Dree. Drake's foreman now." He chuckled inside at Dree's elation over the compliment. The ex tight end sure took pride in his vittles.

"As of yet, ain't a one of the boys calls me boss."

Useless coughed out a patronizing laugh. "And we ain't a-going to neither, Drake. Hell it was a toss up between you, me, or Tray as to who was going to replace the sausage king as foreman. We cut cards for it, remember?"

"Yeah well, maybe the good Lord knew who was best suited for the position and saw to it I won, reckon?"

Useless hung him the bird and went back to eating.

Drake reciprocated and did likewise, taking in a mouthful of chili-soaked cornbread.

Jasper thought back to when he'd taken over after Red died. It was Useless that had first started calling him boss, but he'd done it only as a nickname at first, like dubbing Dree Thor. He winked at Drake. "Well if a man can't handle being called by his own name, he must be ashamed of it."

"That's the way I see it."

"That's good, Drake," spouted Useless sarcastically, "because there ain't nobody here gonna call you boss, except maybe Billy. Right boys?"

Drake flung his right hand in the air, extending the middle finger. "Jump on it and rotate, ghost face."

"Well now, if you're propositioning me, Drake, I need flowers and candy first. Useless Horton may be easy but he ain't cheap."

Laughing, Jasper got up from the table. "Thanks for supper, Dree. Guess I'll head on back to Arlington before Useless gets his ass kicked. Sure was good to see you boys."

* * * *

Jasper woke up the next morning in his bed instead of the couch, but it still took him awhile to ascertain his location. It was Friday and he hoped Peggy Sue had weekends off. After breakfast he called her work number.

The phone rang several times before she answered.

"Peg Drinkwater." Her voice sounded professional and devoid of emotion.

"Peggy Sue? Jasper here."

"Well good morning, what a pleasant surprise!"

He grinned. Her voice had plenty of attitude now. "Are you ready to show me around town tonight?"

"I certainly am."

"Good. Pick me up at seven?"

"I'm taking off early, so can we make it six?"

"Six is fine . . . ."

Scouting out his neighborhood, he found the supermarket Peggy Sue had told him about—bought bread, baloney, cheese, milk, eggs, cigars, and beer—dropped them off at his apartment, and drove to the plant.

Peggy Sue's desk sat vacant. The sounds of power tools, men shouting, and other noises pertaining to construction lured him to a vast area being divided into sections. Workers wearing plastic hard hats were fastening metal studs to the floor and ceiling with pneumatic screw-guns, driving nails into plywood forms, running electrical conduit through prefabbed holes in the studs, taping-and-bedding drywall, and the like. One of them spotted him. Yelling over the racket he hollered, “Can I help you?”

“I’m looking for Peg Drinkwater!” Jasper yelled back.

“If she’s not at her desk I don’t know where she is.”

“Mind if I look for her?”

“Wait for her in the lobby. You don’t need to be wandering around the plant, you could get hurt.”

“I won’t get hurt. I’ll be careful.”

“Unless you work for Cross Enterprises you need to wait out front.”

“I’m the reason you’re doing all this remodeling.”

“Huh?”

“I’m Jasper Miller. It’s my sausage that’s going to be processed here.”

A grin replaced the man’s irritated glower. “Sorry, Mister Miller, my bad. The plant’s at your disposal. Let me get you a hard hat . . . .”

Receiving a yellow head protector that fit too tight, Jasper adjusted the band and went to look for Peggy Sue. Laborers scurried to and fro. Strong smells of wet paint, drywall mud, saw dust, melting welding rods, and freshly poured concrete hung heavy on each breath he took. The whole place looked disorganized and chaotic. Jasper marveled at the way the craftsmen were able to carry out their individual tasks. Welders were fastening steel I-beams to metal supports up towards the ceiling, the embers of their welds almost hitting workers down below, where plumber’s sweated copper lines and electricians wired outlets within walls not yet covered.

Drywall men screwed sheetrock onto metal studs as soon as the plumbers and electricians moved to the next section of wall.

He ventured to the end of the plant and back but never found Peggy Sue. Her desk remained unoccupied when he made his way back to the front. Figuring she must have taken an early lunch, he found the man he'd talked to earlier and returned the hard hat . . . .

Back at the apartment, he ate lunch and scanned the yellow pages, looking for a stable to keep No Name. After calling several places and wincing at their rates, it occurred to him T. Wayford might let his horse remain on the Double Cross for a reasonable monthly fee. Hoping so, he dialed the billionaire's cell number.

"Hello?"

"T. Wayford?"

"Well hello, Jasper. What's up?"

"I called a few places to house my horse, and man are those people proud of their services. I was wondering what you'd charge me to keep No Name on the ranch."

"Don't be silly, I'm not going to charge you a cent. I don't reckon the boys are going to mind feeding your horse."

"No, wouldn't think they would."

"I'll give them a call and tell 'em your mount is a permanent resident. Anything else I can do for you?"

"Nope, that's all I needed. Thanks a million."

The phone rang right after he hung up with T. Wayford. It was Peggy Sue.

"I understand you dropped by to see me."

"Sure did, but couldn't find you so I figured you must have gone to lunch early."

"I did, sorry I missed you. Steve said you checked out the plant. So what do you think?"

He laughed. “Pure pandemonium, that’s what I think.”

“Sure what it looks like now, but give it a few weeks and you’ll be amazed at the end result.”

“I found the store you told me about and am starting to learn the area near here.”

“Great.”

“So what did you have good for lunch?”

“Chef salad,” she said unenthusiastically. *“What did you have?”*

“Oh I had a gourmet delight.”

“Really? What?”

“Baloney and cheese sandwiches.”

A giggle rang out. *“Well you can’t get any more gourmet than that.”*

“For sure. Well I won’t take up any more of your time. See you at six . . . .”

* * * *

Peggy Sue walked into his apartment at six sharp, all decked out in a slinky black dress and high heels. He was wearing his usual snap up shirt and jeans.

“You’ll need to change clothes, Jasper. The place I want to eat won’t let you in dressed like that. No blue jeans, and you’ll have to wear a tie.”

“Well pick another place then.”

“Too late, I made a reservation. I’ll just help myself to a beer while you change.”

He followed her to the kitchen. The dress really showed off her hot figure, making him recall how sexy she’d looked wrapped in that towel. “What if I don’t want to change?”

“Then you can just show yourself around town.”

“Is that a threat?”

"Sure is."

"You've got me at a disadvantage and you're exploiting it."

"Sure am . . ." she opened the icebox and reached inside.

Heaving an exaggerated sigh, he turned and made for the stairs.

Begrudgingly he changed into the western outfit T. Wayford bought him, fetched the blue hat, and went downstairs. She wolf-whistled when he got to the bottom. "All right, don't make this any worse than it is. I feel like a clown."

"You look like a handsome, successful Texan."

"Mm hmm," he mouthed sarcastically while opening the front door. "Shall we go?"

They strolled to an area on the highway side of the security booth, designated VISITORS. She drove a silver BMW Roadster two seat convertible and had the top pulled up.

"Well now, that's what I call a set of wheels."

"You like it . . .?" she pressed a button on her key ring and both doors unlocked.

"Sure do." He finagled his way into the passenger seat, holding the Stetson because his head barely cleared the top. "You never would have made it through that snow in this."

"Be a good boy and buckle up." She fastened her seatbelt and he did likewise.

Commenting on this and that point of interest, she drove for several miles before they arrived at a restaurant named Lou Chong's which had valet parking. He got out of her car and plopped the cowboy hat on his head. A guy wearing an orange blazer drove off in it and they entered the restaurant.

A long line of people stood waiting for a table. She grabbed his arm and led him to a black man attired in a white tuxedo, standing behind a podium. "We're the Miller party."

The slicked-up dude consulted a list and smiled. "Right this way, please . . . ."

His hat got confiscated, then they were seated at a table for two. An oriental woman appeared and doled out their menus. "May I get you something to drink while you decide on your order?"

"We'll have the house wine please."

Jasper cringed. "The hell we will, I don't like wine."

"Trust me," said Peggy Sue through a forced smile that conveyed he'd embarrassed her. "Open your mind a little, expand your horizons. Miss, bring us the house wine."

He opened the menu and almost gagged upon seeing how much everything cost.

"Pricey, isn't it," she said knowingly.

"Pricey ain't the right word. This is highway robbery. Why the hell did you choose this joint anyway?"

"To introduce you to a new way of life. Consider this a foray into the world of the upper class. A lot of Metroplex elite eat here. You're one of them now and even if you never dine here again, you'll always be able to say you did."

"Who cares about that?"

An impatient sigh flew out of her pretty mouth. "Jasper, this is all new to you. A ways down the road you'll be able to settle into it. Your new life is going to differ radically from the one you knew. Tonight's dinner is on me, so quit worrying about the bill."

"Like hell it is. I said any place you liked and I'm no Indian giver."

"In that case I'll let you decide what we're having."

"No, that would be reneging too. You do it."

The waitress brought them two small glasses and a white bottle covered in brown netting. "Are you ready to order?"

Peggy Sue nodded. "We'd like the Peking duck, shrimp soup, stuffed mushrooms, sweet-and-sour pork, fried rice, and egg rolls please."

Biting his lip, he looked towards the ceiling. This promised to be the worst meal of his life. Though he'd never eaten Peking duck, he could only stomach four types of fowl—chicken, turkey, quail, and dove—so he didn't hold out hope of finding it very palatable. The sweet-and-sour pork, fried rice, and egg rolls were the only things she'd ordered that suited him.

When the waitress left, Peggy Sue filled their glasses. The so called wine looked like pale beer to him.

"Taste it. I think you'll be surprised." She took a generous drink.

Cautiously imbibing a small sip, he immediately thought of Ginny's opinion of Lone Star. "This has to be the worst tasting booze I've ever drank."

"Come on, Jasper, don't beat around the bush, tell me what you really think. Seriously, it's an acquired taste. All I ask is that you finish that glass. If you still don't like it by the end of it, I'll never ask you to drink it again."

Surprisingly, after fulfilling her request it didn't taste half bad. The stuff had a kick to it that went straight to his head. He grabbed the bottle for a refill.

"Told you so . . ." she slid her empty vessel towards him. "Me too please."

By the time the food arrived he had a nice buzz and managed to tolerate the duck, soup, and stuffed mushrooms. Though the other items tasted good, they were nowhere near savory enough to justify those jacked-up prices. The waitress gave them each a fortune cookie and presented him the bill.

Peggy Sue busted hers open and read the small strip of paper. "Tonight is favorable for romance."

He did likewise and had to laugh. "Good fortune is soon to overtake you."

It hit her funny bone too.

The wine, meal, and tip seriously lightened his wallet. He'd stuffed it with cash after having trouble with his new debit card at the supermarket. On the way back to his apartment Peggy Sue stopped at a liquor store because she wanted to make margaritas. She insisted on buying the tequila and mix instead of letting him do it like he wanted. "No, Jasper, this is on me. I meant to pick it up beforehand but got behind the eight ball and didn't want to show up late."

When they got out of her car at the visitors' parking lot, she took a small bag from the trunk. Answering his puzzled stare she said, "It's glasses for the margaritas and a change of clothes. I don't want to wear this damn dress the whole evening . . . ."

As he swapped the blue suit for his usual attire, Jasper wondered what she might be expecting from him by trying to culture him up. Peggy Sue would learn quick enough she'd be able to change the weather sooner than him. Heading down the stairs, he could hear his blender whining, but it went silent before he made it across the living room. Now wearing a gray sweatshirt, jeans, and sneakers, Peggy Sue was cutting up limes when he entered the kitchen. The way her breasts captivatingly bounced in rhythm to the movement of her arm revealed they were no longer encased in a bra. Once finished with the limes, she rubbed one around the rim of the glasses and turned them upside down, swirling each in a pile of salt. She then flipped the crystal vessels upright, filled both with her icy concoction, and handed him one.

He raised the glass to his lips. The cold salty mix went down smooth and flavorsome. Eyeing the tequila bottle, he thought of the night Ginny had pulled out her tit, the prelude to what happened the next day when she'd lured him to bed. Facing her wouldn't be easy, but it had to be done. They were through—they had no future. He'd fallen in love with Peggy

Sue.

She'd waited until now to have her after dinner cigarette. He joined her with a cigar. They smoked, chatted, and sipped margaritas. A lighthearted air had surrounded her since leaving the restaurant, but it dissipated as a serious expression overtook her. "There's something I need to tell you, Jasper. I wanted to do it before we turned in night before last, but couldn't work up the nerve."

His heart rate quickened. She'd fallen too and wanted to tell him so. Unlike his feelings for Ginny, no ambiguity existed with Peggy Sue. He didn't merely lust after her. The time had come. She'd tell him first, then he'd confess his love for her. Afterwards they'd take their margaritas to the bedroom and merge their bodies together in blissful consummation. Life couldn't be any sweeter than it was at this precious moment. No wonder so many songs and poems and books and movies centered around the concept of falling in love. For the first time in his life he truly had, and the feeling exceeded any expectations he'd ever imagined.

"What is it you need to tell me?" he tried to sound nonchalant.

"I'm a lesbian . . . ."

* * * *

Drunk and bawling, Jasper switched off *Amarillo By Morning* at two a.m. of the worst night of his life—even worse than the last rodeo in Pecos when he'd dove off Diablo Toro after the buzzer signaled eight seconds had passed. The bull had spun around, caught his right leg between its horns before he hit the ground, and in a violent twisting motion, forced his knee to bend ninety degrees opposite the direction The Man Upstairs designed those joints to work, ripping it apart.

Peggy Sue had gone home right after dropping the bomb because he'd told her to get the hell out of his apartment. The cruel unrelenting pain stabbing at his soul hurt a thousand times worse than the physical agony he'd suffered from Diablo Toro. Such misery defied reason. He now understood why a broken heart could drive a man to suicide. The easy way out wasn't an option for him though. A feller had to be able to take the bitter with the sweet, that's what being a man was all about. But *man* was this bitter . . . .

14

Four months had come and gone since Peggy Sue Drinkwater turned his whole world upside down. He hadn't laid eyes on her since. Each time she called—which she did at least twice a day—he hung up on her. T. Wayford saturated the television and radio stations with commercials, put up billboards all over the place, and not long after making its supermarket debut, the sausage began outselling all competitors. Jasper hadn't gone to the plant since that day Peggy Sue had taken an early lunch. Five days after his heart got shattered, Ginny returned from Hawaii. He'd asked her pick up the first sausage for him to test, and she'd done it for him ever since. Thus far there'd been no deviation in quality, each batch tasted as good as the one before. Ginny always got the receptionist to fetch the sausage, so she never interacted with Peggy Sue, who'd long since moved into her new office.

He hadn't shaved since the night Peggy Sue devastated him, and now sported a thick beard a couple of shades darker than his overgrown curly brown hair, which hadn't seen the inside of a barber shop in that length of time either. Ginny hated the beard, said it hid his pretty face, but he gave her the finger each time she begged him to shave it. He'd confessed he didn't love her, only lusted after her, but she refused to give up on the two of them. When the mood suited him he gave her a good screwing, otherwise he never succumbed to her seductions, and none of her shenanigans could coax him into it. She'd pitched one hissy fit after another, threatening him, begging him, trying to bribe him, but none of it had worked. After a while she'd learned to read his moods and go along with them, so they seldom squabbled anymore.

The commercials were great. A twenty-one-year-old actress had landed the role. With a white wig shaped in a bun, loads of makeup, lots of padding to make her shapely body look fat, granny glasses, and a frumpy dress with a frilly apron, she looked like an eighty-year-old grandmother. T. Wayford's advertising plan played out exactly as the tycoon had envisioned it.

His mother and sister were proud and excited for him, neither accusing him of betraying the real Grandma Miller since he'd improved her recipe, a fact which had really lifted a burden from his shoulders. They didn't like the beard though. Jasmine claimed it made him look like a brain-fried hippy. His pussy whipped brother in law had sided with her opinion, but behind her back, told him he should keep it. The boys all got a kick out of it, especially Dree, who'd said, "It gives you a certain je ne sais quoi," whatever the hell that meant.

He managed to get out to the ranch at least once a week. Sometimes he helped out when everyone was too busy to visit, but occasionally he'd saddle up No Name and take a leisurely ride through the hills, valleys, and plains of the Double Cross. Something he'd dreaded, but thought lay several years down the road, transpired a few weeks after Peggy Sue so rudely awoke him to the fact she'd never be his. Banger contracted distemper and didn't pull through. Dree buried him at the top of a hill overlooking the stream, made him a grave marker out of a large rock, and chiseled his name on it.

Unable get very excited about anything after his initial

exhilaration over the sausage doing well, he merely trudged along from one day to the next. He'd quit kidding himself about cigarettes, and it hadn't taken long to get back to smoking almost three packs of Marlboro reds a day. Ginny had taken him shopping, talked him into to buying some fancy duds he never wore, and new furniture, which he enjoyed. He donated his old kitchen and living room furnishings to the Salvation Army. Now he had a long couch with built in recliners on both ends, very comfortable armchairs, nice coffee table, fancy desk, and dining room set consisting of a rectangular walnut table with six snazzy chairs. He'd purchased a new bedroom suit as well, moving the old one into one of the spare bedrooms. The desk he'd replaced occupied the other. His entertainment center got bumped upstairs to his bedroom. The new one in the living room boasted a huge plasma television set. When the royalties started coming he planned to trade in his pickup. Until then, he figured he'd best only buy necessities with the rest of T. Wayford's advance.

Now well acquainted with all the thoroughfares of Arlington, he didn't bother eating at any of the swanky joints, despite what Peggy Sue had told him at that Chinese restaurant. He'd found a truck stop he really liked and went there whenever he wanted to eat out. Ginny accompanied him once but bitched about everything, so he never invited her again.

The doorbell snapped him from a half doze. He'd been lounging on the couch with his boots off, waiting for a Saturday western matinee to commence. Wondering why security hadn't buzzed him like they always did when he had a visitor, he got up to answer it. An absolute stunner with a ton of red hair bunched atop her head, wearing a green satin robe and no shoes, stood on the other side of the threshold. Though barefoot, she was only a couple of inches shorter than him. He guessed her age to be in the mid thirties.

"I live next door and I hate to trouble you, but I've locked myself out of my apartment. Can I use your phone so I can call the super to let me back in?" Her purring voice sounded as sultry as she looked.

"Sure. Come on in."

"Thank you."

"Phone's over there." He pointed at his new desk.

She went immediately to it.

He listened to the bombshell explain her predicament to the superintendent and that she'd be waiting for him in apartment 101.

When she hung up the phone he extended his hand. "I'm Jasper Miller."

"Selma Russell," she said while shaking it. Her palm felt soft and inviting.

"I assume someone's coming to unlock your door?"

"Yes. I told the super I'd be here, hope you don't mind. I was just about to take a bath when someone rang my doorbell. When I answered the door there was no one there, so I stepped outside trying to let whoever rang know I was home, but they'd already gone and the stupid door closed behind me. I hate that damn automatic lock."

That explained why her hair was piled high—she hadn't wanted to get it wet. It also accounted for the bare feet. They were alluringly slender with toenails painted a deep red. She had a long pretty face with an elegant nose perfectly situated between full red lips and sexy turquoise eyes. The robe she wore couldn't disguise a killer body. Tray, who loved tall women, came to mind. Chuckling inside, he imagined him ogling her with a lusty walrus smile. The cowpuncher refused to give a ten, so he'd have to rate her as a solid nine, the highest ranking Tray allowed. Realizing his examination was becoming obvious, Jasper figured a few words might be in order. "I moved in here back in December and you're the first neighbor I've met. Lived here long?"

"A little over a year." She was boldly probing his face as if trying to memorize his features.

"It seems odd we haven't run across each other before now, living right next door to one another and all. I've never seen a car in your carport, or the drapes pulled apart, so I thought that place was vacant."

The turquoise orbs continued scrutinizing him. "I don't own a car, I use a limo service. As for the drapes, well I like my privacy. What do you do?"

"I'm Grandma Miller's Superior Sausage. Maybe you've seen the commercial."

Her face lit up with surprise. "You're kidding! Why are you living in an apartment instead of a mansion? I mean, you must be rich."

"It's just getting off the ground. The man who backed me rented this place for a year so I'd be near the plant."

"The plant's near here?"

"Yeah, Cross Enterprises on Beacon."

"You don't say . . ." she gripped her waist with both hands, long red nails standing out against the deep green satin of her robe. "I pass that place every day on my way to work."

"Where do you work?"

"I run a modeling agency."

The doorbell rang, announcing the arrival of the superintendent.

Her luscious lips spread into a dazzling smile. "Thanks again for everything. Drop by sometime, maybe we can have dinner or something."

Jasper cleared his throat. "What are you doing tonight?"

* * * *

Selma Russell had invited him over to her place for supper. He'd called Ginny, told her he didn't feel like company, and put on some of his new clothes—a black western suit and matching cowboy boots. The whole getup cost only about a third of what T. Wayford paid for the blue one, though he hadn't bought a hat to go with it.

His hormones surged when Selma answered the door. She'd let her hair down and it stopped at her smooth shoulders in waves of red splendor. Rubies sparkled from earrings, necklace, bracelets, and rings, enhancing her flawless pinkish-pale skin. No longer barefoot, she wore toeless green shoes that sexily accentuated her svelte crimson toenails. Their two-inch stiletto heels would have made her his height if he wasn't standing there in cowboy boots. A low-cut green dress showed an obscene amount of cleavage. She gave off a regal air that reeked with raw sexuality, enhanced by a touch of beguiling perfume.

Her apartment mirrored his. The furniture looked feminine and very expensive—most of it green, contrasting Christmas-like with the scarlet carpet of her living room floor. Her dining table was covered with a cherry tablecloth, punctuated by dark green placemats. Flames danced atop long red candles in a candelabra of gleaming silver, placed in the center. Chrome chairs with green padding on the seats and backs, surrounded it.

"Please make yourself comfortable while I finish getting everything ready."

A savory aroma emanating from the kitchen teased his nostrils as he sat down on a green couch with red throw pillows. "Sure smells good."

"Thank you. Would you like a cocktail before dinner?"

"Sure."

"There's ice in the bucket, help yourself." She pointed at a portable bar while heading for the kitchen.

Perched behind a row of eight ounce highball glasses turned on end, a sealed bottle of Wild Turkey looked tempting. Opening a small refrigerator at the bottom, he spied a two liter bottle of cola. Turkey and coke used to be his drink of choice during his rodeo days when he had a mind to tie one on. He poured a stiff mix and went back to the couch, whereupon he noticed a crystal ashtray on the coffee table, resting beside a candy dish loaded with mints. It likely served merely as an ornament, but he decided to take a chance. "Mind if I smoke?!"

"Not at all!" she yelled back from the kitchen.

Relieved, he reached inside the black coat and pulled his cigarettes and lighter from the pocket of a hundred dollar dress shirt Ginny had insisted he buy to wear with the suit.

Selma walked into the room brandishing a glass of clear liquid as he lit up. "Dinner will be ready in just a few minutes. I'm letting the main course cool down a bit."

"Smells wonderful. What are we having?"

"Chateaubriand, stuffed artichokes, scalloped potatoes, and steamed broccoli. I made a chocolate fudge cake for dessert, which I promise will be to your liking if you have any form of sweet tooth."

Steamed broccoli didn't float his boat at all. Simmered with a bucket-load of cheese was the only way to eat the stuff, to his way of thinking. "You shouldn't have gone to so much trouble."

The statement apparently made Selma think he didn't care for any of the food choices—her stately, erotic facade took on a worried frown. "You do like beef, don't you?"

"It's my favorite food."

Smiling with relief, she took a quick pull from her drink and returned to the kitchen.

By the time he finished his smoke Selma beckoned him to the table. He carried his drink with him and emptied the glass before sitting down. Concentrating on the cuisine to keep from staring at her, he politely forced down a modest portion of steamed broccoli while truly enjoying a hefty helping of meat, potatoes, and artichokes, followed by a generous slice of her sumptuous cake.

"Thanks for a great supper, that was dandy . . ." he daubed his lips with a colorful green napkin trimmed in red.

"You're welcome. So glad you liked it."

"You live here by yourself?"

She nodded. "And you?"

"Yeah, all by my lonesome."

"I like the freedom of being able to come and go without having to account to anyone. I'm fiercely independent. That intimidates a lot of men." She gave him a discerning look. "How about you?"

"Doesn't bother me none."

"Good." Her eyes lowered to his empty tumbler. "Where are my manners? Let me fix you a another cocktail. What were you drinking?"

"Turkey and coke."

"Let's adjourn to the living room . . . ."

Once again perched on her couch, he eyeballed the voluptuous redhead while she made his drink. If Selma Russell had any physical deficiencies, they were well hidden beneath the satiny dress clinging to her delectable bulges and curves.

"My height doesn't bother you, does it?"

"Nope."

A husky laugh rose from her ruby-laced throat. She handed

him the drink and sat down to his left. "You're not just saying that to be polite are you?"

"Not at all." He sampled her mix, finding it a tad stronger than the one he'd made.

"I have a confession to make."

The word *confession* brought Peggy Sue's earth shattering revelation painfully to the forefront of his mind. "Oh?"

"I already knew you liked tall women, or at least tolerated them. I've been watching you for some time. I locked myself out of my apartment on purpose, just so I could meet you."

Flattered, yet confused, he couldn't withhold a frown. "Why didn't you just come over and introduce yourself?"

"Because I know you have a girlfriend, I've seen her—that beautiful blonde that drops by from time to time. She's almost as tall as me."

"You mean Ginny," he said dryly. "Well, she's more of a pest than a girlfriend."

"So her name's Ginny, huh . . .?" she sipped her drink. "I knew if she was there she couldn't fault me for locking myself out, and it would all appear very innocent. I didn't think she was there—I mean I was really hoping she wasn't—but I couldn't be sure, so that's why the ruse. Forgive me?"

"Sure."

"You mean it? You're not just saying that?"

He grinned. "Yeah. I'm tickled you went to such lengths to meet me. Hell if I'd ever seen you I'd have bopped right over and introduced myself."

Her stunning visage blossomed into a sexy smile. "I'm sorry you didn't then. We wouldn't have wasted so much time."

"Me too."

"I like your beard but I think you look better without it, though growing your hair long suits you well."

"You *have* been watching me for awhile then," he said with a laugh.

She nodded and took another nip of whatever she was drinking. "I talked to the men who moved your furniture in, wondering who my new neighbor was. I planned to introduce myself, but then I saw you walking with another woman besides the blonde, back when we had that snow storm. I figured the two of you were married at first. But after awhile, when I never saw her again, I started to approach you and darned if I didn't see you with the blonde woman."

Jasper heaved a big sigh. "You won't be seeing that other woman again. Ginny, now, that's a different story. I could shake my shadow easier then her."

Leaning forward, she took a mint from the candy dish, exposing her large breasts all the way to the rims of her nipples. He knew she'd done it on purpose. Confident she wouldn't take it as being too forward he said, "You have a beautiful body. Matches your oh-so-pretty face."

A light blush filled her cheeks as she gave him a slow, deliberate smile. "Would you like to see it?"

Though he'd figured Selma to be on the fast side, that shockingly surprised him. "Trick question, right?"

She rose from the couch and leisurely slipped out of her dress, letting it fall to the floor, revealing the woman had no imperfections at all. Wearing panties but no bra, she leaned down to pull them off—the movement of her arms and legs causing her beautiful tits to sway sensuously, making his mouth water. Now naked except for the heels, she posed for him like a model, giving him every conceivable view of her breathtaking body. If Selma Russell dyed her hair, she did the same with her midsection: a lush, dense carpet of red curls covered her crotch.

Never taking his eyes off her, he repeatedly turned up his

glass.

Clapping her hands once, she held out her arms invitingly as violin music filled the air. “Shall we dance . . .?”

They moved to the slow rhythm of a violin playing on an unseen stereo as she kept her body pressed against him. Looking into his eyes, she parted her lips seductively. He shoved his mouth against them, plunging his tongue between her teeth with raw passion. Wantonly returning his kiss, she unzipped his pants and pulled out his dick. After goading it to a full erection with her fingers, she eased down on her knees and slid her beautiful lips over the shaft. When he reached the brink of climax she pulled away and started pumping it with her hand, guiding his violent ejaculation onto her quivering breasts.

A lust-ridden grin spread across her face as she stood up and went to the kitchen, immediately returning with a hand towel. Wiping semen off her stiff cherry-red nipples she said, “Now that we’ve got the preliminary jitters out of the way so you won’t have to try so hard to hold back until I come, what say we go upstairs and make love . . .?”

She woke him up at four a.m. and told him it was time to go home. He limped back to his apartment exhausted. Selma Russell had insatiably devoured all his energy. Sweet, replenishing sleep commenced the moment his head hit the pillow.

15

Jasper didn't get out of bed until noon. An hour later he went next door to invite Selma over to his place for supper, but she didn't respond to the bell. Noticing the door lacked a fraction of an inch from being latched, he pushed it open, planning to holler "Is anybody home?" But the words froze in his throat. Before him lay nothing but barren red carpet. Her living room furniture, portable bar, dining table and its chrome chairs, were gone. Stupefied, he pulled the door to, heard the automatic lock kick in, and went back to his apartment.

Unable to find Selma Russell in the phone book, he buzzed the security booth.

"Yes, Mister Miller?"

"I met the renter of one-o-two yesterday, the apartment next to mine, and it appears she moved out some time this morning. Would you check and see if she left a forwarding address or a phone number where she can be reached?"

The clacking of a computer keyboard filled his ear and the guard said, *"That apartment's been vacant for several months."*

"That can't be right."

"According to the computer no one's lived there since last October."

"That has to be a mistake. Her name's Selma Russell. The records must have her living at the wrong apartment. Would you check and see?"

More typing.

"There's no Selma Russell listed, Mister Miller."

"Give me the number of the superintendent . . . ."

Radically bumfuzzled, he hung up the phone after a short chat with the super. No one had called the dude about being locked out of their apartment yesterday, and none of his three helpers could have opened anyone's door because he possessed the only master key and hadn't lent it to any of them. He too said apartment 102 had been unoccupied for a good while.

Jasper again buzzed security.

"Something else I can do for you, Mister Miller?"

"Did a moving van come through there any time today?"

"Not during my shift."

"How about a truck?"

"The only truck I've seen today was a Fed Ex truck which entered before my shift started at noon. It left at twelve thirty."

"Thanks."

Jasper went to the kitchen, popped open a too early in the day Lone Star, took a swig on the way to his new dining table, and set down. The Fed Ex truck apparently carried Selma's furniture away. Whatever was she up to her motives couldn't have been good. But what did she want? All she'd gotten from him was sex. He'd used a condom each time they screwed, so she couldn't be planning to slap him with a paternity suit. Blackmail? That had to be it. She must have had an accomplice taking pictures the whole time, probably the same guy that posed as the superintendent. Her partner in crime may even have been playing the violin instead of the music coming from a recording. He let out a humorless laugh and took a long pull from his beer. She'd picked the wrong cowboy to blackmail. Selma Russell could post pictures of the two of them on every billboard in Arlington for all he cared. It wasn't like he had a wife and kids to worry about losing in some messy divorce. She couldn't do anything more harmful than embarrass him.

The phone rang.

"Hello?"

"Jasper, this is Peggy Sue, please don't hang up—"

He slammed the receiver on the hook and went back to the table. The nerve of her, using his pet name instead of referring to herself as Peg like she'd always done before. Shaking that off, he refocused on the scheming redhead.

How did Selma manage to get in that apartment and stay for so long without getting caught? She had to have been there since I moved in or she couldn't have known about Peggy Sue . . . Wait a minute, she said she saw us walking together back when that arctic snap hit. She might not have saw us within the apartment complex but on our way to or from the Seven-Eleven, or even at the store itself. Hell I've been with Ginny away from here a ton of times, Selma could have seen us on any number of occasions. She must have lied about living here for so long. She's probably only been in that apartment for a couple of days. Somehow she got access to it, moved her furniture in, and then moved it out using the Fed Ex truck.

Once again he buzzed security and asked who last occupied 102.

"I don't have that information, Mister Miller. Sorry."

The superintendent didn't know either.

After stewing on the situation for almost an hour, something dawned on him. The blackmailing bitch probably already knew what he did for a living before asking about it. Reluctantly, he dialed Peggy Sue's home number.

"Hello?"

"It's me."

"Jasper?"

"Yeah."

"Listen, Jasper, I'm really sorry—"

"Don't go there!" he screamed into the receiver. "I'm only calling because I need a favor. If you don't want to do it, just say so."

"Of course I'll do it! What is it?"

"I assume you can locate a list of everybody that works for T. Wayford?"

"Yes."

"The woman probably lied about her name, but just in case would you see if there's a Selma Russell employed by Cross Enterprises?"

"Sure, but why?"

He grunted and ran a hand roughly over his face. "Look, will you do it or not?"

A moment of silence passed. *"Okay. It will only take a few minutes to access it on my computer. Do you want to hold or have me call you back?"*

"Call me back . . . ."

About ten minutes later she did.

"There's an Emma S. Russell that works in Human Resources."

"What's Human Resources?"

"What used to be called Personnel."

"Okay, give me all the information you have on her."

Peggy Sue gave him a home number, work number, birth date, and address. He scribbled it all down on a note pad. "I don't suppose you happen to know her?"

"No, sorry. But these files have a picture. I'll email it to you, what's your address?"

"Don't have one. I don't cotton to electronic mail."

"I could print it out and bring it to you."

The hopefulness in her voice sickened him. "Is she a redhead?"

"No, brunette."

"Okay. Yeah, print it out and bring it over . . . ."

The age would be about right, according to the year Emma S. Russell was born, and she could have dyed her hair in both places. The picture would tell the tale.

Forty minutes went by before the buzzing intercom announced Peggy Sue's arrival. He opened the door and stood at the threshold, waiting for her to walk up from the security booth. His heartstrings yanked his soul into a black hole of excruciating devastation when she came into view. Why the fuck did she have to be a lesbian? Directly, she crossed the porch, handed him the picture, and nervously said, "May I come in?"

"Yeah . . ." he closed the door while looking at the color depiction ink-jetted onto a sheet of printer paper. It wasn't Selma Russell.

His tormentor took off a rainbow colored windbreaker and draped it on the back of his desk chair: beige t-shirt straining over breasts his hands would never fondle, jeans glued to hips whose wondrous nakedness would forever be hidden from his view, torturing him in the process. Her agonizingly gorgeous eyes cut his way. "I see you got some new furniture."

"Yeah, figured it was about time."

Sitting down on the couch, she donned a rigid posture—hands on lap, thumbs nervously encircling each other. He turned his attention back to Emma S. Russell.

"Is that her?" she meekly asked.

"No."

"Sorry. How long have you had the beard?"

He scratched at it absent mindedly, still looking at the copied photograph. "A while now."

"I like it."

"How could you . . .?" he sneered at her derisively. "Oh, I guess you play the female role, huh?"

Face contorting as if she'd been slapped, Peggy Sue started crying. "That was uncalled for."

"Well if you play the male role I don't see how you could like my beard."

She buried her face in her hands.

"Stop it." He tried to sound hard and cold.

"I can't help it!"

"Can't help crying, or can't help that you're queer?"

Slowly she raised her head and stared at him with tear soaked eyes that begged for compassion and understanding, neither of which were his to give. His gaze must have conveyed the fact because she covered her face again.

He wadded up the picture and threw it on his desk. "Man this is a crazy world. I guess people need to start wearing signs saying whether they're hetero or homo, or bi or tri or quad, or just plain weird."

A small laugh escaped her. She sniffled, dug into her purse for a handkerchief, and blew her nose. "I'm afraid it's not as simple as that. People are complex. They can't all be put into a nice, neat category."

"You put yourself in that category, I sure as hell didn't."

"God put me in that category."

That pissed him off royally. "Oh don't go to blaming God or I'll kick your butt right out of here!"

"Sorry . . . ."

Several minutes passed before she spoke again. She'd collected herself somewhat and had quit crying, but her face was a portrait of emotional torment. "I've never felt this way about a man before, and it's not that I like women per se. It's just that I can't tolerate intercourse because it hurts too much. And so I consider myself a lesbian, even though I don't pursue women."

He started scratching his head. "What do you mean you don't pursue women? Don't you have girlfriends?"

"No. I've never had sex with a woman."

His jaw fell. "Then how the hell are you a lesbian? I don't get it."

When she didn't answer he shouted, "Tell me dammit!"

She leaned forward and shrieked into her palms as if the wailing could somehow release all the frustration she'd ever felt over the issue. Then she jerked upright and yelled, "I masturbate, okay!"

"Huh?"

"I don't have sex with anyone, I just masturbate. I don't want to grow old alone so eventually I'll have to seek a lover, and it will have to be a woman. Satisfied?"

Now completely dumbfounded he said, "Why couldn't it be a man?"

Hands clinching into fists, she screwed her eyes shut as her bottom lip started quivering. "I told you why. Because it hurts too much."

The pain on her face made it clear she viewed her sexuality as an awful burden, one she'd apparently never planned to share with anyone. "You say it hurts too much, so you have been with a man, I take it."

Her lids finally parted. Glistening with tears, the beautiful hazel orbs now looked solid green. "I had a steady boyfriend all through high school. Our senior year we had sex and it was the most horrible experience of my life. I broke it off with him and vowed I'd never go through anything so horribly painful again for as long as I lived."

"Are you telling me that one time with your boyfriend is the only time you've ever had sex other than masturbating?"

"Yes."

"Holy shit . . .!" he rammed his forehead with the heel of his right hand. "Didn't your mother or older sister or some friend in the know warn you it would hurt the first time?"

She slowly shook her head. "All my mother ever told me about sex was that I should save myself for my husband like she did. My older sister had been married for two years when I slept with my boyfriend, and I confided it to her. She told me that she didn't enjoy intercourse at first, but had only felt some discomfort rather than any real sense of pain. I don't know what's different about me, but something obviously is because my younger sister is now happily married too. My friends all said getting laid was wonderful, yet for me it was awful."

Not as awful as being told by the woman you love she's a lesbian. He thought of how her words had crucified him, turning a night that had promised to be so magical into a nightmare he hadn't been able to wake up from. "Why did you pick the night you were last here to tell me you were a lesbian?"

Sniffling, she adjusted her position on the chair and wiped her eyes. "Because I knew you were expecting us to make love."

"Why didn't you just tell me you don't like conventional sex, why call yourself a lesbian?"

"Because I'm bound to be a latent lesbian since I have no desire to ever have a man's penis inside me again and will never allow such, so I was just being as forthright as I could, since honesty's so important to you. I knew you were falling for me as hard as I was falling for you, and it would have been cruel to tell you how things stood after you finally made a pass. I'm sorry, falling is the wrong word. I *fell* in love with you, but I can never have intercourse with you. And what man wants a woman who can't have sex with him?"

Elation flooded him like a torrential rain saturating a thirsty desert. Peggy Sue was no lesbian, just a naive woman, sophisticated in all the ways of the world except one. Somehow, despite being so intelligent, she didn't know all she had to do was give it a few more tries and the pain would have turned to pleasure. He stepped to her, got down on his good knee, and grabbed her hands. "I love you, Peggy Sue, and I want you to marry me."

"I love you too . . ." she started sobbing. "But I can't marry you."

"Why not?"

"I told you why not!"

"Hey, I can masturbate same as you. We'll be the Masturbating Millers. No one will ever know we're not your every day husband and wife. What do you say? Will you marry me?"

Incredulity laced with fervent hope captured her face. "Are you saying you'd actually marry me without ever expecting us to have intercourse?"

"Yep . . ." he rose to his feet and grinned down at her.

"You wouldn't have to masturbate," she said excitedly. "You could have a mistress on the side. I'd let you, so long as I know you love me and not her."

"So when do you want to tie the knot?"

"Five minutes ago . . .!" she lunged from the chair and locked her arms around his neck. "Oh, Jasper, I love you! I love you! I—"

He shut her up with a compulsive kiss, unable to refrain, despite longing to hear her keep saying it. The taste of her lips, and the hungry way she kissed him back, gave him an instant hard on. Peggy Sue might be afraid of having a penis inside her vaginal canal, but she obviously loved the feel of his tongue invading her oral cavity. He ran his hands through her pretty hair as they ravaged each others' mouths.

Suddenly she pulled away. "Can you fondle my breasts without trying to force me to make love? I'm aching for you to."

Immediately groping them with eager hands, he kissed her again and she moaned with pleasure. Their exquisite fullness and firmness made his passion soar towards the point of no return. Having no choice but to either back off or rape her, he released Peggy Sue's marvelous tits and took a step back.

Disheveled hair covering her eyes, cheeks flush with heat, pretty mouth sucking wind, she gasped, "Oh my god, that felt wonderful!"

"Yeah," he said, catching his breath. "Felt good on my end too."

She unfastened her jeans and slid her right hand inside them. "Please . . . kiss me and feel me up again, and I'll make myself come."

Taking her in his arms, he did as she asked. Before long she cried out as her knees buckled and she fell back on the couch with him on top of her. He could feel her fingers moving furiously over her crotch. "Oh Jasper, I love you so much!"

The motion stopped, and she sighed in his ear. "That was the hardest I've every came. Now show me how to satisfy you with my hands and mouth, I've never done either . . . ."

* * * *

For a first timer she'd handled herself real well. Jeans and underwear pulled down to his knees, he lay across the couch with her stretched out on top of him, repeatedly saying, "I love you." Each time she did, he reassured her he felt the same.

They remained that way for awhile, then she got up and started taking off her clothes. "I want to be naked with you."

Gawking at Peggy Sue's fantastic body, he tore off his shirt, kicked off his boots, and stripped his jeans. He lay back down and she flung herself on top of him. The sensation of having the woman he loved pressed against him, skin to skin, made withstanding the urge to penetrate her almost overwhelming, even though he'd shot his wad into the air after forcing her pretty mouth off his dick only a few minutes ago. Thankfully, he had a handy excuse to break away from the temptation without having to explain the real reason. "I hate to spoil the mood but I'm getting hungry."

"Want me to cook something?" The words came out in a sleepy, lazy drawl.

"No, it would take too long. I found a truck stop that serves real tasty grub. Let's go there."

* * * *

Chicken fried steak had never tasted so good, but the credit didn't belong to whoever cooked it. The beauty sitting in front of him enhanced the flavor by her mere presence. Peggy Sue made everything magically wonderful beyond description. *This*, he thought to himself, *is what true happiness is.* He could lose everything and it wouldn't matter, so long as he had her. And he could tell by the look on her face she felt the same. She'd killed him inside with three cruel words that fateful night. Now she'd resurrected him with three others—"I love you."

Swallowing a bite of mashed potatoes, she reached for her iced tea. "So what's the deal with that woman Selma Russell?"

He didn't want to hurt her but Peggy Sue had a right to know the truth because she was his woman. Phrasing it as delicately as possible, he told her everything.

Pain and anger radiated from her. "How could you have sex with her when you just met her?"

"Oh it wasn't hard because of the misery I was feeling over you at the time. But in fairness to myself, she seduced me."

Though obviously still smarting over it, he could see she was trying to be objective by the expression she wore while mulling it over. At length she said, "Well I agree with you. It sounds like you were being set up for blackmail. What made you think she worked for T. Wayford?"

"When I realized she must have lied about living next to me for so long, I got to thinking. She knew too much not to have been connected in some way. She knew about me and you, and me and Ginny—"

"You and Ginny?" Her eyes shot wide with rude surprise.

He heaved a sigh. "Yeah. She said she saw Ginny and me coming and going from the apartment. She didn't call her by name but I know that's who she meant. Ginny's T. Wayford's daughter, and you work for him, so I thought maybe Selma worked for Cross Enterprises too—learned I was the inventor of Grandma Miller's Superior Sausage and thought she could blackmail me because of the image T. Wayford's presenting to the public."

She stewed on that a spell, then let out a short laugh. "Now if she could have gotten Grandma Miller to have sex with her, she might have gotten some good blackmail material."

The notion made him chuckle.

"And you're sure she's not the woman in the picture I gave you."

"Positive. But that doesn't mean Selma doesn't work for Cross Enterprises. She most likely made up the name."

"What does she look like, besides having red hair?"

He hoped the description wouldn't reopen the wounds Peggy Sue had apparently sutured in her mind. "She's a good looking tall woman. Somewhere in the neighborhood of six feet. She's real classy and appears to be in her mid thirties."

"The only woman I know of that tall who works for Cross Enterprises is a black lady."

"Well that obviously can't be her."

She lit up her after dinner Marlboro light. When he unsnapped the flap on his shirt pocket and pulled out his pack, a frown jumped on her face. "Where's your cigars?"

"Finally gave up. Been back on cigarettes for a good while."

"I thought you'd switched from cigars to cigarillos when I noticed that bulge on your chest." A remorseful pout came over her. "It was because of me, wasn't it."

"Yep."

"I'm sorry."

"Nah, you should feel proud, darlin'. I was so overwhelmed with seeing you again I'd forgotten all about cigarettes until now . . . ."

They said goodnight at ten because Peggy Sue had a six o'clock meeting tomorrow morning with the people T. Wayford had chosen to run his other food production outfits. Five minutes after she left, the doorbell rang. He answered it and there stood Selma Russell.

16

Having enjoyed pleasuring her as much as he did Ginny, who topped the list of every woman he'd ever bedded down, Jasper hated that Selma had only been using him. If she'd really wanted him they could have continued sleeping together until Peggy Sue finally decided to give intercourse another try. Curious as to how his blackmailer planned to go about it, he thought about playing dumb and let the redhead enact her devious plan. Not knowing he'd gotten a peek at the empty apartment, she mistakenly thought her cash demand would come as a big ugly surprise. Admiring her physical splendor, he tossed the idea and decided to shoot straight. "Let me guess. You're here to blackmail me."

The glamorous vixen laughed as if he'd only been popping off. "Um, no, I just dropped by to ask you over for a nightcap."

"To your place?"

"Of course. Where else would I mean?"

Shocked and confused, he followed her to the apartment next door.

Creepy chills slithered up and down his spine. Red candles burned on the dining table, the bottle of whiskey he'd opened sat atop the portable bar, his cigarette butts still littered the crystal ashtray. All the furniture sat right where it had the night before. He stood in front of the couch, watching her make his drink, head spinning with puzzlement. "I came by earlier and the door wasn't closed all the way. Your furniture was gone."

Selma handed him the tumbler and took a slow pull from hers, which once again contained some form of clear liquor that she'd poured before inviting him over. The corners of her mouth turned up slightly as she swallowed. "Some things are hard to understand at first."

The statement unnerved him, then he realized something that brought on more unease. Selma looked exactly as she had last night—same green dress, same green shoes, same fiery rubies, same lipstick and eye shadow—nothing had changed. While he wouldn't expect her hair and makeup to look different, women were famous for refusing to wear the same formal attire two nights in a row, especially in front of the same man. Ominous wonderment storming his thoughts, he swallowed a mouthful of booze, trying to steady his jumpy nerves. "According to security and the superintendent, this place is supposed to be unoccupied."

"You don't say. Well everyone's entitled to their opinion. What's yours? Do you think I live here? Silly question, isn't it. But I've got a serious one for you. Would you like to know why I was so willing to pose for you au naturel last night?"

Seriously not liking the mysterious gleam in her eyes, he weakly nodded.

"I am the body."

A cold blast of fear swept over him and he almost dropped the tumbler. Adjusting his grip, he quickly guzzled over half its contents. Adrenalin competed with the whisky as to which inflamed him more, but neither held a candle to the firestorm of fearful perplexity blazing in his psyche. When time kept passing without the veiled woman manifesting, he'd finally concluded he would never have to deal with the paranormal again. Now it seemed to have returned in an intensified state. How much further would it escalate? "A-Are you the woman I saw at the ranch?"

Her ruby lips spread with a seductive smile. "So many questions. For now, all you need to know is I am the body and I need help."

Jasper fell back on the couch, barely able to hold the shallow drink shaking in his hand. The veiled woman had frightened him when she'd vanished in the rain, but the horror gripping him now made that emotion seem trivial. Selma's voice didn't match the veiled woman's, and she was much taller, but a dark intuition assured him they were one and the same. "Are you a ghost?"

Still wearing the seducing smirk, she turned up her glass and swallowed sensuously. "Did I feel like a ghost when I was in your arms last night? Drink up, we have the whole night ahead of us."

Terrifying bafflement flooded his brain. She'd felt like flesh and blood when their bodies were fused together, but saying the exact words as the vanishing female on the Double Cross couldn't be coincidence. Selma Russell might not be a ghost, but whatever she was didn't fit the schematic of being altogether human. "What do you want from me?"

She threw her head back and laughed before sternly gazing down at him, ravenous passion radiating from a face whose sexy exquisiteness now intimidated him. "I think you know the answer to that question, lover."

"N-No I don't."

Clasping her tumbler with the fingertips of her left hand, she stirred the clear liquid with the middle finger of her right. The long blood-red nails glistening against the glass looked menacing and claw-like. "Don't be foolish, Jasper, you know what I want. I want you."

He hacked a nervous cough and cleared his throat. "About that . . . earlier today I got engaged to a wonderful girl named Peg Drinkwater. I-I should be getting back home."

Totally unfazed, she slid the wet finger into her mouth and languorously withdrew the slender digit from her puckering lips, sucking the liquor from it. A wicked smile emerged—evil, yet all too alluring. "Nonsense, the night is young. One woman will never be enough for you. Deep inside your heart you know it. Engaged or not, you'll always have need for a woman like me, who worships your penis, and doesn't waste a moment of your time with frivolities."

Hastily downing the rest of his drink, he barely felt the whiskey go down his throat. "Who are you really?"

"Selma Russell, just as I told you."

"Why was your furniture gone, and how did you get it back here?"

Turning towards her front door she said, "Perception is a relative thing. People see what they want to see, and sometimes—" she faced him again "—what they don't. I'm here and you're here. That's all that matters for the moment. Let me make you another cocktail."

The mystifying redhead took the tumbler from him, strolled to the bar, and soon brought it back full. He downed a big swallow and ran a shaky hand over his face. "Are you the woman in white I saw at the ranch?"

"I'm a woman in green with red accessories. Do you see anything white on me?" Though she spoke it humorously, her expression appeared enigmatic, shrewd, and threatening.

Remembering Dree's advice, he responded to her earlier statement. "How can I help you?"

She stared at him a long time without speaking, turquoise orbs decadently sweltering with carnal desire. "By keeping me satisfied."

Macabre apprehension, perplexity, and mounting frustration whirled within his head like three opposing windstorms. Why had this nymphomaniacal waif chosen him to haunt? He wanted answers not sex, but she seemed unwilling to provide anything but the latter. "The woman at the ranch said the same words you did. *I am the body and I need help."*

"Perhaps she does."

The spinning trio of emotions turned him flush—he felt his face burning.

"Oh, dear Jasper, I'm frightening you. I'm sorry. But it's like I said—some things are hard to understand at first."

"Damn you, tell me who you are! Are you the woman I saw at the ranch or not?"

Once again laughter poured out as Selma lifted her chin high. Then—soberly locking eyes with him, mouth held lustfully ajar—she traced the crack of her cleavage with her free hand, the long scarlet-tipped fingers moving sensuously between her breasts. He managed to take a couple of belts before she finally spoke. "I am the body. I'm here to give you pleasure with it, and to have you pleasure me with yours. I want you to possess me. I want to possess you . . . forever. I want us to be one flesh, one mind, one spirit floating on a cloud of endless orgasmic ecstasy. I want to take you to a place from which you won't be able to return."

Her chilling words, and the fact she never once questioned him about the veiled woman, flustered him. Gut wrenching with panic, he rose unsteadily to his feet. "I'm going home now. I don't know what's going on but I'm leaving, and don't you try to stop me . . . ."

* * * *

His apartment door locked automatically, but it also had a keyless deadbolt which he'd never used. Until now. The lighter shook in his hand as he fired up a cigarette while heading to the fridge for a beer. Jasper sat down at the dining table and kept staring at the front door, frightened as hell she'd walk right through it. He wanted to call Peggy Sue and tell her what happened but couldn't. She needed her sleep because of that six o'clock meeting. And tomorrow being a Monday meant the boys at the ranch would be sacked out by now. Mondays were slaughtering days and always hectic. Though he desperately needed to talk to someone about the strange woman next door, he wasn't going to bother them. Scared and too full of energy to sleep, having only been up since noon, he decided to guzzle beer until numbness overtook all emotion and brought on drowsiness.

That solution only half worked. Two hours later he'd managed to get pretty numb but the fear remained. The veiled woman and Selma Russell might not be the same ghost or spirit or whatever the hell they were, but they were damned sure connected or Selma wouldn't have said the same words. Though she'd certainly felt real, he suspected she was as ethereal as the woman in white. Thinking of her beautiful body, Selma's strange declaration sprang to the forefront of his mind: *One woman will never be enough for you. Deep inside your heart you know it.*

At the moment that was true enough, since the woman he loved couldn't tolerate intercourse, and said he could have a mistress. Impetuous, sexy, insatiable Ginny had really never been anything more than that to him anyway. If she didn't want to play second fiddle to his wife, he could always screw the redheaded phantom next door, provided he could overcome his trepidation. Even if she wasn't human, she'd felt as hot blooded as any woman he'd ever made love to. He certainly hadn't said anything to her, seeing as how nobody would ever hear about it from him, but Selma had spoke as if being aware of Peggy Sue's sexual hang-up. If she did know about it, she'd obtained that information supernaturally.

He thought about how exciting last night had been: the incredible physical compatibility between them, how much it resembled his carnal oneness with Ginny, her total lack of inhibition, also like Ginny. The memory aroused him, feverishly—to the point lust completely overrode his anxiety. Had Selma Russell cast a ghostly spell on him, causing him to want her in spite of his fear? Or was the passion now engulfing him simply a natural result of recalling her saying she worshipped his dick? That place she'd spoken of taking him had put bubbles of terror in his blood, but all the bodacious specter seemed to want from him was sex. How dangerous could that be?

Three hours after fleeing her apartment, certain he'd never return again, he stared at the front door of apartment 102. Common sense dictated he shouldn't do it, yet he felt compelled to. Almost of its own accord his finger pushed the button and the doorbell chimed.

A naked redhead answered and let him in . . . .

* * * *

Jasper felt someone shaking his shoulder. He woke up to see Selma hovering over him. "Time for you to go home, lover. It's almost dawn."

He dressed, kissed her goodbye, went to his apartment, and collapsed in his bed.

* * * *

Shortly after waking in the early afternoon, he returned to Selma's mysterious abode and rang the bell. Like yesterday, no one answered, and the door once again stood slightly ajar. He pushed it open. There wasn't a stick of furniture to be seen. Giving the vacant living room one last look, he closed the door and went back to his apartment with a macabre cyclone whirling in his brain.

He'd been sulking for a couple of hours when Peggy Sue pulled him from a deep well of morbidity. She'd called to ask him over to her place for supper. His handwriting reflected the confusion he felt over the ghost next door—the directions to his fiancé's apartment were barely legible. After they hung up, he refused to let his brain cast him back into the pit of darkness he'd been dwelling in since crawling out of bed. Peggy Sue made him drunk with happiness in every aspect of his life except one. He wished she'd been educated on what to expect the first time she took on a penis, so the experience wouldn't have gotten her all twisted up about it. Then again, maybe he should get down on his knees and thank God she hadn't known the full facts. Peggy Sue might have wound up marrying her boyfriend if she had. Reflecting on that, it dawned on him he had some unfinished business to tend to. Grabbing his hat at the door, he stepped outside and headed for his pickup, planning a trip to a jewelry store.

* * * *

"What price range are we talking, sir?" said an effeminate man wearing a broad smile on his narrow face after Jasper told him what he wanted.

Gazing at a glass display case filled with dazzling gems, he pointed to a diamond ring that had Peggy Sue's name written all over it. "Let me have a look at that one."

The skinny dude pulled it out and handed it to him. "That twenty-four carat gold bridal set boasts a three carat princess cut diamond with half carat clusters on the engagement ring, and four full-carat stones on the wedding band. It lists at ten-five if you choose the twelve month installment plan. Otherwise it will run you fifteen thousand, payable in twenty-four months."

"Shit, I didn't know I had such an expensive taste in wedding rings." He started to tell the clerk to show him something around five hundred, but it dawned on him he was thinking like a hayseed again. Peggy Sue would probably never say anything but she'd feel insulted since he was supposed to be a millionaire soon. "Um, what kind of discount can you give me if I pay for it in one lump sum?"

The thin man's beady eyes twinkled excitedly. "Oh I could come all the way down to seven-five in that case, sir."

Jasper frowned at him. "That's a helluva leap. You have the authority to do that?"

"Sir, I own this place."

"Oh, well in that case we've got a deal. I'll take it."

"What size is your fiancé's finger?"

"Aw hell, I don't know . . ." he smacked his forehead. "Dang it, I should have snuck that out of her somehow before coming here. What time do you close?"

"At six."

"All right, here's the deal. I'll pay you half now and give you the other half tonight after you size it for her. I'll call and let you know when we're coming, but it'll be some time after seven, probably around eight or so. You'll have to reopen, or hang around and wait on me."

The jeweler cleared his throat. "I'm afraid I can't do that, sir."

"Is that a fact. Well in that case I'll find out her ring size before taking my business to another jewelry store. You have a good 'un." He started for the door.

"Uh, sir! I suppose I could make an exception this one time, let me give you my business card . . . ."

Jeweler's phone number in his pocket, Japer drove home to get ready for a dinner date with his betrothed—the woman he loved, but couldn't make love to.

* * * *

Peggy Sue's apartment had flowers everywhere—sprouting from vases and clay pots, arranged in wicker baskets, dangling from sconces, beautifully arranged on the fireplace mantel. Her furniture wasn't as chic as he'd anticipated but blew his out of the water. The sofa and chairs had the same floral designs of swirling tulips and daisies. So did the tablecloth they dined on. She'd made salmon steaks for supper. He liked them okay, but when it came to fish he preferred cat, bass, crappie, or perch, breaded and fried. Nonetheless, he made a big deal about how delicious hers tasted. Being in her presence had put him in a bright cheery mood, but a black claw lurked beneath the surface of his thoughts, threatening to pull him back into the dark perplexing world of Selma Russell.

When she finished her after dinner cigarette he said, "Come on, we need to go somewhere."

Disappointment flooded her pretty face. "I was hoping we could spend a quiet evening here. You know, in bed."

"Sounds great to me too, but this is something that can't wait. But first I need to use your phone."

"Why?"

Instead of answering, he called the jeweler, ignoring her contemptuous glare . . . .

* * * *

His future wife sat on the passenger side of his pickup, arms folded beneath her breasts, pouting over his unwillingness to relive last night's passion, angry with him for not giving a reason for his noncompliance. "Who was that you called? I don't understand why you won't tell me where we're going."

"You will," he said with a grin.

Peggy Sue continued to sulk until he pulled into the jewelry store, whereupon she turned towards him with gleeful surprise, her expression depicting the awestruck portrait of a little girl's dream coming true. "Does this mean what I think it does?"

"Uh, probably not. I bought a Rolex here earlier today and had them put my name on the back, but they screwed up. The jeweler stayed open late to fix it because I told him I wanted it done today or I'd buy one somewhere else."

She snorted a laugh and squinted at him. "Somehow I just don't see you buying a Rolex, Jasper Miller."

"Ahem, just decided it was about time I started living the high life like you wanted me to."

"Why don't I believe you?" she retorted with a giggle.

Following the instructions he'd given the jeweler before leaving the store, the thin man handed him a fancy box that had *Rolex* emblazoned on it. "Sorry about the mishap, sir. We got it right this time."

"I appreciate it. Call me a sentimental fool, but being this is my first Rolex, I wanted my name engraved on it." It was almost impossible to keep a straight face because of the gross disappointed radiating from Peggy Sue's. "Here, darlin', would you open it for me?"

An angry tear trickled down her cheek as she accepted the

box. Upon seeing what it contained, a slew of them started flowing, and he nearly suffered a busted lip when she rammed her mouth against his. Her joy almost made him forget how bizarre and complicated his life had become.

The jeweler cleared his throat. "Ma'am, I need your ring size please . . . ."

Jasper pocketed the wedding band and drove away from the store with his giddy fiancé snuggling next to him, proudly wearing her engagement ring. He smiled at the way she kept admiring it, refusing to let the mysterious Selma Russell ruin the moment for him, despite not being able to free his mind of the weird predicament the redhead had sucked him into. "Now we can go to your place and fool around . . . ."

* * * *

Jasper got home at eleven, feeling bad for Peggy Sue and horribly frustrated. She was too apprehensive to allow his fingers near her twat, and wouldn't let him use his mouth for fear it would make her feel like a lesbian again. Though she'd once again brought herself to the mountain peak while he kissed and held her, he'd been unable to climax. She'd blamed herself until he lied, saying it was just one of those things that sometimes happen with men. It had never happened before, and would have worried him if he hadn't known why. His aching desire to consummate their love by depositing his seed inside her womanhood wouldn't allow her mouth or hands to open the floodgate, even though they'd made him stiff as a board.

He felt like a split personality. The side of him desiring love and romance belonged exclusively to Peggy Sue, while the other—driven by lust—craved Ginny and Selma in equal measure.

The doorbell rang at eleven fifteen and he allowed himself to be coaxed next door. Not long after that, he spewed his pent up load inside Selma Russell's thrashing body. Around four that morning she woke him up and told him it was time to go home.

17

It was three in the afternoon. Peggy Sue would be at the plant for another two hours and Selma Russell wouldn't return from her unknown haunt until nightfall. Deciding it was time to quit putting off the inevitable, Jasper had agreed to meet Ginny at a motel she'd called from, being in one of her kinky moods. They'd used the room several times after she came back from Hawaii. The last occasion took place two days before he met Selma. It had a heart-shaped hot tub and mirrored ceiling over a vibrating bed they were presently lying on. But the mattress wasn't pulsating at the moment, and the lights were off. He'd told her about his engagement to Peggy Sue and she took the news extremely hard.

"So where does that leave us?" she sobbed, finally able to speak after bawling hysterically for the last ten minutes.

"You can be my mistress, but you've got to be discreet."

"But I want to be your wife, Jasper! Can't you understand that? I'm so tired of having to hide my love for you from Daddy. He'll give his blessing if you'll only ask him, but he'd have a cow if he knew we were carrying on outside of wedlock."

Groaning with frustration, he leaned over on his side and lit a cigarette. "I just don't feel that way about you, Ginny, and I've told you that. If you want to call it quits I understand. And

I sure don't blame you if you do."

"You know better than that, dammit!"

He exhaled a stream of smoke and cleared his throat. "There's something else. I hate to bring it up now, with you being so upset and all, but I want everything squared away. Here recently I've wound up with another woman on the side besides you."

"What?!"

Turning over to face her, he grimaced. Ginny's livid features looked hot enough to fry an egg. "Look, there's nothing going on between her and me but sex."

"Who is she, what's that bitch's name?"

"Doesn't matter . . ." he settled on his back. "I think she's a ghost."

"A ghost?"

"Yeah, just like the woman in white. Only this one lets me touch her."

"Oh now I've heard it all." She got out of bed and started pacing in front of the window, her naked body silhouetted against sunlight peeking around the closed curtains. "Do you know what a cheap whore I feel like right now, Jasper?"

"There's nothing cheap about you, Ginny. You're as high-dollar and spoiled as they come."

"What can I do to make you love me the way I love you?" The semi-darkness enhanced the angst on her face.

"I don't think you love me. I think we both just have a case of the hots for each other."

"You're dead wrong on that, I *do* love you, even if you don't love me. Just what is it your little Miss Drinkwater has that I don't?"

"Hell I couldn't explain it if I tried. There's just a chemistry between us I've never felt before. I fell in love with her. Didn't plan to, it just happened. Now I'm being honest with you. I don't want to hurt you, but it has to be this way or no way. The choice is yours."

Ginny stopped walking the floor and glared at him for several moments, looking wounded and desperate. Then her eyes shifted into predatory mode and she started towards him, her wondrous body crying out to be adulterated. Blowing out a deep breath, she kneeled beside the bed and lowered her face to his mid section. "Well I can't give you up. If this is the way it's got to be, then this is how it will be . . . ."

* * * *

At four o'clock he'd left his blonde mistress at the motel, trying unsuccessfully to coax her redheaded rival's name from him the moment she finished administering a stupendous blow job. At seven his fiancé had taken him to a French restaurant. The cuisine had tasted pretty good but didn't beat the truck stop's. They'd had sex the Peggy Sue way—no intercourse. She snuggled beside him, running her fingers through his chest hair. "When we're ready to have kids, we'll use artificial insemination. I just hate that I can't tolerate coitus."

Jasper wanted to tell her all she had to do was grit her teeth and bear it a few times and she'd learn to enjoy it, but didn't for fear it might drive her into a shell of inhibition. She'd become more daring with each sexual interlude, even rubbing his dick against her vulva. He'd bide his time, figuring sooner or later she'd develop a desire to feel him inside her and find the sensation pleasurable. Until then he had to fight the desire to screw her and take out his frustration on Ginny and Selma.

Peggy Sue was spending the night, so he'd have to send Selma away when she made her nightly call. He anticipated the doorbell would ring any second.

But it never did . . . .

He woke at eighty thirty to find Peggy Sue gone. It was the earliest he'd risen from bed since spending his first night with the ghost next door.

After breakfast he drove to the plant. He hadn't been there since Peggy Sue broke his heart, so he'd never gotten to see what it looked like finished. This time the woman at the front desk really was a receptionist. The young blonde had cherub cheeks on a face that looked freshly scrubbed. "Hi there, I'm here to see Peg Drinkwater."

"And you are?"

"Jasper Miller."

"The Jasper Miller?"

He nodded.

She quickly hit an intercom and a woman answered. "Yes, May?"

"Jasper Miller is here to see Miss Drinkwater."

"Well send him up!" The voice sounded Texan and humorous.

"If you'll follow me please."

May led him into an elevator and they exited on the second floor, stepping into a lobby surrounded by several offices, all but one having glass walls. A door in the midst of the solitary stretch that wasn't transparent had a sign that read Peg Drinkwater with an inscription beneath, denoting her as vice president. He followed May through it and saw an elder fat woman with blue-black hair sitting at a desk. She quickly got up and shook his hand.

"I'm Martha Spate, Peg's personal assistant. It's a real pleasure to finally meet you, Mister Miller."

"Call me Jasper."

"Well thank you." She aimed an index finger at a door several feet behind her desk. "Just go right in, she's expecting you."

He walked in to find Peggy Sue on the phone. She smiled and pointed towards an armchair near her desk. Listening to her instruct somebody on the proper procedure for filling out some type of form, he made himself comfortable, grinning when he saw the big diamond on her finger. A few minutes went by before she hung up.

"So what do you think, Jasper? Look any different than the last time you were here?"

"I'll say it does."

"Come on, I'll give you the grand tour . . . ."

The chaotic mess he'd encountered when last at the plant now looked orderly, expensive, and impressive.

"No one's allowed on the line without a safety hat," said Peggy Sue, selecting two from a row of a dozen hanging on hooks horizontally arranged along a wall beside a steel door with a sign above it containing her statement in condensed form. He followed her through it.

"Grandma Miller's Superior Sausage is made exclusively from hogs raised on organic feed on a farm outside Dallas. Cross Enterprises acquired it when T. Wayford first laid out his vision for your delicious breakfast ware. We receive their de-boned carcasses within forty-eight hours after each hog is slaughtered. First the pork has to be ground, then it's dumped into that hopper up there which evenly distributes it onto the conveyor." She pointed to an expanse of shiny metal hanging on the ceiling with a wide chute running up to the floor above, where a loud grinding noise emanated. The machine sounded mean and hungry. A narrower chute, a few feet above the conveyor, endlessly dumped freshly ground pork onto it.

"Then the product has to be mixed with your seasonings." Several feet ahead the conveyor emptied the pork into a vat with spinning blades that blended in his grandma's enhanced recipe, streaming down like a heavy rain from a device above it. "A computer controls the spice drop in proportion to the weight of the meat."

The conveyor and spice rain stopped when a robotic arm attached to the vat flipped it over, emptying its contents into a tank with a worm gear running through it. Then the arm swung sideways and held the mixing tub above mechanized steam guns that cleaned the blades whereupon another set of nozzles blasted them with dry air until all moisture was eliminated. That accomplished, the vat was repositioned to accept another load, causing the conveyors to start moving again. Meanwhile the worm gear further mixed the meat while forcing it through the tank, where the sausage emptied onto a lower conveyor. Several workers manned this station insuring everything worked properly.

"Once mixed, it then has to be separated into one pound increments." She led him further down the line where the conveyor dumped the pork into a metal contraption that spat sixteen ounce piles of sausage into a rotating apparatus from which they emerged wrapped in plastic tubes with a picture of an old white haired woman standing beside the name Grandma Miller's Superior Sausage. These were carried by conveyor to a bin whose purpose was to catch any packages that got past workers busily piling them into boxes, which another crew sealed and stacked on crates that were carried by forklift to a refrigerated warehouse to await transport to their final destination.

The whole process amazed him.

Peggy Sue smiled proudly, eyes radiant beneath the rim of her hard hat. "Now you know how your sausage is made."

"Yeah, and I'm blown away by it. Hell all I ever had was a fork and bowl to mix mine with."

"Humble beginnings. Those days are forever behind you."

"Well you'd best give me a pound so I can test it."

Snatching a tube from the conveyor, she motioned for him to follow.

They wound up at the warehouse. A forklift stacked with boxes rolled towards a refrigeration truck with the sausage logo painted on both sides of it. "That particular load is on its way to Arkansas."

"How do you know that?" he asked.

"Look at the license plate."

The truck had an Arkansas tag alongside its Texas plate.

Up until now it had seemed surreal, like a dream he might wake up from any minute. But witnessing the actual process caused reality to set in. Seeing the name Miller on the sides of those trucks and on the countless packages of sausage, knowing that all those workers were there because of his experimentation with his grandma's recipe, filled him with a tremendous sense of pride and accomplishment. Each one of those tubes represented fifteen cents in his pocket, or would when his advance was paid back. He could now see with his own eyes that T. Wayford's experts were right.

He'd soon be a millionaire.

They said goodbye in the parking lot and Jasper drove back to his apartment, stopping at his mailbox along the way, located within a rectangular cluster of the other locked boxes belonging to residents of Water Crest Manor. He dropped the mail on his desk and fried up two sausage patties. A single bite from one assured its quality, so he put both between two slices of bread and made a sandwich for lunch. Afterwards, he sat down at his desk, called Peggy Sue, and gave her a thumbs up report.

Still at his desk, he sorted through the mail, all of it junk except for an envelope from Cross Enterprises. He opened it and removed the contents. It was some sort of sales report, and along with it came a check made out to him. For at least a full minute he gaped at the bank draft with disbelief. The amount written thereon was eighty-five thousand dollars and thirty-two cents. A euphoric laugh blasted from his mouth as he pounded out a drum roll on his desk, feeling almost as victorious as he used to when the eight second buzzer sounded and the crowd roared.

Almost.

Fooling around with ground pork didn't quite carry the same exhilaration as defying the will of an angry bull. So excited he found it hard to write, Jasper made out a check to his mother for ten thousand dollars. He wanted to send more but knew he'd be lucky to get her to accept that much. After composing a short letter, telling her to spend the money however she wanted, he made out checks for one thousand dollars each to all the boys at the ranch except Billy Culpepper. Collecting his envelopes, he got up and headed for the door.

The time had come to trade in his pickup for some new wheels . . . .

* * * *

Jasper drove home in a brand new silver Dodge Ram. He called Peggy Sue to tell her about it, knowing she'd be real proud.

"You bought a what?"

"A Dodge Ram pickup, it's real swank."

"Jasper, that sort of vehicle is for blue collar working stiffs. You're white collar now. When is that going to get through your thick head? I can't believe you."

Her incredulous tone blew his mind. "Excuse me. I must

have dialed the wrong number."

A sigh of irritation filled his ear. *"What made you decide to trade in your old pickup anyway? I thought you were going to wait until you started getting your royalties before taking that step."*

"I got my first royalty check today, that's why. And after seeing all those fifteen cent tubes at the plant, I figured it was time to move on up."

"What are you talking about, fifteen cent tubes?"

"I get fifteen cents off every pound of sausage you make."

"What am I going to do with you? You get fifteen cents from every dollar *the sausage makes. It sells for more than a dollar a tube, you silly nitwit."*

Peggy Sue wasn't talking to him like her fiancé, but dressing him down like one of her underlings at the plant. Jasper felt like a hayseed again, the way he had when the lawyer told him he'd be getting a copy of the contract. T. Wayford told him his percentage was on the dollar. How had he come up with fifteen cents a tube?

"Look, I'm sorry I was sharp with you," she said in a more civil tone. *"If you want to drive a Dodge Ram, that's your business. I shouldn't have criticized you and I'm sorry."*

He started scratching his head. "No, you're probably right. Maybe I'd better see how the other half lives before making any other large investments."

"That's all I'm asking you to do. Don't cheat yourself. You can't know for sure you won't like being upper class if you don't investigate it a little. I mean, you may not like it and fine if you don't, but at least see what you're missing."

"Okay. Well I'll let you get back to your rat killing. Love you."

"Love you too."

"Snotty bitch," he mumbled with a grin after hanging up.

Rubbing his hands together he hurried outside, making for the carport. The glistening silver pickup was beautiful. It reminded him of the one Chuck Norris drove on *Walker: Texas Ranger.*

After cruising around Arlington for almost an hour, relishing the feel of the new truck, he saw a sign advertising cell phones. "That's what I need, a cell phone . . . ."

Forty-five minutes later he was back behind the wheel talking to Peggy Sue on his new cell.

"Well now that was *a good investment,"* she cheerfully allowed.

"I'm not too good at dialing and driving at the same time. Would you call T. Wayford for me and give him my cell number?"

"Jasper, I can't call T. Wayford over something trivial like that. I'm his employee. You'll have to call him. You're his colleague, you can call him over trivial matters."

He chuckled. "So my cell number's a trivial matter, huh?"

"No, of course not, I didn't mean that. But when I call T. Wayford Cross I'm an employee taking up his valuable time, so I damn well better have something more important to tell him than a cell number, even if it is his sausage magnate's number."

"Okay, okay. I'll pull over somewhere and call him. See you tonight." He started braking as he spoke, and slowed to a stop on the shoulder of the street . . . .

"T. Wayford? Jasper here." He gassed the new Dodge back onto the highway.

"Hey, cowboy, how's it going?" T. Wayford sounded jovial as usual.

"Great. Got my first royalty check in the mail today."

"Yeah I saw the report and told accounting to get it to you ASAP. You don't lack much getting the advance paid back.

The bulk of your next check will be fifteen percent instead of ten."

Jasper grimaced, recalling his miscalculation on tube verses dollar. "Listen, the reason I called is to give you my new cell number."

"You went and got yourself a cell phone, that's good. I got your number right here on mine already, it always tells me who's calling. I'll save it. Now you have a real nice day, hear?"

"You too."

To his surprise the phone rang right after he hung up. T. Wayford called back to make sure the number saved. *". . . dang thing disappeared from the screen, then popped back up."*

"Well I reckon it must have saved it since you got me."

They said goodbye and a few minutes later the phone rang again. He laughed, wondering what T. Wayford was calling for this time.

"Hello?"

"Hello, Jasper."

The voice was feminine.

"Yes?"

"It's Selma."

Jasper hung up on her and almost sideswiped a van. Droplets of sweat popped up on his brow as nausea rose from the pit of his stomach. The cell phone started ringing again but he didn't answer it—the impossibility of her knowing his number proved once and for all that Selma Russell was not of this world, and that confirmation terrified him. He realized at that moment that his suspicions of her being supernatural had been buffered by an equal possibility she was merely an eccentric mortal, despite the mystery of her furniture not being there those two times. Now that buffer had been completely vaporized. She had to be the woman in white. How many other ways could she appear? Did she always manifest in feminine form or could she turn herself into a man as well? Numb with shock, he drove aimlessly from Arlington to Fort Worth—no destination in mind, only the burning question of why she'd picked him to haunt.

He stopped at a red light. A car pulled next to him. The woman behind the wheel looked familiar and was staring at him. By the time the light turned green he recognized her. When she drove through the intersection, he swerved to the next lane, determined to follow her. The woman was none other than Lorraine Bradbury, the girl who'd claimed to be his daughter . . . .

She pulled into the driveway of a single storey house in a neighborhood with similar structures, denoting their owners' social status lay midway between lower and middle class. He switched off the engine and got out of the truck. "Hello, Lorraine, remember me?"

The young woman studied him a moment. "Mister Miller?"

"Yeah, it's me behind this beard."

"I'm sorry I troubled you . . ." she started stepping back, eyes wide with fear. "I promise I won't bother you again."

"No, don't be afraid. I want to talk to you."

Her feet stopped moving but she still looked petrified. "How did you find me?"

"I wasn't looking for you, it was just a coincidence we wound up at the same red light."

"I'm sorry I was staring at you at the intersection, but you looked so familiar I was just trying to figure out who you were."

He gave her a warm smile. "Mind if I come in and visit a spell?"

She eyed him suspiciously.

"Look, I don't mean any harm. I'm not mad at you, I just

want to talk. Would you please relax?"

Several seconds passed before she reluctantly turned and started for her door.

Judging by the business dress she wore, he figured she must have driven home from work. No longer pinned in a bun, Lorraine's hair hung past her shoulders, making her look older than she had at the ranch. Once inside the house, she adjusted her glasses and nervously said, "I'm going to have a Dr Pepper. Would you like one?"

"Sure." He followed her to the kitchen.

She took two cans from the fridge and handed him one. "We can talk in the living room . . . ."

An upright piano had pictures of Lorraine and her parents neatly arranged across the top. She sat down in a wooden rocking chair facing it from across the room. Leaning against the left side of the entryway, he opened the soda pop and took a drink. It tasted sweet and cold, reminding him of how much he enjoyed the soft drink in his school days. "This sure hits the spot. Haven't had a good ol' DP in ages."

Lorraine began nervously rocking back and forth. "This is sort of awkward, Mister Miller. That lady at your house really scared me. I don't want any trouble."

"Aw don't worry about Ginny. She scares everybody."

Looking anxious in spite of his encouragement, she took a drink and swallowed. "Well she sure frightened me."

"Do you still think I'm your father?"

"I don't know why my mother would lie to me," she said defensively.

"I don't either, and that's what makes me curious. I told you the truth. I can't be your father because I never had relations with your mother, and for the life of me I can't figure out why she'd tell you I was."

"You seem sincere, Mister Miller, but I hope you can

understand I choose to believe my mother over you."

He nodded. "I can understand that. But it's not like I'd have to pay child support since you're obviously over eighteen. Why would I lie about it?"

"I don't know."

"How old are you anyway?"

"Twenty-one."

"Hmm, let's see . . . Tulia and I graduated together but she was a year older than me because she flunked sixth grade. I'm forty so that puts her having you at twenty. The last time I saw her she was eighteen going on nineteen, so I couldn't be your daddy even if we *had* been intimate." Wandering over to the piano, he perused the pictures and pointed at a snapshot of Tulia. "These are some real nice photographs, that's an especially good one of your mother."

"Yes, I like that one too. She was a pretty lady."

"She was for a fact. Is this where she lived?"

"Mm hmm."

"So what do you do?"

"I work thirty hours a week keeping the books in order at a pet store, wait tables on weekends, and go to school part time."

"College, huh?"

"Yes."

He downed some more DP and wiped his mouth. "Let me ask you something. What were you hoping to get out of me, assuming I was your father? I'm just a poor cowpuncher. At least that's all I was when you came to see me."

Instead of answering she turned up her can.

Her hand caught his eye, igniting a strong sense of déjà vu that made him realize something that hadn't occurred to him before. Not only did her pretty fingers look like the ghost's on the Double Cross, Lorraine Bradbury's voice would probably sound quite similar to the apparition's if she were to cry out in distress. He gave her a good going over. Take away the glasses, put a veil on her, and she might damn well be the woman in white. It now struck him as an awfully odd coincidence she'd turned up at his door only minutes after the phantom female last appeared, and it was mighty peculiar the ghost hadn't turned up since. An idea came to him and he decided to try a bluff. "Do the words *I am the body* mean anything to you?"

Jasper thought he saw a nervous twitch on her bottom lip. When she didn't respond he said, "How about *I am the body and I need help*?"

This time the lip tightened.

"Well?"

"No," she finally said. "Those words don't mean anything to me. Why would they?"

"I bet you'd look real pretty in a white dress with a veil."

She stopped rocking. "It's time for you to go, Mister Miller."

"It's time for you to come clean with me, Miss Bradbury."

Lorraine arched her brows with angry insult, but the action failed to disguise the fact he'd rattled her. "If you don't leave right now, I'm going to call the police."

"Okay I'm leaving." He set the Dr Pepper on her piano. "But if I find out you *are* the woman behind the veil that I've seen several times on The Double Cross Ranch, I'll be the one calling the police . . . ."

Jasper drove to the store where he'd bought the cell phone. The puzzle began to fall into place. Selma Russell was no more a ghost that Lorraine Bradbury, who he now knew to be the woman in white because of her reaction. Someone had gotten her and Selma involved in an elaborate scheme to convince him they were ghosts. Either that, or the two women planned it on their own for some crazy reason. He didn't know all the why's or how's, but one *how* was about to be solved. A young black man had sold him the phone and he spotted him immediately upon entering the store.

"Howdy, remember me? I bought a cell phone from you a couple of hours ago."

The clerk frowned. "Yeah, I remember you. Is something wrong with it?"

"No, just curious about something. After I left, did a good looking redhead come in and ask for my cell number?"

A big grin overtook the frown. "So she did call you. Congratulations, man, what a catch."

Careful not to be appear as confused as the statement made him, Jasper played along. "Yeah, thanks. The way you're talking she must have told you about it."

"Yeah. She said she saw you leaving the store and asked if you'd bought a cell phone. When I told her you had, she told me how you'd proposed to her and she'd told you she needed time to think about it. She begged me for the number so she could surprise you by calling you on your new cell to say she'd marry you." He suddenly looked concerned. "We're not supposed to do it, but under the circumstances I figured you'd want me to give her your number, so I did. It's cool I did, right?"

"Sure, no problem. Just wanted to find out how she got it because she wouldn't tell me."

The clerk smiled with relief. "If you don't mind my saying so, that lady could make it in Hollywood she's so beautiful."

"Oh that's not the only reason she could make it in Hollywood, hoss. She's also quite an actress . . . ."

He got into his new pickup and waited, studying the rearview mirror for any signs of Selma Russell, but didn't see her anywhere. She apparently wasn't following him this time like she'd been doing when he'd bought the cell. At some point Lorraine Bradbury had picked up his trail and made the mistake of letting him see her. The two women were definitely in cahoots, but he couldn't figure out what they were up to.

Back at his apartment, he called the superintendent. "This is Jasper Miller in one-o-one and I've got a proposition for you. I'll give you fifty bucks if you'll unlock one-o-two and let me have a look around . . . ."

The apartment looked exactly as he'd last seen it.

"I don't know whose furniture this is," said the dumbfounded super, "but this apartment is supposed to be vacant and unfurnished."

At six o'clock, with a cigarette and Lone Star, Jasper sat on his couch, thinking about the scam. Selma had left her door only partially closed on purpose, hoping he'd open it, see the empty apartment, and think she was a ghost when she asked him back for an encore. She'd counted on him not going inside, for if he had, she'd have been exposed if he explored the upstairs, where the furniture had undoubtedly been stored in the two spare bedrooms he'd never entered, as they always had sex in the master bedroom. The furniture had never been taken out of the apartment, simply hauled upstairs and back down before she came to call. Since Selma thought she had him convinced, the furniture didn't have to be moved again because there was no further need to leave the door ajar for him to push open. The heavy drapes made it impossible for someone outside to see the lights turned on, thus assuring 102 appeared vacant. Selma obviously didn't live there. That apartment had been procured for the sole purpose of convincing him she was a ghost.

Jasper planned to act normal, not let on he was wise to her. Lorraine had probably called Selma and told her about their conversation the minute he left her house. The redhead would be suspicious if he acted different in any way. He'd phoned

Peggy Sue to say he couldn't be with her tonight, using the excuse of needing some time alone to sort things out over getting his first royalty check. She'd told him she understood. Not wanting to alarm her, he decided not to say anything about Lorraine Bradbury or Selma and the cell phone until he knew more.

At eleven o'clock the doorbell rang and there stood the seductress, all decked out in the same low-cut green dress and ruby accessories. The evening went well, with him still badgering her about whether or not she was a ghost, her still giving him the same old tease: "Some things are hard to understand at first." The sex was great like always, and when she ushered him away a little before four, he obediently left. But this time after returning to his apartment he snuck back out, went to his carport where he could peek around the corner, and waited.

It paid off. Less than ten minutes went by before Selma crept outside and turned right at her empty carport. He hurried to it and saw her make another right at the far end, where the vehicle belonging to whoever lived in 103 was parked. Rushing to that corner, he watched her stroll to the duplex right behind his. She unlocked the door of apartment 104 and went inside.

18

Jasper took a catnap after spying on Selma, and called T. Wayford at eight a.m.

"Why'd you choose Water Crest Manor to house me in?"

"It was recommended to me. Why, is there a problem with the apartment?"

"No. Who recommended it?"

"Peg Drinkwater. I told her to find you something middleclass."

Stunned, he looked towards the ceiling, brain whirling with confusion. Why didn't she tell him she'd picked out his apartment? "Can I ask a favor, T. Wayford?"

"Sure."

"Don't tell Peggy Sue you told me about her recommending the apartment."

"All right. Is something wrong?"

"No, but you know how women are. She didn't tell me she picked it out, and I'm afraid it might embarrass her that she didn't if she was to find out I knew."

"Hmm. Wonder why she didn't tell you?"

"Who knows? Anyway, I'd really appreciate it if we could just keep this between us."

T. Wayford snickered. *"My lips are sealed."*

"Thanks . . . ."

He smoked and paced for half an hour after talking to T. Wayford. More of the puzzle seemed to be coming together with one major piece missing. The woman in white bullshit started long before anyone knew he'd wind up becoming a sausage tycoon. That meant there was some motivation to get him cornered way back then, and for the life of him he couldn't figure out what that incentive could be.

Peggy Sue called to check up on him. He told her he felt better after thinking things through, and knew he'd have to adjust to the fact a simple cowboy's life could no longer be his. She wanted to know if she could come over after work and fix dinner for him. He told her she could.

Though he needed to find out who rented 104, the apartment Selma went to after he left her in 102, he didn't want to ask security, having no idea who all might be involved in this complicated scam. The superintendent appeared to be a straight shooter. Deciding to take a chance on him, he called and made the inquiry. Jasper thanked him for the information, hung up the phone, and plopped down at his desk, unable to wipe a scowl off his face . . . .

* * * *

Peggy Sue arrived with two bags of groceries and whipped out a meal of veal scaloppini and eggplant parmesan. As she enjoyed her after dinner cigarette at the dining table, he grabbed a Lone Star and started pacing around the living room.

"You seem agitated, is something wrong?"

He shook his head. "Just the same old change of life jitters. Wonder if I shouldn't just give my share of the sausage to my mother and go back to the Double Cross. Hell I don't need to be a millionaire. To tell you the truth, I'm not sure I even want to be. We'd be just as happy out on the ranch, living from paycheck to paycheck. You'd stand by me if I made such a decision, wouldn't you?"

Brows elevated, she belted out an incredulous laugh. "You'll never get me to live the life of a simple cowgirl, Jasper. I may be a Texan but I'm a city girl just the same."

A bitter sigh vacated his lungs. "I hate to hear that."

"It's the truth. You wouldn't want me to lie to you would you?"

"No."

"Want your ring back?" she said with a giggle.

"Do you want to give it back?" he replied seriously.

"Of course not. Jasper, what's wrong . . .?" she stubbed out her cigarette and stood up.

"It's that weird Selma shit and that apartment next door. Wonder why T. Wayford picked this apartment for me in the first place?" He came to a standstill, closely watching her face, waiting for her to say she had no idea, which would be a lie and put an end to their relationship.

She became pensive. Several seconds went by before a look of resignation signaled she'd come to the end of a mental wrestling match. "He didn't, I did."

"You did?" Her admission shocked him, he'd fully expected a lie to flow out of her mouth.

"He asked me to pick something middleclass. I would have told you before but I figured T. Wayford wanted you to think he picked it out personally. Please don't tell him I told you. I still can't believe I got you an apartment without a fireplace. Sorry, I just wasn't thinking. I liked this one, the blue color scheme sold me on it. It seemed sort of masculine."

"Thanks for telling me the truth."

"I told you, I always tell the truth."

Her saying she'd never live the simple life of a cowgirl still bothered him in spite of the relief he felt over her not lying about the apartment. He started pacing again. "Do you know anyone at these apartments?"

"I know a lot of people so it's possible. But if anyone I know lives here, I'm unaware of it."

If it wasn't for the renter of 104 she'd have his complete confidence again. Somebody might be trying to frame her, but Selma Russell letting herself into that apartment meant it couldn't be mere coincidence. Caution dictated he keep his mouth shut and not tell her that the superintendent informed him the renter of apartment 104 went by the name P. S. Drinkwater. The dude didn't know the renter, had never seen P. S. Drinkwater, and had never been called to 104 to fix anything.

"Is this the only apartment you looked at or did you check out some others first?"

She cupped her hands and inspected her nails. "I checked an apartment complex north of here but didn't particularly like them, and they were asking far too much money for what they were offering."

"Was this the only apartment you looked at in this complex?"

"Yes. Like I said, the blue carpet and walls sold me. And again I'll ask you to please not tell T. Wayford I told you I picked out the apartment. If he wants you to think he did it, you might get me in trouble with him. He counts on his higher-ups being discreet."

"Don't worry, it won't be a problem. Do you know anyone named Bradbury?"

"Bradbury?"

"Yeah."

"Hmm . . . no, I don't think so. Why?" Her reply seemed innocent enough.

"A young woman named Bradbury came to see me at the ranch when I was still foreman. I went to school with her mother, and she told her I was her father."

"Well you're not are you?"

"No, and I told her so. I never had sex with her mother."

Suspicion rising in them, Peggy Sue narrowed her eyes. "Why are you asking me if I know her? What's going on, Jasper?"

"Some sort of conspiracy it seems like."

"And you think I'm part of it?"

"I sure hope you're not, but I honestly don't know. Anyway, I ran into her yesterday while I was cruising around in my new pickup, and I looked her over real good. She could be the woman in white I saw at the ranch."

"Exactly where do I fit in with all this?" she said angrily.

"Like I said, I don't know."

"Look, I don't know the girl and I'm not part of any conspiracy. I love you. I want to spend the rest of my life with you, but you're going to have to trust me or we're never going to make it."

"I know . . ." he ran a hand over his face and exhaled a harsh breath. "I guess we'd better back off from one another till I get to the bottom of this weird shit. It's about the only thing I know to do."

Her jaw dropped with alarm. "Jasper—"

"No, don't say anything. It's for the best. Let me solve this thing, it's the only way. Until I find out more, it's impossible for me to trust anybody because I just don't know what's going on or how many people are involved. All I know is someone's out to get me for some reason, and since this thing started before the sausage deal, it can't have anything to do with money. Someone wants revenge, that's the only thing I can figure. But for what, I don't know . . . ."

He sent Peggy Sue home at ten. Forty minutes later Selma rang his bell. Like always, he went next door, sat on the couch, and enjoyed a turkey and coke while smoking. Selma hovered by the portable bar, trying to look mysterious.

"You know, I bet I could shoot you and it wouldn't even faze you would it?"

She gave him a puzzled smile. "Why would you want to shoot me?"

"To prove you're a ghost."

"Oh, dear Jasper, you're still confused aren't you? Give it time and you won't be. As I told you before, it's just that some things—"

"Are hard to understand at first," he finished the sentence for her. "Who's P. S. Drinkwater?"

The drink fell from her hand but the glass didn't break on the thick carpet. She grabbed a towel from the kitchen, got on her knees, and began drying the spill.

He took a sip from his own. "Hit a nerve with that one, didn't I. What are you up to? I know you're not a ghost like you're trying to make me think. The guy that sold me the cell phone ratted you out. And I had the superintendent let me in here yesterday and you know, the funniest thing—all the furniture was still here. Who helped you move it upstairs those two times I saw this place empty, besides that dude pretending to be the superintendent the day we met? P. S. Drinkwater or Lorraine Bradbury?"

Selma kept scrubbing the carpet, looking down at the spill as she worked.

"Tomorrow I'm going to find the person renting one-o-four."

She looked up in a panic, a thick lock of red hair straying across her face.

"That's right, I saw you go there. And I know it was rented

by P. S. Drinkwater. But that's you, isn't it. You're P. S. Drinkwater. Of course that's not your real name any more than Selma Russell is. Now you've got two choices. You can tell me who you really are and what you're up to, or I'm going to hire a private investigator to find out, then I'm going to the police."

Standing up slowly, she put her hands on her hips and sighed. "All right . . . ."

* * * *

Last night the redhead hadn't bothered waiting until four in the morning to return to 104. They'd left apartment 102 at the same time, parting shortly after midnight. The clock had just struck nine a.m. and Jasper was sitting at his dining table, smoking, sipping coffee, thinking everything over.

Selma Russell was really Catrina Smith, a hooker who worked exclusively from the internet where she had her own website called Fantastic Fantasies. Someone going by the name Bomber hired her via email to convince him she was a ghost. She knew nothing about her employer other than the fact he or she had to be loaded because Bomber rented the two apartments, paid extra to have 102 listed as vacant, furnished it, and sent her the cash to have her furniture moved into 104.

Having been instructed to somehow get his semen on a towel and leave it in the kitchen, she'd accomplished the mission by doing the oral number on him that first night. She claimed everything else had been her choice because she enjoyed making love with him. Though she'd been told it would be done, she had no idea who moved the furniture upstairs, nor who took the towel. Her employer warned her she'd breech their agreement if she ever went inside apartment 102 between 6 a.m. and 6 p.m. without being told to. She'd been receiving two thousand dollars a week in cash, deposited in the mailbox for apartment 104 every Monday. It made for a lucrative deal for her because she could still run her business from her computer in 104, which was much nicer than the apartment she'd lived in before.

The food they'd eaten for dinner that first night was obtained from a restaurant and she'd only pretended to cook it. In reality she was a lousy chef, or so she claimed. She'd been given the pseudonym Selma Russell by Bomber, who'd informed her the lease went under the name P. S. Drinkwater. One of her regulars pretended to be the superintendent the day they met and had no idea why she'd asked him to do the favor.

She'd been told to use the term *I am the body and I need help* after he became suspicious she might be a ghost. Otherwise her job called for her to freelance, come up with anything on her own that would help convince him she was other worldly. She kept her car in the carport of 104 and followed him every time she spotted him leaving the complex. She'd been tailing him when he bought the new pickup and tracked him again when he wound up at the electronics store with a sign out front advertising a special on cell phones. Correctly guessing he'd purchased one, she'd manipulated the number from the clerk, knowing it would further convince him she was supernatural if she called his cell right after he bought it, without being told the number.

After she'd finished laying it all out Jasper had said, "If you're telling the truth, then you really don't want this gig to end do you?"

"Not at all! This whole deal has been great for me."

"Okay. No reason to end it then. Don't tell Bomber I'm on to you. Make out like I'm becoming more and more convinced you're a ghost. String it along and let me try to get to the bottom of this. If you're telling the truth you've got nothing to worry about when I finally figure this out. You're just a pawn in this game and I won't hold it against you."

"Can we still have sex?" she'd asked with pleading eyes. "I love making love with you."

He'd grinned and said, "Sure, why not? I like you too."

Jasper ambled over to the sliding glass doors and gazed idly through them, still thinking. Lorraine Bradbury didn't appear to have any kind of money, making it very improbable she hired Catrina Smith. Peggy Sue had told him she made six figures a year, but what would her motive be? And if the six figures were low numbers, the strain of paying ten grand a month for two apartments, plus Catrina's weekly two thousand, would seriously drain her piggy bank. There were only two people he knew that had the kind of money to foot a bill of this magnitude, and they were both named Cross. T. Wayford wasn't even a consideration so that left dear ol' pathological liar Ginny. But why the hell would she do it? And why would she want his sperm on a towel when she had so many opportunities to get it without going through a third party? That fact alone pretty much crossed her off the list of suspects. Since the scam started long before he met Peggy Sue, if his estranged fiancé was in on it, someone had hired her to do it.

He examined the prospect. Besides having no apparent motive, the main flaw in her being involved was the use of the name P. S. Drinkwater. Peggy Sue would know he might find out, so why take such a risk? The apartments were secured so the landlord probably required proper identification, but with access to that kind of cash, why not just pay someone else to rent the apartments or procure fake credentials under a phony name? It seemed logical to assume Bomber wanted him to think Peggy Sue engineered it all. That brought Ginny back to center stage via jealousy, but the notion still didn't make any sense because he didn't know Peggy Sue existed when the apparitions first started on the ranch. In order to learn the truth, he had to find a way to make Bomber come out of the woodwork.

* * * *

"Tell Bomber you're getting me convinced but that it's taking more and more of your time, so you need an extra five hundred a week. Say you expect the first installment by three tomorrow afternoon or you're going to tell me everything and pull out of the deal."

Sitting on his couch, wearing a green jogging suit, Catrina Smith, aka Selma Russell, smiled seductively. "That won't be a lie, sugar, because you *are* taking more and more of my time. Of course Mama wants you to . . . ."

19

Jasper used binoculars on the ranch to check cattle from a distance. But standing at the adobe fence surrounding Water Crest Manor, he had them focused on a group of mailboxes, the one marked 104 in particular. It was nearing the three o'clock deadline and he'd been waiting for over two hours. Finally a car pulled up. A hand reached through the window and unlocked box 104, deposited a white envelope, relocked the box, and sped away. He pulled out his cell, called Catrina, and told her to check and see if the deposit had been made because he couldn't tell due to several cars driving by the mailboxes. It was a lie of course. Lorraine Bradbury had dropped off the envelope . . . .

Back in his apartment, he again called Catrina, this time from his house phone. "Did you get it?"

"Got it right here," she said excitedly. "Five hundred dollars, just like I asked for. So you weren't able to tell who left it?"

"No, couldn't make it out because of those damn cars."

"What a shame. See you tonight?"

"Not tonight. Got some stuff I've gotta do. I'll give you a call tomorrow . . . ."

Waiting long enough to allow time for Lorraine Bradbury to get home, he drove to her house, hoping that's where she'd gone.

When the conniving bitch opened the door and recognized him, she tried to slam it shut but he got a boot across the threshold and forced his way in.

"Okay, Lorraine—" he kicked the door closed behind him "—it's high time we had a heart to heart."

She backed away, face colorless with panic.

"I saw you put an envelope in a mailbox at my apartment complex. Who told you to do it?"

"I don't know what you're talking about!"

"Cut the bullshit, I've got you dead to rights. Now who told you to do it?"

"I'll-I'll call the police, I swear I will!"

"Call them, let's get this out in the open once and for all. Then I can charge you with conspiracy to commit blackmail. Go ahead, call them!"

Still stepping backwards, she started bawling. They wound up in the kitchen and she cried, "Please leave me alone! I don't want any trouble!"

"Oh you're a tad late for that. Trouble's here and it ain't going away till you tell me what I want to know."

The petrified girl began to hyperventilate and her glasses fell to the floor.

Unable to find a bag of any kind, he pulled a small plastic bowl from a wall cabinet and thrust it to her. "Cup this over your mouth and nose, and try to seal it with your hands."

Leaning over, she buried her face in the container.

"Keep it there until you start breathing normally."

A few minutes later the panic attack subsided.

Rummaging through her cabinets again, he fetched a glass, filled it with tap water, and commanded her to drink it.

She complied with a grateful expression.

He picked up the unharmed spectacles and handed them

over while guiding her to the living room. She sat down in the rocker and put them on.

"You're in way over your head, Lorraine. Someone's trying to do a number on me, and they're using you to do it. Your mother never told you I was your father, did she."

Her face was etched with desperation. "No."

"I know she really died, but was it suicide?"

"Yes, she took her own life but not because of my dad, he got killed in an oilfield accident four years ago. She'd been stricken with pancreatic cancer and didn't want to face the pain."

"Someone paid you to lay all that bullshit on me, didn't they."

"Yes."

"Who?"

"I don't know. A few days after my mother died I found an envelope on my front porch containing five hundred dollars and a typed note saying it was a consolatory gift from Bomber. Nobody I know uses that nickname, so I was pretty nervous even though I was glad to get the money. Then I got a condolence email from Bomber, containing a proposition. I was offered a thousand dollars if I'd be willing to be in a short film that wouldn't take more than a few hours of my time. I was worried about how Bomber knew so much about me, my email and home addresses and everything, but I was really in a bind—I desperately needed the money. I emailed back that I would do it, and Bomber sent me an address, telling me where to go and what time to be there. When I arrived to do the film I was offered another thousand dollars if I'd tell a man named Jasper Miller that Mother claimed he was my father. There were only two people there and I don't know if either of them was Bomber. They coached me on what to say and gave me the diary and laptop with the photographs I showed you that day I went to see you. I asked why they were doing it and they said it was a practical joke. Since I got another thousand dollars for doing that besides the film, I didn't push the issue."

It dawned on him he still had his hat on. Taking it off he said, "Did Bomber tell you to drop off that envelope?"

"Yes. There was a package on the porch when I got up this morning. It contained a sealed envelope, a note with instructions for me to deposit it in box one-o-four at Water Crest Manor by three o'clock, the key to the mailbox, and a thousand dollars cash."

"Were you following me when I saw you the other day?"

"Yes."

"Per Bomber's instructions?"

Nodding, she pressed her dry lips together and swallowed hard. "Would you like a Dr Pepper? I need one bad."

"I'll get it for you, keep your seat."

He brought her the soft drink and settled on the couch. "Did Bomber have you dress in a white dress with a veil for the film you were asked to do?"

She nodded and took a long drink.

"I thought so. What was the film about?"

"It was weird. I only had three lines—*Help*, *Help me*, and *I am the body and I need help.* They had me stand in front of a large green screen and say them all while posing with my hands held out and looking straight ahead, lowering them and looking down, and standing with arms at my side. Then they made me rehearse what I was supposed to say to you."

"Do you have a copy of that film?"

"No."

"You didn't ask for a copy?"

She shook her head. "I didn't want one. The whole thing was creepy, but I needed the money."

"Do you have the dress and veil?"

"No. They handed them to me when I got there and told me to put them on. I never saw them again after changing back into my clothes."

The rim of his upper lip developed an itch. He rubbed it away with the side of his index finger, ruffling his moustache in the process. "Where's the studio?"

"It wasn't a studio, they had me come to a hotel suite and filmed me there."

"Did you ask what they planned to do with the film?"

"No. I didn't want to rock the boat. I was just relieved they didn't ask me to do porno like I was afraid they would. They were wearing ski masks and gloves and baggy raincoats. It was really weird, and scary. They were both tall so I assume they were both men, but I only know for sure that one of them was because he did all the talking. He had a French accent."

Wondering if the silent one could be Ginny he said, "Was that the only film you made?"

"Yes."

"What about when you came to see me, what happened over that deal?"

Lorraine took a deep pull from her can before answering. "I emailed Bomber, told him what happened, and that your lady friend ran me off. Bomber said that was okay, that I had fulfilled my end of the deal. I found the money on my porch the next day. That was the last I heard from Bomber until I was asked to follow you."

An itch crawled under his chin. Scratching it through his beard, he began to think it might be time to mow the damn thing off. "How did that go down?"

"I got a call at the pet store from someone saying they were calling for Bomber. They said Bomber would pay me a thousand dollars if I'd leave work immediately and wait in my car until they called me on my cell phone. I did and they called, saying you were headed for Fort Worth in a silver Dodge Ram. They directed me to where you were and I was told to make sure you spotted me. The caller was obviously trying to disguise her voice, but I could tell it was a woman pretending to be a man."

"Did you tell Bomber I came here?"

She took a another drink, holding the can with both hands. "No."

"Why?'

"I was afraid I might not get paid."

"Okay. Don't tell Bomber I'm on to you, just act like everything's normal. I won't hold you accountable when I finally find out who Bomber is—and I *will* find out. Can you do that, just make out like everything's normal?"

She gave him a meek nod.

"What's Bomber's email address?"

"Bomber at Plex Net dot com."

He'd already gotten the address from Catrina but wanted to see if Lorraine would tell him the truth.

She had.

20

When he got home from Lorraine Bradbury's, Jasper called Ginny.

"Hello?"

"Hey, Ginny."

"Jasper! I've been on pins and needles waiting on you to call after you told me at the motel not to call you again until you told me I could."

"You know what, Ginny?"

"What?"

"Since we started fooling around together there's something we've never done."

She gurgled an erotic laugh. *"Honey, they haven't invented what we haven't done to each other."*

"No, I'm serious. You've never asked me over to your place. Why is that?"

"Because of Daddy of course."

"Well I want to come over."

"Jasper, you can't! Daddy would have a cow if he caught us together."

Her panicked voice made him grin. "So who's gonna tell him? He won't know."

"Jasper, the one place I always behave myself is at my house because I never know when Daddy's gonna pop in to

say hello. It's just too risky, sorry. I could come over, or rent a motel room if you're just wanting to get out of your apartment for awhile."

"Naw, I want to come to your place."

"Well you can't and that's final."

He snickered. "Quit being so paranoid. T. Wayford isn't going to think a thing about me dropping by to visit you."

"The hell he won't! Now you drop that foolish notion right now, you hear?"

"Ginny, you're being unreasonable."

"No I'm not. If you want to fuck, pick somewhere besides my place."

"Forget it. Talk to you later . . . ."

He hung up the phone and grabbed a Lone Star. His scheme had failed. After Ginny fell asleep he'd planned to sneak a peek at her computer in the hope of determining whether or not she was Bomber. Though her being Bomber didn't make a lick of sense, all signs pointed to her and an accomplice. He set down at his desk and switched on his computer. As it booted up he tried to think of what password Ginny would use. Not having much use for the internet, he seldom messed with it. Back on the ranch he used his computer to keep a log of worming and slaughter dates, meat deliveries, state inspections, and the like. Since he no longer dealt with such things, he seldom turned it on anymore.

The busy light on his hard drive settled down, he directed the search engine towards *Plex Net*, soon had the website on his monitor, and saw he had two options—sign in or create a new account. He decided to get an email address and see exactly how those things worked before trying his hand as a hacker. Unable to get one using his name because it had already been taken, he chose the top title from a list of suggested combinations of Jasper Miller and numbers that were available. His new email handle was Jasper_Miller_44.

Trying to think like Ginny, knowing he was looking for a needle in a haystack, he attempted to break into Bomber's email, but kept getting a red notice saying *Invalid ID or password.* Giving up on that, he rummaged through his desk and found the piece of paper Peggy Sue had written her email address on. He sent her a short note to let her know he'd finally given in and joined the throng of electronic mailers, logged off, and called Ginny back.

"Hello?"

"All right, haul your butt over here."

She squealed with delight. *"Be there shortly . . .!"*

As soon as Ginny arrived he cautioned her he wanted to talk and wasn't in the mood for sex.

"Okay—" she plopped down on the couch with a pout "—let's talk." She was wearing jeans and a frilly pink blouse. Stretching her long arms sensuously along the couch's back caused the fabric to tighten against her breasts while she slowly crossed her legs in an obvious ploy to turn him on.

"Got myself an email address today."

"You did?"

"Mm hmm. What's your email address?" He went to his desk and grabbed a pen as she answered. Then, at his insistence, she spelled her funky computer nickname while he jotted it down. "Okay, *Ginny girl luvs pink*, I'll email you, then you'll have my address."

"Great," she said dryly. "Maybe we can have cyber sex since you no longer seem interested in the other kind."

"You know better than that. I'm just not in the mood tonight, that's all. Know anything about Plex Net dot com?"

"No. Why?"

"Know anything about bombs?"

A shocked laugh blew out of her mouth. "Bombs?"

"Yeah. You know, those things that go boom."

"I know what bombs are, Jasper Miller. Why the hell are you asking me about them?"

He eyed her closely. If she was Bomber she hid the fact damn well. "Just fooling around. I'm in one of my oddball moods."

"Do tell," she spouted sarcastically. "So where's little Miss Drinkwater tonight? Don't tell me the poor dear has a headache."

"Me and Peggy Sue are cooling it for the time being."

Her face ignited with jubilation. "I knew you'd come to your senses! When did this happen?"

"Never mind," he said somberly, his expression letting her know not to pursue the matter any further.

She obviously picked up on it for the next words she uttered were, "So when are you going to get rid of that disgusting beard?"

He grabbed a handful of chin hair. "You really hate this thing, don't you."

"With a passion."

"I'll probably shave it off here pretty quick. Itches me something fierce sometimes. By the way, I got a new pickup."

"You did? Let's go look at it."

"All right . . . ."

The carport was equipped with tube-lights that came on at dusk and went off at dawn, the silver pickup gleamed in fluorescent radiation. He admired it with a smile that faded when Ginny said, "Why in hell did you buy a Dodge Ram?"

"What's the matter with it?"

"When are you going to learn that you're no longer a poor cowboy riding the range on my daddy's ranch? Dammit, Jasper, I talked you through some new duds, helped you pick out some decent furniture, and now you go and do this. Why didn't you let me help you choose a new vehicle? You should have gotten one of those huge tacky double-cabs covered in chrome that scream 'I've got money to burn!' if you just had to have another pickup. What you really need is a Vette or a Jag."

"Yeah well," he scratched at the back of his neck, "I don't have money to burn. At least not yet, and I like my new pickup just fine."

Back inside, he went to his desk and swiveled the chair around so he could sit facing Ginny, who returned to the couch and crossed her legs. "You remember Lorraine Bradbury, that woman who thought I was her father?"

"That little bitch better not have come to see you again!" Ginny's eyes swore vengeance.

"No, but I ran into her the other day when I was driving around Fort Worth. I followed her home and the girl has quite a story to tell."

She wriggled her dangling foot from side to side. "Like what? She wants to do a DNA test?"

"Not exactly."

"Then what?"

"Remember our ghost, the woman in white?"

"How could I ever forget that?"

"Well, turns out the ghost was her all along."

"What . . .?" Ginny leaned forward with a fallen jaw.

"She had a film made of herself dressed in white and wearing a veil, saying 'Help me, I am the body' the whole nine yards."

"You're kidding. She told you that?"

"Mm hmm."

"Did she tell you how she was able to come and go, how she was able to just vanish right before our eyes?"

"No. But the ghost is a projection of the film she made, I'm sure of that. There never was a ghost, just someone projecting

Lorraine Bradbury's image and playing a recording of her voice."

"How can that be done? We'd have seen a projector, and you know we didn't see anything of the sort. I don't know what she's pulling but the woman I saw damn sure wasn't her."

If Ginny wasn't such a good liar he'd be convinced by her reaction she had nothing to do with the scam. That not being the case the jury was still out. "She told me she got paid to make the film. Made quite a bit of money for doing it as a matter of fact. And the ghost was wearing a veil, remember? You can't be sure that wasn't her we saw."

"Who paid her?"

"She doesn't know."

An incredulous glower erupted on her face. "She made a film for money and doesn't know who paid her? That doesn't add up. She's lying to you. I don't know what that little bitch is up to, but she's lying out her ass."

"No. Her mother never told her I was her father. She got paid to say all that bullshit by the same person who faked those pictures of me and her mother. And remember my other mistress I told you about? She's being paid by the same person that paid Lorraine."

"Paid for what? To screw you?"

He got up and stepped towards her—eyes narrowed, teeth bared. "More like screw with my mind."

Rearing back from his accusing expression, she shouted, "Oh I get it now! You think I'm the one behind this, don't you!"

"Are you?"

"Hell no! Ghost or no ghost, that bitch in white scared the shit out of me. I didn't have a damn thing to do with that, or that bitch Lorraine saying you were her father. And whoever this mistress of yours is, I damn sure didn't pay her to fuck you. If I was going to pay her, it would be to stay the hell away from you, dumbass."

She seemed totally truthful, but this was Ginny Cross, the gal who believed her lies while spouting them out. He decided to let it rest a spell, then see what she had to say.

Still fuming, she got up and went to the kitchen. "Got anything to drink besides cow piss?"

He ambled in and pointed to the icebox. "There's some leftover margarita's in a pitcher in back. Give it a good stir and it should taste close to decent."

Fetching a spoon from the silverware drawer, Ginny stirred the liquor mix vigorously and grabbed a highball glass from an upper cabinet. She'd bought him a set in order to have something besides jelly glasses to drink from when she came to visit. "Tell me about this mistress of yours that you refuse to name. What does she look like and why do you think she's a ghost?"

The last part of her question dangled in his ears, elevating his pulse. That slipup meant she had to be the one behind it all. But what the hell prompted her to do it? He glared at her while loudly clearing his throat. "Uh-oh, bad mistake, ol' girl. I never said she was a ghost."

"Yes you did, when you told me about her at the motel."

"Huh?"

"When I asked her name at the motel, you said it didn't matter because she was probably a ghost. Remember?"

Damn, she's right! Her statement refreshed his memory, instantly removing the guilty tag, sending him right back to square one. "Sorry, I'd forgotten."

"I'll ask again," she said impatiently. "What does she look like?"

He shrugged. "She's close to six feet tall, fantastic build, dark red hair, real classy. Likes to wear green and tons of rubies."

"Humph, sounds like my cousin Catrina." Ginny spouted the words disdainfully, appearing to be talking to herself more than him, obviously not thinking it could possibly be her.

"You have a cousin Catrina?"

"Yeah. Catrina Canton, she's my second cousin. Willis is her dad. We were real close when we were kids, she was like my older sister. But we had a serious falling out and we've hated each other ever since. To show how close we were, until Blane and I came out to the ranch that weekend, she's the only one I ever told about my feelings for you. I was fourteen at the time and she was nineteen. She moved to France with some guy years ago, and as far as I know she's still there."

Rubbing his hairy jaw, he stared blankly into space. He knew Willis Canton had a daughter but he'd never laid eyes on her, and didn't know her proper name until now, having only heard her referred to as Sugar Plum. Willis had several stepchildren, but she was his only blood offspring. His first wife had borne her, and they'd divorced before Red took him aboard as a tenderfoot. *I was at the border of the Canton Ranch when I first heard the cry for help. Lorraine Bradbury said the man who did the talking while she was being filmed had a French accent. Could Catrina Smith be Catrina Canton?*

Ginny snapped her fingers. "Hello! Over here please!"

"Sorry . . ." he flexed his face as if just waking. "So your cousin, did she ever marry or does she still go by Canton?"

"Seems like she did marry that guy. Let's see, what was his name? Leonard something."

"Could it have been Leonard Smith?"

"Hell I don't know, possibly. Why?"

Adrenaline raced through him. Willis Canton had more money than God, so his daughter would most likely have a hefty bank account like Ginny did because of her dad's generosity. If Catrina Smith was Ginny's cousin, the cash spent on the scam wouldn't amount to a drop in the bucket to her, provided she hadn't gotten on her rich daddy's bad side. "Your cousin Catrina, does she have money?"

"Uh-yeah!" she belted out caustically. "Willis set up a trust fund for her the day she was born, and the poor dear only inherited seven hundred million when it matured on her eighteenth birthday. Yes, the bitch has money. Anyway, back to your mistress. Who is she? Why won't you tell me her name?"

He couldn't hold back a taunting grin. "What if I was to tell you I suspect she might just be your cousin Catrina?"

"Huh?!" Ginny's features were twisted into such a nauseous contortion of shock, she looked like she might throw up. "It damn well better not be her!"

"If you're game we can find out. She lives at this apartment complex. I'll call her and invite her over. You hide in the closet under the stairs and hold the door open a crack. I'll lure her close enough so you can get a good look at her. Then I'll say I want to go to her place, find an excuse to cut the evening short after we do, and come back here."

Brows irately arching over them, her predatory eyes looked more savage than ever. "Call her, I'm dying to find out . . . ."

Catrina answered on the second ring and said she'd be right over.

21

Ginny fled to the closet when the bell rang. Once she got situated he answered the door. Catrina walked in wearing a green pant suit, beautiful ruby choker with matching earrings, and bracelets covered in the red gems, all differing from the ones she'd worn with the ghost dress. Her thumbs were the only digits not adorned with scarlet jewelry closely matching the color of her long nails.

He invited her inside. "Got some news about the person who deposited the envelope."

"Great, what is it?"

Apparently all Ginny needed to determine her identity was to hear Catrina's sultry voice, because she burst out of the closet and ran towards her screaming, "You fucking bitch!"

"Ginny?!" The fake ghost staggered back, reeling with shock and alarm as if she'd just seen a real one.

Grabbing Ginny before she could claw the redhead's eyes out, he drug her to the couch, kicking and screaming like a snared alley cat. "Now sit there and let's talk this out!"

Catrina then decided to bail, but he snatched her left hand before she could step through the door. Yanking her inside, he slammed it shut. "Not on your life, sister! The three of us are going to have a pow wow."

Cursing at the top of her lungs, Ginny attempted another

assault . . . .

* * * *

After forcing Ginny back to the couch again while warning Catrina to stay put, he finally got the fuming blonde to promise she'd stay there by threatening to never speak to her again if she didn't. During her second attack Ginny had inadvertently clawed him above his right eye. Though only a scratch, it bled tiny droplets. He periodically daubed it with a fingertip and wiped the blood on his jeans. Doing so now he said, "Okay, Ginny, now that we've established that she's your cousin, let's hear what she has to say."

Catrina wouldn't speak, just stood in front of the door with arms crossed beneath her breasts, glowering at Ginny, who glared back menacingly.

"Okay, let's break the ice with this. What happened to make you two hate each other so much?" He suffered their silence for a few more minutes before angrily screaming, "Would somebody please talk?! What happened to you two?"

Still boring down on Catrina with hate-filled eyes, Ginny crossed her legs and shoved her forearms under her breasts. "She caught me fooling around with her boyfriend. We got into a fight and the fucking bitch called my mama a whore!"

"And I told you I'd get even, didn't I, Ginny." Catrina's icy tone reflected the loathing on her face.

He heaved a raw sigh. "Okay, you're speaking, that's a start. Now, what I want to know is how the hell I figure into all this."

Catrina finally broke off her laser stare aimed at Ginny and looked at him. "I've been living in France for the last ten years. I wouldn't let my daddy talk about Ginny when he called because I didn't want to so much as hear her name.

You're all Ginny's wanted since she was a kid. She always gets what she wants, so I knew she'd find a way to win you. When I got back to the states I was shocked and quite delighted to learn she hadn't already succeeded. I knew she still wanted you or she'd have married someone else long before now. And so, to rain on her parade big time, I set out to convince you that she was behind the haunting of The Double Cross Ranch. Once you started suspecting she planned the whole thing, you'd naturally confront her, and the more she protested her innocence, the less enthralled you'd have been with her. The plan called for you to eventually think she was insane so you'd wash your hands of her totally. She thought my boyfriend—the one she seduced behind my back—was just one of my many flings of those days. But she was wrong. I loved him." She cut her eyes to Ginny with contempt. "He was my Jasper Miller."

Ginny gasped and covered her heart with both hands. "Oh, Catrina, how could I have known?! I thought he was just another hard dick for you to play with, another heart you'd eventually break. If I *had* known, I never would have done that to you."

"Yeah, you're a real angel, aren't you, Ginny."

"I mean it! I never—"

"Can it, Ginny, I'm not buying it!" She refocused on him. "Everything was going precisely as planned until I met you. Then I got confused . . . my emotions started getting the better of me, and I started falling for you myself."

Ignoring her adoration, which he took to be a farce, he said, "You're Bomber, aren't you."

The redhead laughed. "There is no Bomber. I made all that up."

He gently fingered the scratch over his eye to find the bleeding had stopped. "But Lorraine Bradbury told me—"

"She told you what I told her to tell you. You, of course, were supposed to think Ginny was Bomber."

Ginny gasped with fury. "So that's why you were asking me about bombs! You bastard!"

"Aw shut up, Ginny!" he yelled back. "You've told me so many lies you're lucky I even talk to you. I didn't think you were Bomber because it didn't make any sense, but all the evidence pointed to you so—"

"Just as I planned," Catrina interrupted with a sinister smile.

"And P. S. Drinkwater?" he asked, noting the daggers Ginny kept casting at him with her angry eyes.

"To make you think Ginny was trying to frame Peg Drinkwater. Make her appear all the more despicable. Which she is."

Ginny launched from the couch and Catrina started towards her. He got in between and grabbed each of them by the throat. "I'm going to choke you both to death if you don't knock it off—that's enough!"

Receiving slaps to the face from both of them, he squeezed tighter to show them he meant business. When they finally lowered their arms he let go. Catrina marched towards the door, but he jumped in front of it. "Oh you're not going anywhere, girl! How did you project the woman in white at the ranch?"

She merely glared at him disdainfully.

"Answer me. You're not leaving here till you do, I guarantee you."

"You can't hold me here against my will!"

"The hell I can't. Now answer my question."

Catrina swooped back a stray lock while exhaling an angry breath. "I didn't, a friend of mine did. I met him in France. He's a genius with sound, photography, and holograms. I financed him and he filled a van with all kinds of high tech equipment. We did it all from the edge of my daddy's ranch. He planted these tiny wireless speakers in several locations on the Double Cross. They're amazing—they look just like a blade of grass but can transmit sound like a large speaker. Along with the speakers, he dispersed tiny optical devices that can scan three-hundred-sixty degrees and transmit pictures to monitors in the van with crystal clarity. The gadgets used to produce the hologram are similar. Both are no bigger than a nail head, and that's just what they look like when you stick them to a wall. That's how we were able to see you and know where to place the hologram. We had every square inch outside of the ranch house, bunkhouse, and slaughterhouse monitored. Since you always left your doors unlocked, while you were out slopping hogs or whatever, he was able to place some inside. He invented the devices, as well as the speakers, and has a patent pending on all three. When they finally reach the marketplace I, as his backer, will receive fifty-two percent of every dollar he brings in."

Jasper thought back to that day Useless couldn't get in the backdoor to deposit the Lone Star. Catrina's accomplice must have inadvertently locked it on his way out.

"We started with another cowboy who was replacing a busted post on the fence near where we were parked. He never saw us. We knew he'd have to come back because several more posts needed replacing and the bottom three strands of wire were broken. My friend planted some transmitters and sure enough he came back to the same spot the next day."

"That was Drake Jensen," he said with a sigh, marveling such technology existed.

"Well we freaked him out good. We were going to give the cowboy another round of vocals, knowing he was bound to tell you about it and you'd already be concerned when we started in on you. I didn't want my friend to start using the hologram until you were convinced an unseen woman was crying for help. When you wound up finishing that part of the fence instead, I figured we must have scared the other poor cowpoke right off The Double Cross Ranch until we played a recording of him telling you his father had died. It was hilarious watching you look for that poor damsel in distress. After you went home, we flashed the hologram around to get your attention, but far too quickly for you to tell it was a woman."

"The woman is Lorraine Bradbury, right?"

"Yes. Before we started with the fence-mending cowboy we'd already put most of the transmitters and optical sensors at various places on the ranch while you and the other cowboys were partying in town one Saturday night. All told, I spent almost a million dollars to produce that ghost. And it would have been worth every penny if you hadn't found out, because you'd have wound up thinking Ginny was a loon."

"You bitch!"

"Shut up, Ginny!" he shouted without taking his eyes off Catrina. "How did you hook up with Lorraine Bradbury, and how did you know I went to school with her mother?"

Catrina stretched her ruby lips into a sly grin. "Classmates dot com. I researched you thoroughly. Ginny had told me you were raised in Waco, and it wasn't hard finding the year you graduated. I made out like I'd gone to high school during the same time you did but moved away before graduation. I got a few nibbles and asked each one if they knew Jasper Miller. Tulia Barella Bradbury responded and told me the two of you had dated in high school. The ghost had to be someone you'd eventually recognize, so you'd hunt her down and she'd confess her trickery. And of course she'd claim someone named Bomber paid her to do it, dropping enough clues for you to eventually conclude Bomber was Ginny. Tulia was going to be my ghost, but before I could approach her with the offer she committed suicide after being diagnosed with pancreatic cancer. I heard the sad news from Lorraine, who answered the phone when I called Tulia to make the proposal. Learning she was Tulia's daughter, I offered her the role instead, and came up with an alternate plot to get you on Tulia's trail. Lorraine was in dire need of money, so she was basically putty in my hands. Of course I never told her my name. She knows me only as Casper.

"Once you were convinced Ginny orchestrated the whole deal, you'd have no choice but to think she was insane. Only a mad woman would pay someone to haunt you as a ghost and have her pretend to be your daughter at the same time. I instructed Lorraine to tell you Bomber had someone call her at work and offer her money to follow you, and though the caller was obviously disguising their voice, she thought it was a woman. The truth is she knew it was me directing her by cell phone while I was following you. I told her to make sure you spotted her. All this was done to start bringing Bomber into the picture.

"Lorraine was going to be well compensated for calling you to say she'd gotten another package from Bomber and had spotted a woman getting into a pink Stingray after depositing it on her porch. She would have told you that although she hadn't gotten a clear look at the face, the woman was tall and shapely with strawberry blonde hair. The package would have contained pictures of Peg Drinkwater two-timing you with another man, composed just clumsily enough for you to tell they were fakes, accompanied by instructions for Lorraine to mail them to you. If you hadn't asked me over tonight you'd have wound up convinced Ginny was a hopeless nutcase with a sick obsession of tormenting you while trying to possess you. Now you know the truth, and Ginny fucking wins again."

Jasper couldn't believe his ears. All this over a catfight that happened years ago. He needed one more question answered. "Is Peggy Sue involved in any of this?"

"Peg Drinkwater? Hardly."

"Well I'm confused. She picked out this apartment, and it's a damn strange coincidence she chose one with a vacant apartment right next door, where you could pretend to be my neighbor."

"You underestimate my cousin," said Ginny with guile. "She probably bought these apartments and paid whoever lived next door to move out."

Catrina let out a sarcastic snicker. "No, Ginny. The apartment next door just happened to be vacant and so was one-o-four. Due to the owner's unwillingness to lower the rent during these tough economic times, thirty percent of the apartments in this complex are unoccupied. I simply rented them both three days before Jasper moved in, and was delighted to learn one-o-two had red carpet. I paid the apartment manager five hundred dollars to keep her mouth shut about me renting one-o-two and insisted it remain listed as vacant.

"I had some of my furniture moved to one-o-four and the moving van also contained the furnishings I bought for one-o-two, which I had the movers put into one-o-four. I hired some men to move the new furniture to one-o-two after midnight, so no one would see them doing it. Security merely thought they were my guests. This was all done within forty-eight hours after I rented the apartments."

She turned her attention back to him. "The day after you told me of your engagement I did some research on Peg Drinkwater, learned her middle name was Sue, and had the lease for one-o-four switched over to the name P. S. Drinkwater. It's amazing how easily money can get you around legal technicalities. I'd planned for you to see me leave one-o-two and follow me to one-o-four so you'd start digging around and find out who rented it, but you did it before I was ready."

"How did you know I was moving to this apartment in the first place?" he asked, amazed at the intricacies of Catrina's diabolical plan.

"T.W. had your furniture moved right after that limousine brought you to Dallas. It was simply a matter of following the moving van. We could eavesdrop on the ranch as well as transmit. Every conversation in the ranch house was recorded and we had your phone tapped. I've known about your sausage every step of the way. When T.W. called you and said you two were going to be partners, and you needed to train a replacement because you'd be leaving the ranch, I decided to put Ghost Lorraine on hold and devise a scheme that involved me so I could sweeten my revenge by seducing my treacherous cousin's heartthrob the way she did mine. I knew I had a good chance of succeeding because of what you'd told her about your personalities clashing. You'd have met Selma Russell not long after you moved in if urgent business hadn't forced me back to France and kept me there for almost four months." She gave Ginny a haughty smirk. "By the way, that was an interesting conversation you had with Jasper about your tits, Ginny dear. It inspired me to suck his cock and pump his hot semen all over mine the first time we were together."

"You *fucking* bitch . . .!" Ginny shot towards her.

Lowering his shoulder, he leaned into her stomach as she tried to run past, heaved her over his back, and deposited her on the couch. "Now you sit there, Ginny, until I hear it all!"

Catrina folded her arms beneath her breasts and shot him a defiant smile. "If you're thinking of reporting me to the police for trespassing, think again. That ranch belongs to my dear first cousin once removed—T.W. would never press charges. And any other legal shit you try to pull, my lawyers will have swept under the rug in less time than it takes you to scratch your balls."

He shook his head wearily. "No, wasn't thinking along those lines. Just want the truth, that's all. It's not like anyone's been murdered or anything, although your hologram damn near gave me a heart attack. Where's your accomplice?"

"In apartment one-o-four. He's who pretended to be the superintendent the day we met. His name's Francois. It was a stereo he designed to turn on by a handclap that played the violin music we danced to when I had you over for dinner. It was hidden beneath the bottom of the cocktail bar so that it would appear I'd summoned the music supernaturally after you started thinking I was a ghost."

"Who all was involved?"

"Just the three of us—me, Francois, and Lorraine."

"No one else knows about this?"

"No. Though I did hire some men to move the furniture upstairs between five and six a.m. and back downstairs between nine and ten p.m. two days in a row. I had them come and go through the patio so you wouldn't see them. They think they did it so Francois could do some trick video shots where it looks like the furniture disappears. I put the ashtray in a drawer right after you left that first night, leaving it littered on purpose to enhance the ghostly effect when you saw everything back in place."

"This Francois, is he your lover or what?"

That ignited a short round of hysterical laughter. "Francois is gay."

"What made you come up with the idea of a ghost? There must have been cheaper ways to get even with Ginny."

"Francois loves to play with holograms. One day I was watching him produce this ghostly looking image from a photograph he had, and the idea just came to mind. And there could be no sweeter revenge on Ginny than for the love of her life to write her off as a psycho."

Glancing warily at Ginny, afraid she might launch another attack, he relaxed. She still looked pissed, but remained seated, so he refocused on the redhead. "Is Smith really your last name?"

"No. I married a sweet older man named Leonard White, who treated me like a queen. We were true soul mates. He was extremely wealthy and couldn't care less about my money, nor I his. Sadly, I wound up with his fortune because I lost him to leukemia eighteen months after we moved to France. I met Francois during that time."

"So you're Catrina White?"

"Mm hmm."

"And Fantastic Fantasies?"

"No such thing. However, as a safeguard I had Francois put up an actual website named that in case you checked it out. How sad I had to tell you about it before I was prepared for you to catch me. Believe it or not several idiots actually tried to pay the one thousand dollar membership fee. Each received an automatic reply that explained the website was being renovated, and not accepting new members until completion."

"Why the name Selma Russell?"

"I'm a natural redhead like Amanda Blake, who played Kitty Russell on Gun Smoke. Selma is my middle name and I always loved Miss Kitty. Now I'd like to ask you a question. Why did you call me over here tonight with Ginny here?"

"I'll answer that one," hissed Ginny venomously. "He was describing you and I said you sounded like my cousin Catrina, never dreaming in a million years it was really you."

He nodded. "And that's why I called you here—so Ginny could get a peek at you from that closet on the stair wall."

"So that's what you meant a while ago about establishing we were cousins. I shouldn't have used my real first name but you caught me by surprise, and I hadn't decided on what to call myself when I lured you into exposing me. I started to make one up on the spot while you were demanding to know who I really was but nothing came immediately to mind other than Smith, and I knew you'd get suspicious if I took too long to answer." She uncrossed her arms and sighed. "I need a drink."

"I think we all need a drink, but all I've got here is beer and some leftover margaritas."

She gave him an ironic grin. "Shall we reconvene next door?"

* * * *

Jasper sat in an armchair of apartment one-o-two with a turkey and coke in one hand, a Marlboro in the other. The second cousins, each brandishing a drink, circled around the living room, stalking one another like two angry cats with claws fully extended. Ginny had slapped Catrina, immediately got slapped back, fired another round, and received a second blow. Their cheeks still retained the red imprints of a female hand. He'd started to intervene but it became evident after their mutual face-slapping the fight would remain only a verbal duel. Silently he observed, sipping his drink, smoking his cigarette, letting them scream it all out.

". . . Oh yeah? Well I don't care if he did start it, Ginny, you're still nothing but a two bit whore! You knew damn well I was in love with him!"

"I did not know that, you slutty bitch! If I had known I

wouldn't have fucked him as I've already told you! Besides, you fucked Jasper so I guess that makes us even, doesn't it, skank!"

"I loved you, I trusted you, and you betrayed me!"

"How many times do I have to tell you I would have rejected his come on if I'd known how you felt?"

"Did he really come on to you, or are you just saying that? Tell me the truth dammit!"

"I swear to God he came on to me! If I'd known you loved him I'd have slapped his face and told you what a bastard he was right away! And you had no right to call my mother a whore, Catrina! I was only three years old when I lost her! Can't you understand how cruel that was for you to say that?"

The redhead's stormy countenance mellowed. She stilled her feet and placed her free hand on her hip—standing there for several moments, catching her breath, large breasts heaving. "You're right. I should never have said that and I'm sorry. She was like a second mother to me and I loved her very much. I'll never forget that horrible day the accident happened. I was only eight when she died but I miss her to this day. I said you were a whore like your mother because I wanted you to hurt the way you made me hurt, and I knew that would do it. Now I'm dreadfully sorry I did it, and I take it back. Please forgive me."

Ginny's rapacious eyes misted over and turned penitent as she began to sob. "Me too . . . I'm so sorry I hurt you . . . can you ever forgive me?"

Tears streamed down Catrina's cheeks as she set her drink on the coffee table and held out her arms. "Come here, dear."

A moment later the two raving beauties were locked in a tight embrace, declaring their undying love for one another, each promising never to hurt the other again. Hair mussed, mascara running from tracking tears, hand prints on their faces, they looked comical yet incredibly sexy. When the stream of apologies and declarations of devotion finally stopped, they gathered their drinks and nestled on the couch, hip to hip.

Catrina took a sip of the clear liquid he now knew to be vodka and vermouth, then turned towards Ginny. "So what do we do about him?"

Jealousy clutched Ginny's visage for a stark instant before a diplomatic smile overtook it. "Isn't he everything I told you he was?"

"And more."

"He made it clear to me he plans to marry Peg Drinkwater. Even so, I can't give him up, though I'll never be anything more than his mistress."

"Please don't be angry with me, Ginny, but I can't give him up either."

An uneasy silence filled the room as Ginny absorbed Catrina's declaration. He feared the truce had just been broken and the years-long feud was about to resume. When she finally spoke, her tone was bitter but acquiescing. "Then I guess that makes three of us that have to be willing to share him."

Irritated, he snuffed out his smoke and frowned at the presumptuous second cousins. "Quit talking about me like I'm not here. Reckon I have a say in this."

"Well of course you do," said Catrina, brows raised over two turquoise pools glistening with concern. "You're the only man I want and I'll take however much of you I can get. I'll settle for being one of your two mistresses if you're determined to marry Peg Drinkwater."

Things would be so simple if Peggy Sue wasn't afraid of intercourse, because then he could tell them both to shove off. But the way things stood he wasn't about to. Maybe the day would come when she'd let him guide her through it and they could have a normal relationship. Then again, maybe she never would. Catrina's statement about one woman not being enough for him sprang to his mind, and a cold hard fact dawned on him. Even if Peggy Sue did learn to enjoy spreading her legs, he knew it wouldn't kill the fiery passion he felt for the second cousins. He took a long pull from his glass and wiped his mouth. "You'd better understand something, Catrina. If you're going to be my mistress, I expect you to be true to me and not mess around with other men."

"Of course," she replied with a shrug. "I'm not interested in any other man."

Ginny glared at him angrily as if he was to blame for Catrina's avowal. "Well there's damn sure no one else for me."

"Reckon I know that."

"No you don't. You're just saying that, but it happens to be the truth."

"Uh-uh. You've convinced me of one thing, Ginny. Whether it's love or lust, you don't want anybody besides me. Been sure of that for a good while."

Her expression shifted into a simper of surprise. "So you really believe me then?"

"Yep."

Swallowing a nip of booze, Catrina kissed her cousin on the cheek and draped her arm around Ginny's shoulders. "Just so we understand each other, Mister Miller, we expect you to be faithful to us as well. Any woman besides the two of us and Peg Drinkwater is off limits to you."

"Goes without saying." He fired up another Marlboro. "Just don't think you're going to change me in any way and we'll all get along fine."

"Then we have a deal? Other than your fiancé, Ginny, and me, you promise not to touch another woman?"

"You've got my word, but I don't know if Peggy Sue will still want me after I told her we needed to back away from each other until I could find out what the hell was going on with this ghost shit."

Catrina sighed. "If she's a real woman she'll want you. But don't blame us for hoping she doesn't."

"Amen to that," said Ginny, giving the redhead a love pat on the thigh. She looked pacified but not totally acceptant of the situation.

He took a drag and eyeballed Catrina. "Speaking of women, something's bugging me about Lorraine Bradbury. You said she only told me what you told her to say. Was she supposed to tell me that one of the two people wearing disguises while filming her was a man with a French accent?"

"Lord no," she laughed. "Lorraine doesn't know it was Francois and I that filmed her. I screwed up there, didn't I. I should have done the talking. I guess it's true there's no such thing as a perfect crime. If Ginny had learned Lorraine told you the guy sounded French she might have suspected I was behind it since I'd moved to France. Anyway, all's well that ends well as they say . . . ."

At midnight he left the reconciled cousins. They had a lot of lost time to make up for, so Ginny decided to spend the night with Catrina.

22

Jasper enjoyed the best night's sleep he'd had since Selma pulled the disappearing furniture act. After breakfast he decided it was time to figure out the trash compactor. The phone rang before he succeeded.

"Hello?"

"Hey, Boss. It's me, Drake."

"Good to hear from you, hoss. How's it going?"

"Fine. Just wanted to call and thank you for me and the boys."

"Thank me for what?"

"Well hell, the grand apiece you sent us, that's what."

"Oh that," he laughed. "Not a problem. Glad I was able to do it."

"And I've got some news."

"What's that?"

"Dree's leaving us."

He couldn't imagine what would tempt Dree to leave the Double Cross. Despite the frequent ribbing's he had to take from the boys, especially Useless, the big blonde loved his job and T. Wayford paid him a generous wage. "Why's he leaving?"

"Seems he feels the call of God on his life to be a preacher."

"You're shittin' me."

"Nope, and get this—the money you sent somehow validated it all for him."

"No kidding?"

"Nope. Here, he wants to talk to you . . . ."

"Hey, Boss," said Dree excitedly.

Jasper stroked his chin, trying to digest the shocking news. "So you're going to be a man of the cloth, huh?"

"I've felt for some time that God was calling me to preach, but I kept it to myself. I checked out this Bible college and it was going to take me six months of saving my pay to manage tuition along with room and board for the first year.

"Well, I laid out a fleece and told the Lord that if He wanted me to preach He was going to have to somehow get me into that school. But the second I laid the fleece I felt in my spirit He was telling me not to worry with Bible school, that He'd be my teacher as well as provide the means for me to leave the ranch after giving my two weeks notice. Then Drake checked the mail today and your checks were there. It validated everything and I can't thank you enough. I just gave Drake my two weeks notice and he, Useless, and Tray are each going to give me a hundred dollars from the money you sent them. I tell you, Boss, God sure does *work in mysterious ways."*

Deeply concerned, he took a moment to let everything sink in before voicing it. "You're not making a mountain out of a molehill, are you, Dree? I sent that money because I got my first royalty check and it was a humdinger. Just wanted to do something nice for you boys. I didn't feel no call from God to do it."

"Oh ye of little faith," Dree replied after a big sigh. *"Just because you didn't feel the hand of God on it doesn't mean He didn't put it in your heart to do it. I know what I'm doing, and I don't want you to worry about me."*

Disguising his anxiety that Dree was being too impulsive, he forced a chuckle and said, "So you think you can preach as well as you cook?"

"Maybe not at first, but I know God's calling me. He'll give me the tools I need."

"You're going to be hard to replace. The boys are sure going to miss your cooking. I'm surprised they didn't try to bribe you to stay."

Dree laughed. *"As long as the next cook knows how to make good chili they'll never even know I'm gone."*

"Preachers aren't supposed to fib, Dree, and you know what you just said is an outright lie." He mouthed it light-heartedly, still covering his apprehension, but his next statement was dead serious. "Just promise me you won't turn into one of those sleazy TV preachers who's only real call is love of the almighty dollar."

"Like I told you that day when we were talking about what the ghost meant, The Body of Christ does need a lot of help. I agree with you about those television shysters. For every soul that might get saved through their ministry, they drive at least ten away. God will provide for the call He's placed on my life, I'm never going to ask for a red cent."

"Glad you brought up the ghost, Dree . . ." Jasper explained the whole phenomenon, but lied about Catrina's motivation, saying she'd merely done it as a lark. When he finished, Dree surprised him again.

"Well the lady didn't know it, but her having that girl say I am the body and I need help *was part of God's divine plan because that very statement is what got me to wondering how I could possibly help The Church, and eventually led to my realizing God was calling me to the ministry. Can I tell the boys about it, or are you reserving that honor for yourself?"*

"Nah, tell 'em all about it, and pass on an 'I told you so' to

Billy . . . ."

* * * *

"Miss Drinkwater's busy at the moment, can I take a message?" said Martha Spate.

"This is Jasper Miller, just have her call me back . . . ."

Mere seconds after he hung up from Martha Spate, the phone rang.

"Peggy Sue?"

"Don't be disappointed," said T. Wayford with a laugh. *"It's just me."*

"Never disappointed to hear from you. What's up?"

"I want you to come to my office at two o'clock. You'll never guess who you're going to meet."

"Who?"

"Now if I told you it wouldn't be a surprise. Be here at two sharp . . . ."

* * * *

Jasper drove away from the high rise building containing the opulent office suite of Theodore Wayford Cross knowing his life had radically changed. The billionaire had introduced him to Jerry Jones, the owner of the Dallas Cowboys. T. Wayford had apparently known the man for years and chatted with him like an old beer buddy. Nervous and tongue-tied, Jasper hadn't said much past how great it was to meet the icon. To top it off, T. Wayford had given him an open invitation to sit with him in his luxury suite any time the Cowboys played at home.

Grinning with heady elation, he wanted to tell the boys about it but it was only four o'clock, they wouldn't be near a phone this time of day. Then again, Dree might if he was cooking something for supper that took a good while to make. He pulled over, punched in the bunkhouse number, and goosed the accelerator, prodding his new wheels on down the highway. To his surprise, Drake answered.

They swapped hellos and he said, "Tell the boys I actually shook hands with Jerry Jones."

"You're shittin' me, Boss!"

"Nope. If I'm lyin' I'm dyin'." He heard Drake pass on his message and a couple of voices commenting on it. "Who all's there with you, Drake?"

"Useless, Tray, and I stepped in for a coffee break. Dree and Billy are over by the hog pens working on the windmill."

"Well tell Useless and Tray to eat their hearts out."

Drake passed it on and came back with, *"Useless says 'Fuck you very much for your kind consideration.'"*

Jasper snickered. *"Tell Useless I said fuck him very much too . . . ."*

He drove to the plant. Peggy Sue was aloof, and he didn't blame her.

"Can we go some place where we can talk in private?"

"Look, I'm really busy, Jasper. I'll give you a call when I get home . . . ."

Six o'clock rolled by, then seven, then eight, and finally a little after nine she called. He laid out everything about Catrina's failed plot to convince him Ginny was nuts. "Now that I've found out the truth about everything, I know I can totally trust you. I'm ready to pick up where we left off."

Several seconds passed without her responding. "Did you hear what I said?"

"I heard you." Her voice sounded distant, making his stomach tighten.

"Okay, what's the matter, Peggy Sue?"

"What's the matter? I'll tell you what's the matter. I'm not someone you can just write off then write back on when the mood suits you. I'm sure you're used to women fawning all over you, asking how high when you say jump, and making your wish their command every time you snap your fingers, but I'm not one of them."

"So," he sighed out, "what are you saying?"

"I'm saying I expect to be treated with respect and as an equal, and if you can't do that, then there's no point in going any further."

He lowered the receiver, recalling her statement about never being able to live the life of a simple cowgirl. Taking a deep breath, he brought it back to his ear. "Goodbye, Peggy Sue."

The phone rang immediately after he hung up. He knew it was her calling back but he grabbed his hat, walked out the door, and into the night.

Driving through downtown Dallas, he took in the pretty lights of the skyscrapers, feeling bad about hanging up on Peggy Sue, but knowing they'd hit the end of their road. She was too headstrong and wanted him to change too much for things to work out. It didn't hurt like it had when she'd told him she was a lesbian, and he wouldn't be lacking for female company since Ginny and Catrina were adamant about not giving him up. Still, he felt sad. He loved her, and had really looked forward to one day helping her blossom into true womanhood. Now that task—if it ever happened—would fall to some other man.

Nothing on the radio suited him, so he turned it off, wishing he'd thought to bring some CD's along. That old classic by The Rolling Stones *You Can't Always Get What You Want* filled his mental ears and he sang a line, though it was a stretch to call it singing. Passing another skyscraper, he realized he'd absent-mindedly arrived at T. Wayford's building. *Maybe I'll get me one of those swank offices some day.* A moment later he shook his head and grinned. *Now why would I need a fancy office just to taste sausage?*

Bob Dylan's *The Times They Are A Changing* sprang up in his mind as he headed back to Arlington. It was still playing in his head when he got to his apartment. Pulling around front, making for the carport, he saw her sitting on the porch, leaning against his door. She'd either bribed security to get in, or had been there so many times the guard figured he'd want him to let her pass. He killed the engine, walked over, and looked down at her. "Hello, Peggy Sue . . . ."

They were sitting at the dining table, drinking Lone Star. He was smoking. Other than asking for a beer when he got his, she hadn't said anything up to that point.

"Did you come here to talk or sulk?"

She silently eyed him with a hurt expression.

"Okay I'll talk then. I don't know that I expect my women to ask how high when I say jump as you said, but here's what I do know. I'm forty years old and set in my ways. Any changing I do will be because I want to change, not because somebody tells me I need to. I can handle the hard times as well as the good, and I can tolerate loneliness. The prospect of dying an old bachelor doesn't scare me none. So any woman who enters my life, better realize she's doing just that—entering *my* life. You'll be stepping into my world, I won't be stepping into yours. If that sounds too ambiguous to you, let me clarify what I mean. If you want to be with me, you'll learn to see things my way. It's the grand American scheme of things for the woman to emasculate the man, use her wiles to manipulate him and eventually transform him into what she wants him to be. That's just what my sister did with her husband, but it ain't happening to me. I got along for forty years before I met you, and I can damn sure make it the rest of the way without you.

"You say you want respect? Fair enough. But let's make sure what you call respect isn't just another way of saying you want to wear the pants, because these pants ain't coming off for nobody, and they're too damn tight to allow somebody to stand in them with me. You say you want to be treated like an equal? Well I just can't do that because you're a woman. Call me a chauvinist, politically incorrect, narrow-minded, hell call me a fucking caveman if you want, but it won't change the fact that you're a woman—you're always going to be a woman—and there's not one damn thing you can do about it."

She took a swig of beer and kept looking at him with the same pained expression.

Exhaling a final drag, he put his cigarette out. "I went through hell and back trying to figure out this ghost crap, and I'm sorry I got suspicious of you—but you would have too if you'd been in my shoes. Well all that's been solved now, it's water under the bridge. I know after the fact it was wrong to suspect you had anything to do with it, but there's nothing I can do about that now. I'll tell you one more thing about me. I love you, and I want to put you on the highest pedestal where I can worship you like a goddess. I don't want you stooping to my level. I've never been in love before, don't much think I ever will be again. You gonna say something, or just sit there like a bump on a log?"

An awkward length of silence crawled by, then she cleared her throat and softly said, "Here's what I know. You may be able to live without me, but I can't live without you . . . ."

They were soon in his bed and he did what he'd promised never to do. He forced himself on her and she screamed in pain. When it was over, he kissed and fondled her, and kept declaring how much he loved her. When his libido revived, he penetrated her again. Before long Peggy Sue tightened her legs around the small of his back, and thrust at him furiously. Gratified moans and thrilled sighs filled his ears. Several times she cried "Thank you!" before yelling "Oh, Jasper!" amidst the womanly sounds of climax streaming from her throat as they reached the mountaintop together.

He held her naked body against his. She kissed his neck and let out a deep sigh. "I'll treasure this night for the rest of my life. I finally became a real woman, and I owe it all to a real man."

Gently stroking her hair he said, "So you're not mad at me for breaking my word?"

A grateful smile leisurely materialized. "Jasper, if ever there was a promise that needed to be broken, it was that one. I can't believe how intense my orgasm was—I've never felt that good before—and it was so beautiful feeling you come inside me while I was going through it. When you first forced yourself on me it was painful, but not nearly as bad as when I was deflowered in high school. The way you keep speaking so tenderly to me, and caressing me afterwards, made me actually want to feel the pain again, because I knew I'd be giving my man what he wanted, and so desperately needed. Little did I know what awaited me. My god, I thought my heart was going to burst it was so thrilling. You're quite a guy, you know that, cowboy?"

Yeah, he thought, *quite a fucked up guy. What am I going to do about Ginny and Catrina?* As much as he loved Peggy Sue the two cousins had gotten so under his skin that the thought of giving them up seemed harder than trying to break his nicotine habit. As he'd feared, Peggy Sue finally putting out hadn't changed the fact one iota. It was time to come to grips with the truth. Though he was in love with her and she owned his heart emotionally, he felt a deep undeniable bond with Ginny and Catrina that he'd never be able to shake. His wife to be had told him he could have a mistress, but that was only because she'd feared intercourse at the time. Now that Peggy Sue relished it, she'd no doubt be unwilling to share him any longer.

The doorbell rang.

He slid out of bed and put his jeans on. "That'll be Catrina. I'll get rid of her . . . ."

Barefoot and shirtless, he opened the door to find Ginny standing there holding an open bottle of tequila with Catrina at her side.

"Peggy Sue's here," he whispered.

"We figured," said Catrina, not bothering to lower her voice. "That's why we're here. It's time we all got acquainted."

"Are y'all drunk?"

Ginny started giggling and slapped a hand over her mouth to stifle the sound. "Let's just say we're not exactly sober," she testified, voice muffled by her palm.

"The mistresses are never supposed to talk to the wife, don't y'all know that?"

"Oh that's all right, we're not married yet, Jasper."

He jerked his head around to see Peggy Sue crossing the living room, wearing only his blue jean shirt and a proud look.

"You girls come on in," she said on her way to the kitchen. A moment later she came back through the dining area holding a beer, spun his desk chair around so it faced the sofa, and set down.

As Ginny and Catrina made themselves comfortable on the couch, he went to the dining table. He'd left his cigarettes on it when he carried Peggy Sue upstairs. Nervously igniting one, he settled on a corner of his desk.

Ginny honed in on Peggy Sue with her predator gaze. "I'm Ginny Cross and this is my second cousin Catrina White."

Peggy Sue donned a dignified smile. "I'm Peg Drinkwater. I see my man has good taste in women. It flatters me to know he wants me too, seeing how beautiful the two of you are."

"You should feel truly flattered then," spoke Catrina, holding her regal head high. "He wants you the most."

Ginny squinted with recognition. "We've met before, at Daddy's office."

"That's right, we have . . ." Peggy Sue turned up her Lone Star.

He went to the kitchen and grabbed a beer, hurriedly downing a bunch of it in an effort to calm his nerves. This situation was an atomic bomb, waiting for one wrong word, a snotty look, the slightest misinterpretation of an expression to set it off. Back at his desk, he resettled on the corner, feeling very ill at ease.

Sensing his apprehension, Peggy Sue cut her eyes to him. "Relax, Jasper, there's not going to be a catfight. Right, girls?"

"Of course not." Ginny took a pull of Cuervo Gold and swallowed. "We're lovers not fighters."

Nodding in agreement, Catrina grabbed the bottle from her cousin, downed a big swig, and made a sour face while swallowing. A grin followed the tequila burn. "Ginny and I have fought enough for the three of us. You look adorable in Jasper's shirt, dear. I'm not being facetious, I mean it. I've seen you from a distance several times and knew you were cute, but my—seeing you up close—you're a pretty thing."

Peggy Sue smiled at the redhead. "Thank you. I love your jewelry. Are those real rubies?"

"Sure are, honey."

"Thought so. They must have cost a fortune."

Ginny giggled and yanked the Cuervo back from Catrina. "She can afford it, believe me."

Jasper examined Catrina, decked out in yet another full compliment of rubies—earrings, necklace, bracelets, and rings. *She must have a vault full of those red gems*, he thought. Like always, she wore green—sweater, slacks, and shoes. Ginny had on a pink sweat shirt and jeans. The only jewels she sported were pearl earrings. He'd never thought about it before but vain, materialistic Ginny seldom wore finger jewelry. He wondered why.

The big diamond and smaller cluster of stones on Peggy Sue's engagement ring sparkled against the brown bottle she raised to her lips. Lowering it she said, "I trust neither of you have any sexually transmitted diseases?"

Ginny's face erupted with a scowl of offense. "Of course not! We're not whores."

"Well in a sense we're all having sex with one another, so it doesn't hurt to ask."

Catrina shot Peggy Sue a cold smile. "I trust the same is true of you?"

"It was, up until tonight."

"Huh?" Catrina's snooty expression transformed into a glower of concern.

Peggy Sue winked at him and refocused on the redhead. "If Jasper's not contaminated, then neither am I."

Ginny imbibed more tequila, handed the bottle to Catrina, and clasped her hands together. "Okay, here's the deal. All of us love Jasper, so we all need to be friends for his sake. Agreed?"

"Here, here," said Catrina, gearing up for another shot of Cuervo.

Peggy Sue tilted her beer in salute.

Apparently trying to silence a burp after swallowing,

Catrina covered her mouth with the scarlet-tipped fingers of her left hand, grimacing in the process. Features relaxing, she lowered them, and sighed. "Okay. Now we all know each other. Question is, do we like each other? I guess we pretty much have to, don't we."

"So it would seem," said Peggy Sue.

Shaking her head back and forth, Ginny sealed her lids, long lashes curling out majestically above high cheekbones. "Nope . . . I saw him first . . . he's all mine."

Jasper hoped she'd said it in jest but couldn't tell. Peggy Sue wore a wary expression, visibly weighing Ginny's words. The spoiled blonde seemed vulnerable, and it surprised him to feel a protective attitude towards her. Her predatory orbs were powerless when closed—the lioness seemed tame, like her teeth had been pulled. He wasn't sure he liked that.

At length Ginny stilled her head and opened her eyes. They'd reacquired their customary carnivorous gleam, but looked out of focus. "We're going to have to go, Catrina. I've reached my limit . . . I may be sick."

"Come on, dear, let's get you to bed." Catrina helped Ginny to her feet, giving Peggy Sue a wink in the process. "Nice meeting you, Peg. Try not to wear him out tonight, okay?"

"I can't promise that," she replied with a grin. "It was good to meet the two of you as well."

When the door closed behind the cousins, he squashed his cigarette and put a hand on Peggy Sue's shoulder. "Sorry about that."

She looked up at him with a helpless smile, eyes shining brightly. "It was odd at first, but I'm glad it happened. I mean, it was inevitable that it would. And now that it has, I'm glad to get it over with."

That floored him. "You knew I was still carrying on with Ginny?"

"I strongly suspected you were, and I could hardly blame you since I wasn't able to . . . you know. But I didn't know you hadn't given up Catrina. She's a real hottie, isn't she."

"Yeah." He didn't know what else to say, now feeling protective of Peggy Sue. Guilt tweaked his innards as he realized the instinct felt no stronger than what he'd previously sympathized towards Ginny. Could it be he had more than a physical bond with the strawberry blonde? Would he have wound up falling in love with her if he hadn't lost his heart to Peggy Sue? It was too late to worry about that possibility now, since nothing could change the fact.

Waiting for his fiancé to draw a line in the sand—demand he choose between her and his mistresses, dreading having to confess he couldn't, fearing he'd wind up losing her—she totally surprised him. Vulnerability gave way to blatant sensuality as Peggy Sue stripped off his shirt, ran a hand through her hair, and started for the stairs. "Well you're mine alone tonight, cowboy. Come on, let's hope you've got at least one more bullet in your pistol . . . ."

23

The morning after Peggy Sue became a real woman, he took off for the Double Cross to confront Dree and lay out his fear the big blonde might be mistaken in thinking God had called him to preach. And if he wound up leaving, Jasper planned to help out until a suitable replacement could be found . . . .

* * * *

Cruising down a ramp from the interstate, Jasper entered the city he now called home. Before departing for the ranch six weeks ago, he'd warned Ginny and Catrina not to call him there because the boys were liable to get wise and it might get back to T. Wayford, who'd brought him some sausage to test on each of his weekly visits. But he'd phoned Peggy Sue every day, while hanging around to feed the crew until a new cook hired on, since Dree did quit. He'd helped out with ranch work between meals, and enjoyed staying in the bunkhouse with Useless, Tray, and Billy Culpepper, turning down an offer from Drake to use the spare bedroom at the ranch house. A fifty-year-old codger named Ed Hopper became the official cook. All the boys liked him and Ed gave as good as he got, so morale was going to be fine. Ed didn't have Dree's diverse culinary expertise, but the more adept cowpuncher really knew his way around a pot of beans, and made good chili. It had tickled Jasper to learn the old boy had been a fan of his way back when, and broke out under Red on the Canton Ranch. Being only eighteen at the time, having to rise at dawn six days a week hadn't suited him, so he'd quit after six months and didn't set foot on a ranch again until twenty years later.

Jasper hadn't been on the ranch more than an hour before it became obvious Dree was hell-bent to preach, so he'd told him, "Go ahead on if you're sure about this. I'll take care of the boys until we can find another cook." Dree had a contact at a Baptist church in Irving and walked right into an associate pastor position. All the boys were proud of him, and he was too, but still had concerns that the young cowboy's motivation might stem from something besides the call of God.

Two days after Dree left, Jasper had called Catrina and told her to have Francois come to the ranch and remove all the listening, transmitting, and optical devices. Before the technical wiz did it however, he gave the boys and him a demonstration of how everything worked. Despite knowing Lorraine Bradbury's image was being electronically generated, the woman in white had still appeared as ghostly as all the other times he'd seen her.

The speakers and optical implements were so small, and so well camouflaged, even Francois wouldn't have been able to locate them without using a device that looked like a metal detector. He'd also shown them the van, jammed with such advanced looking equipment it made all the paraphernalia on the bridge of the Star Ship Enterprise look out of date. Catrina's accomplice had handed over all the disk recordings, which Jasper immediately burned in the slaughterhouse incinerator to keep Useless, Tray, and Drake in the dark about Ginny and him. Useless had mercilessly teased Tray about

Francois having a crush on the mustachioed cowpoke. Fact was, it appeared the Frenchman did.

An itch crawled up Jasper's jaw. While raking his fingers through the irritating forest of whiskers to quell it, he passed a barber shop and decided get the damn thing shaved off. He told the barber to crop his hair short as well.

A pile of mail awaited him when he got home, one piece of which was a royalty check totaling over a quarter million dollars. He made out a ten thousand dollar check to his mom, another grand each for the boys at the ranch, and called Dree at his new address in Irving. Then he changed into his fancy black cowboy suit, and went to the plant to call on Peggy Sue.

"Oh great, you got shorn!" she bellowed with delight when he walked into her office.

"Yeah, figured it was about time."

"I liked your hippy look, but you look so much prettier clean shaven with short hair. And I've been dying to see what it's like to kiss you without being tickled by whiskers." Peggy Sue vigorously rubbed his cheeks before planting one on him in front of Martha Spate.

Unlocking lips with his fiancé, he winked at the snickering fat woman. "Some gals can't resist a smooth face."

"Personally, I think you looked handsomer with the beard."

"Boy, you just can't please everyone, can you? You might as well take the rest of the day off, Martha, because your boss is going to."

Peggy Sue gasped. "Oh I can't, Jasper, I've got—"

"Oh yes you can or I'm going to tell T. Wayford this new batch of sausage I'm taking home with me is way off the mark."

She folded her arms and fired a cocky smile at him. "You wouldn't."

"Like hell I wouldn't."

Martha grinned. "I think you'd better do as he says or we may be out of a job."

His protesting betrothed switched off her computer and grabbed her purse. "You know this is blackmail."

"It is for a fact . . . ."

He took her to the truck stop for an early supper, then drove to his apartment so they could made love, learning along the way that she'd started taking birth control pills, something she had previously thought would never be necessary.

"Do you have any idea how hard it was, doing without you for so long?" she said after their second go round. "I think you've turned me into a nymphomaniac."

"Missed you horribly too, darlin', believe me." Despite knowing she was hoping for a third excursion, he got out of bed and lit up a smoke. "Get dressed, there's someone I want you to meet. Then we'll come back and wear each other smooth out until morning."

Looking up at him with a sated face, she replied in a tone that was only half teasing, "You've got another mistress?"

"No. I want you to meet Dree . . . ."

* * * *

Jasper parked in front of a small house located two blocks from a Baptist Church. Dree, who wasn't expecting them, answered the door.

"I can't believe you actually came to see me, Boss!"

The enormous grin on the big blonde's face made him laugh. "Hell I said I'd drop by some time, didn't I?"

Dree grabbed him in a bear hug. "So that's why you asked what my plans were for this evening when you called earlier today, you sly dog."

Jasper patted him on the back and pulled away. "Yep, and when you said you were just going to lounge around the house I decided to surprise you. Dree, this is Peggy Sue Drinkwater, soon to be Peggy Sue Miller."

Still grinning, the upstart preacher grabbed her hand. "It's so good to meet you, Peggy Sue. I didn't think I ever would."

"Nice to meet you too," she replied with a warm smile.

"She's every bit the beauty you said she was, Boss."

A blush tainted her cheeks. "Thank you, Dree. I think I'm going to like you."

Dree laughed and waved them inside. "It's real humble but it's home for now."

The place was laid out like an efficiency apartment. An ancient couch, small desk, and narrow bed rested on a dilapidated carpet. The linoleum covering the floor of a kitchenette had eroded down to black patches in several sections. A short wooden bar with two stools served as a dining table.

He told Dree about Francois and how they'd gotten to see the ghost projected. Dree filled him in on life in Irving since he'd left the ranch. "I can't thank you enough for covering for me, Boss, especially with you being such a big shot now. Not many people would have done that. There were several guys wanting this associate pastor spot, and I wouldn't have been able to get it, working out my two weeks notice. So once again God has used you big time in my life."

"Aw, I had a fun time doing it. Listen, I got another one of those royalty checks and I brought a little something for you." He dug out his wallet and handed Dree the check he'd made out to him.

His eyes shot wide. "Praise God, another thousand dollars! Thanks so much, Boss!" The big blue orbs looked towards the ceiling. "And thank you, Lord, for putting this man in my life."

Embarrassed and trying not to show it, Jasper glanced around. "You might use some of that loot for new furniture."

"It is pretty modest, isn't it. But I'm real proud to live here because the church owns it and I'm not being charged a dime in rent."

"So you're sure this is what you want to do?"

Conviction riveted to his face, Dree nodded. "More importantly, it's what God wants me to do."

Jasper breathed out a sigh. If The Man Upstairs wasn't calling him to preach, Dree damn sure didn't know it. "Okay. I'll try to help you out from time to time. Reckon you'll be my outlet to donate to the Lord's work, but I'll say it once again—promise me not to become one of those money grubbers that use the name of Jesus to line their pockets and promote themselves instead of the truth like preachers are supposed to."

"Like I told you, Boss, I hate that crap as much as you do, if not more. I'm here to serve the Lord, not my bank account. To quote the apostle Paul, *No man that wars entangles himself with the affairs of this life, that he may please him who has called him to be a soldier.*"

Something stirred him inside as Dree spoke the passage. "You said that with real passion. I bet you're going to be a good preacher. Do you still have my address and phone number I gave you before you left the ranch?"

"Sure do, Boss."

"Good. Well call or drop by any time. If you need anything, don't hesitate to ask."

Dree's smile of gratitude contorted into a frown. "Hey, you shaved off your beard! And look at you—wearing those fancy duds."

"Yeah . . ." Jasper felt embarrassed again. He'd worn the suit for Peggy Sue, and wished he'd changed back into his jeans after their roll in the hay. "I dolled up to take my gal out to supper."

Peggy Sue grinned. "Yeah, it was a real swanky place too. A truck stop."

"Just like you, Boss," laughed Dree. "Get all dressed up for dinner at a truck stop."

Though managing a grin over Dree's remark, Jasper felt foolish for not thinking to take her to a high-priced joint. *Hell, guess I really am just a hayseed.*

"So," Dree turned to Peggy Sue, "I guess you know you're famous."

"Why's that?"

"You're the woman that lassoed Jasper Miller. A lot of gals tried, a lot of gals failed."

"He's pulling your leg."

"I doubt that," said Peggy Sue, half serious, half joking.

"According to Useless Horton, Jasper had to fight them off with a stick during his rodeo days. You really think you can handle this cowboy?"

She cut her eyes to him, then shot Dree a knowing smile. "I don't think anyone can handle this cowboy."

Dree grinned at him. "Well, Boss, looks like she's going into this with her eyes wide open."

"Are you ordained?" asked Peggy Sue.

"Not yet. Hope to be soon."

"Will you marry us when you are?"

"It would be an honor and a pleasure."

The thought hadn't occurred to Jasper but the prospect tickled him. Nonetheless he faked an irritated look. "Um, you think you might ought to consult me about it first, darlin'?"

"No, sweetheart, I sure don't. You may wear the pants on everything else, but our wedding is my baby, you dig?"

He tried not to laugh but couldn't help it. "Well do I at least get to pick my best man?"

"Sure, so long as I approve of him."

That got Dree to laughing too. "So when are you guys planning on getting hitched?"

"As soon as you're ordained suits me. How about you, Peggy Sue?"

Beaming like a lighthouse, she rapidly nodded.

The greenhorn preacher suddenly looked nervous. "I hope I don't mess up."

"Oh you'll do fine." Jasper popped him on the shoulder. "Just don't forget what you promised me about not turning into a money grubber. The gospel and cash mix about as well as ice cream and shit. It was real good to see you, hoss. Guess we'd best be shoving off now . . . ."

When they got in his truck Peggy Sue let out a sigh while buckling up. "That is one *good looking* man."

"Watch it now," he laughingly spouted with a fake scowl. "You wanna walk home?"

She giggled. "Okay, let me rephrase. Man but your friend Dree is a homely boy. Ug-lee!"

Snickering again, he fired up the engine and drove away.

"This seat is comfortable, I'll give you that much."

"You mean there's actually something about this pickup you like?"

"Yeah, I like the passenger seat," she teased.

"Meant to tell you but never got around to it. Guess who I met before I took over Dree's spot at the ranch?"

"Who?"

"The one and only Jerry Jones."

"Oh really? Where?"

"At T. Wayford's office."

"That's nice."

Her blasé reaction made him frown. "You don't seem very

impressed. You do realize who I'm talking about don't you?"

"Yes, the owner of the Cowboys."

"You must not like football."

"I love football and I'm a big Cowboys fan. I just don't like Jerry Jones."

"You know him?"

"No."

"Then why don't you like him?"

"For firing Tom Landry. It broke my father's heart."

Jasper thought back to when that happened and remembered he'd hated Jerry Jones for that too. But he felt the man tried to make up for it after the fact, and told her so. ". . . and he even put up a statue of Tom Landry."

"Too little too late, as the football commentators say."

The look on her face told him there'd be no changing her mind on the matter, so he let it drop. A few miles further down the road she said, "Your mistresses and I got a little more acquainted with each other while you were gone."

His stomach began to churn, sending a sour taste to the back of his throat. Peggy Sue's tone sounded normal, but he braced himself for bad news. "You did?"

"Yeah. We've had dinner together three times. Once at Lou Chong's where I took you, and twice at an exclusive club in Dallas Ginny's a member of. It was very nice."

Relieved she seemed to have enjoyed herself since her manner didn't reflect any jealousy or hostility, he said, "Wonder if it's the same place where T. Wayford took me when I signed the sausage contract."

"No, it's not the same place."

"Well how would you know? You weren't there that day."

"Because I made the arrangements for T. Wayford." Pulling the shoulder strap out a ways, she shifted her hips and positioned herself at a slight angle to face him. "Once you get past her veneer, Ginny's actually a sweet girl, and very vulnerable. She puts up that front to hide it, I suspect. And Catrina's amazing. She's seen it all and done it all. That girl is *so* into rubies. I've yet to see her wear the same piece twice. I'd love to prowl through all her jewelry. I bet she could feed the third world if she ever sold it."

He cleared his throat. "So whose idea was it for you guys to get together?"

"Mine. They made the first move that night they came to your apartment, and I felt I should reciprocate. I invited them to Lou Chong's, then they invited me out twice afterwards."

She seemed totally at ease with the situation, which baffled him. "You talk like the three of you are actually getting along?"

"Oh we are. They've agreed to be my bride's maids while my two married sisters will serve as matrons of honor."

Dumbfounded, he could only gawk at her stupidly. "You're kidding."

"Nope . . . ."

24

One year to the day after he'd signed the contract and met Peggy Sue, her last name became Miller. Though Dree had been ordained before then, she'd sentimentally chosen that date for their wedding because if not for Grandma Miller's Superior Sausage—which had burgeoned his net worth to nine figures—their paths most likely never would have crossed. In four months they'd celebrate their fifth anniversary. He'd bought ten thousand acres of prime grazing land and started his own ranch, which he called The Triple Lady, in homage to his wife and two concubines. Dree explained the term to him when he'd told the big blonde about his love life, wanting to know what the Lord thought about it. While watching one of Dree's television broadcasts Jasper had gotten saved. Worried he might be living in sin, he'd gone to see the cowboy turned preacher and laid out his unusual situation. Dree had told him he simply had two lesser wives along with Peggy Sue. Though no ceremony was required, the preacher advised him to ask for their fathers' blessings on the unions for full sanctification in the eyes of God.

It turned out T. Wayford had known about Ginny's feelings for him since their inception, and went along with the idea: not only because it was what she wanted—it also kept her away from the hordes of fortune hunters who'd been trying to woo her since late adolescence. Willis Canton, on the other hand, had threatened to have him castrated if he didn't leave his darling Sugar Plum alone. Catrina had taken control of that situation. He still didn't know how she'd gotten her daddy to change his mind, since she refused to say, but he figured it involved some sort of blackmail because Willis had given his blessing through clinched teeth. She and Ginny had their surnames legally changed to Miller soon after a marriage license automatically altered Peggy Sue's.

Lounging on a balcony-covered porch stretching across the front of his twenty-room ranch house, enjoying a lazy Sunday afternoon, Jasper watched his two four-year-old boys wrestling with a baby pig in the front yard. Theodore Wayford, whom they called Ted, came into the world through Ginny's womb, and was the first born. Catrina had given birth to his second son only ten days later. He'd given him the middle name Willis in honor of the boy's grandfather, but his first name was Red, dubbed after Red King rather than his mama's hair color, which he'd inherited, as had his baby sister, Jasper's newborn daughter Kitty Amanda. Catrina—sitting on a lawn chair to his left, nursing the little darling—had insisted on the name. His so called legal bride sat to his right, enjoying a neck massage administered by Ginny, who was standing behind her. Peggy Sue had finally decided she was ready to become a mother and had blossomed out with twins. She knew the sex of each through a sonogram but he wouldn't let her tell him their gender, wanting to wait until they were born to find out. They'd be arriving any time now. Not to be outdone, Ginny had recently gotten knocked up again as well.

Dree had gotten booted out of the Baptist church early in his career over doctrinal disputes, and now had a nondenominational nation-wide television ministry, backed by

The Triple Lady Ranch, Catrina, and T. Wayford, who'd also found the Lord after being moved by a soul shaking Dree Gillis sermon. The big blonde kept his promise to never ask for a penny, and reached millions with the pure truth of the Bible. The Double Cross was now totally repopulated because Useless, Tray, Drake, Billy Culpepper, and Ed Hopper had all been shown the light by a former NFL tight end who'd once done the hash slinging there. They lived in Irving now, helping him run his ministry.

Dree's contention that Lorraine Bradbury had carried out God's plan, even though acting on Catrina's orders, seemed to have been validated. Lorraine ran into Dree at a rodeo in Fort Worth, neither of them knowing they had mutual acquaintances. Recognizing the televangelist, she approached him for an autograph. He invited her to his church and she'd attended every Sunday thereafter, meeting Drake when he went to work for Dree. Despite the age difference, they fell in love, and realizing she only had a superficial understanding of the gospel, Drake convinced Lorraine to accept Jesus as her personal savior. "You see, Boss," Dree had said at their wedding, "God really does work in mysterious ways. Drake was the first one to hear her cry for help. Seems to me he helped her pretty dang good, wouldn't you say?"

Like he'd done on the Double Cross, Jasper raised Angus cattle alongside Duroc and Blue Butt hogs, but he had a gang of cowboys living in a ritzy bunkhouse situated a good ways from his hacienda doing all the actual work. Useless, who'd helped him weed out the misfits when he put the crew together, had nicknamed his foreman Gil Favor and the cook Wishbone, because of Jasper's fondness for Rawhide rather than any resemblance. Once in a while he'd head down to the bunkhouse and enjoy an evening of poker with them. They were all fun loving, hard working young bucks, and he'd become quite attached to the whole lot. On the last Saturday of every warm month, he'd throw a big bash, hire some local band, and man the barbecue pit himself while the hands danced the night away in his rodeo arena with some of the pretty girls working under Peggy Sue at Cross Enterprises.

T. Wayford had expanded his restaurant chain beyond the Metroplex and opened a slew of steakhouses across Texas, buying up every ounce of beef and pork the Triple Lady processed. Ironically, Grandma Miller's Superior Sausage still didn't appear in any of T. Wayford's restaurants, as none of them served breakfast. It had, however, gone national, outselling its nearest competitor at a ratio of two-to-one. He faithfully gave the sausage a periodic taste test, and the quality never wavered.

His mother passed away nine months ago, and his sister wouldn't speak to him because he had three wives, though the government only knew about Peggy Sue. He figured his private life was none of Uncle Sam's business. His brother-in-law gave him a call every now and then to let him know how Jasmine was doing. Jasper hoped in time she'd bury the hatchet, but all that rested in the Lord's hands.

The miles were piling up on the Dodge Ram he'd purchased upon receiving his first royalty check. Pretty soon it would be time to trade it in for a new one. His contentment with the pickup, and lack of desire to drive some slick vehicle, baffled his old ladies. When he had a hankering to sit in the saddle instead of behind the wheel of his truck, he strapped it on the back of a beautiful palomino stud named Ventura, in homage to the song *Ventura Highway* by America. He'd turned No Name out to pasture, and the aging paint seemed to be enjoying retirement.

Peggy Sue temporarily quit her three cigarettes a day habit upon learning she was pregnant, but continued running the plant, which had quadrupled in size. She wouldn't hear of giving up her job. Salvation and motherhood had completely transformed Ginny and Catrina from materialistic snobs, demanding to be the center of attention, to down-home country gals with tender caring hearts. On the rare occasions any of the girls could coax him out for supper, he usually chose his favorite truck stop. He still enjoyed Lone Star beer and Marlboro reds, and still broke down bawling every time George Strait wrenched his soul, singing about that broken leg in *Amarillo By Morning*.

About the Author

Arley Owens, Jr. is a musician, composer, author, poet, artist, producer, and rancher who resides in his native Texas with his lovely wife Cristi.
He's a member of the musical group TORN PAGE.
http://www.tornpageband.com

Other books by Arley Owens, Jr.
A Tale of the Mojave
The Cyrus Syndrome
Incident in Baltimore
Death Ranch

Read Arley Owens, Jr. on your Kindle:
http://www.amazon.com/author/arleyowens

SHORTY MAE PRODUCTIONS
P.O. Box 81102
Midland, Texas 79708

www.ingramcontent.com/pod-product-compliance
Lightning Source LLC
LaVergne TN
LVHW020703110826
845149LV00012B/2090

* 9 7 8 0 9 8 4 8 1 9 5 5 3 *